Awakened by the Hidden Poet

A Novel

Roberto Rabago

The Awakened Press

The Awakened Press

The Awakened Press
www.theawakenedpress.com

Cover photo by Mike Levy, Sun Valley, Idaho
Author biography headshot artwork illustrated by Annie Rabago

The references and resources provided are accurate at the time of publication.

For information about special discounts for bulk purchases, please contact The Awakened Press at books@theawakenedpress.com.

The Awakened Press can bring authors to your live event. For more information or to book an event contact books@theawakenedpress.com or visit our website at www.theawakenedpress.com.

Book design by Kurt A. Dierking II

Printed in the United States of America
First The Awakened Press trade paperback edition

ISBN: 979-8-9860377-9-0

ALSO BY ROBERTO RABAGO

Rich Town, Poor Town

Preface

The title of this book is in reference to the eighth stanza of a poem written by Percy Bysshe Shelley, entitled "To a Skylark." The eighth stanza says:

Like a Poet hidden

In the light of thought,

Singing hymns unbidden,

'Till the world is wrought

To sympathy with hopes

And fears it heeded not.

This stanza was chosen because of its very lyrical summary, which is the purpose of this book: to demonstrate by reason and logic that God is always "nudging" or directing you to remember, to sympathize, with the hopes and fears you have always carried within yourself, but heretofore have either forgotten or ignored.

This book is not a "Bible Thumper" text; it is based on scientific facts and logic that is rooted in the thinking of intellectual giants of the last ages, such as Heraclitus, Aristotle, and Aquinas. The author of this book is not an official philosopher or theologian, so has relied on more recent theologians to refute some of the errors discerned in that of Kant and Hegel, whose thinking is more fashionable in our recent times.

The characters involved in the love story are fictional, but all the conclusions that are based on the Shroud of Turin and the Sudarium of Oviedo are scientifically factual. The application of proper reasoning to those facts gives rise to some conclusions that can be very unsettling to us, and our current way of thinking.

But there is peace in becoming aware of a solution that has always been present, but has been ignored or forgotten.

After reading this, the reader will either agree or disagree with its conclusions. Those that disagree will be left with two unresolved and difficult problems to explain: How the Shroud of Turin has come into existence, and how the Sudarium of Oviedo and the Shroud of Turin have come to exactly correspond and verify each other. But those readers that agree will hopefully increase their awareness, on their way to a better life.

—Roberto Rabago

Awakened by the Hidden Poet

A Novel

Roberto Rabago

The Awakened Press

The Corn Goddess

The Aztec priest could read the signs. He knew that many changes were forthcoming; not only for him, not only for the nude young woman who lay unconscious before him on the stone altar, but quite possibly for the entire Universe. This night would be the most dangerous night in his entire lifetime, the night of the New Fire Festival.

The New Fire Festival would start with today's death of the sun, at the exact moment that it dropped below the western horizon, because that would be the time that the two wheels of the Aztec Calendar, the Tonalpohualli and the Xiuhpōhualli, would come into coincidence. Convergence of the two wheels was a rare event that occurred only once in a lifetime; so many months, many Metztli, would come and go before the next New Fire Festival would take place.

The priest knew that tonight would be the only Festival he would experience in his lifetime, but should the Gods consent to renew the entire Universe tonight, he might be able to live long enough to see some of the changes that the Gods would choose to impose in the new cycle.

The priest felt honored that his people had bestowed upon him the trust and responsibility of delivering tonight's petition to their God for the continued functioning of the Universe, and for a plentiful corn harvest in the coming growing season. The priest would make the petition directly to the Goddess responsible for the corn harvest, Chicomecoatl. To assure that she would remain favorably disposed towards them, the New Fire Festival included the sacrifice and offering of a young virgin, the living nude woman who lay peacefully on the altar before him, as if sleeping.

The priest had the self-confidence to perform the sacrifice, which involved removing the woman's heart from her body, and offering her still-beating heart to Chicomecoatl. Of course, that could not be accomplished unless the girl had been properly sedated, to make certain that she would not feel any pain before reaching the next world.

In spite of his confidence, the priest was troubled by some omens that were parts of tonight's ceremony. He hoped that these omens were harmless, and not sinister omens that seemed to foretell a catastrophe in the aftermath of this New Fire Festival. One troubling omen was that the setting sun would mark the end of the cycle known as the coatl, the cycle of the snake. But the name of the Corn Goddess, Chicomecoatl, meant "seven snakes." Did the end of the coatl cycle mean that there would not be a new "seven snakes" cycle? Did that mean that after tonight's event would take place, that the future would no longer hold the Corn Goddess, and no more corn? Did that mean that the Universe would completely end tonight? As far as the priest and the Aztecs were concerned, the end of corn and the end of the Universe meant the same thing.

The priest realized that he would not be able to answer these questions before sunset, and since the sunset was very near, he needed to turn his attention to the conduct of the ceremony.

First, he focused on the beautiful woman who lay unconscious and nude before him. He remembered that when he had first seen her, he knew immediately that she should be the next Corn Goddess. She had been a seller of flowers, where all the flower vendors congregated on the causeway between the Capital and the mainland. Because he was very well known and highly respected as a priest, and because it was a singular honor to be selected as the Corn Goddess, many maidens brazenly tried to attract his attention to themselves. This particular girl, however, had not only avoided calling attention to herself, but had dropped her eyes demurely when she saw that he was assessing her beauty. After he had made the necessary investigations and was certain that both she and her parents were fully informed of all that was to be required of them, all three gladly consented, and he appointed her this year's Corn Goddess.

The time remaining before he should begin the ceremony left the priest only a short minute for introspection, but in that moment, he became aware of something within himself that momentarily unsettled him. Although it took a lot of conscious effort, he admitted that he was beginning to doubt the existence of the all the Gods, including the Corn Goddess and even the Sun God himself. Did the Gods really exist? Did the sacrifices they offered really affect the future of his entire tribe? Did the Gods really interact into human affairs? Could any human, whether they were priests or not, affect the conduct of the Gods? Regretfully, he would have to face those questions in the future, provided that the Universe would continue to exist after tonight.

Now it became time to start tonight's ceremony. First, he verified that the girl's body was completely covered with red dye, and her legs and arms were tied securely to the altar. Very gently, he lifted her eyelids and held a flaming torch close to her eyes. The pupils did not react to the light, so he felt assured that the herbs she had been given had successfully anesthetized her; she would feel no pain. He verified that her virginity was still intact.

As the sun touched the rim of the western horizon, his assistant priests gathered around the altar, and he put on his own elaborate ceremonial headdress of colorful feathers, and placed the headdress of the Corn Goddess on the girl's head. The large crowd that surrounded the pyramid saw the increased activity of the priests, and their agitation and murmurings markedly increased.

When the noise reached a crescendo, the priest placed himself next to the altar, exposed his instrument and, holding the heavy obsidian knife with both hands, completely extended both arms above his head. The knife was held motionless for a brief instant before he brought it down swiftly and buried it into the girl's chest, precisely at the intersection of the cross formed by the line between her nipples and the line between her navel and her throat.

Then the priest quickly widened the incision made by the knife, and blood started to gush out of her abdomen and down her arms, until the blood reached the girl's hands and the corn husks that were tied there. In the wavering light of the torches, the priest saw the color of the individual kernels change from whiteish-yellow to bright red as streams of blood flowed over them. Now the priest could relax a little, because he felt satisfied that next year's corn harvest was being nourished.

One final step remained. The priest thrust both hands and the knife into the initial incision. He then cut through the muscle of the diaphragm, located the heart, then quickly severed its circulatory connections, and extracted it from the girl's body. He held it tightly in both hands, then raised it high above his head in order to offer the still beating heart to the Corn Goddess. His own heart was pounding, since he still believed that the continued existence of the entire Universe depended entirely upon the God's acceptance or rejection of his offering. His mind remained poised at its highest level of awareness, breathlessly awaiting to learn whether the Goddess had accepted or refused his offering. If the Goddess rejected the offering, he expected the entire Universe to collapse in the next instant, probably accompanied by immense thunderclaps, blinding lightning flashes, and violent shaking of the pyramid and the entire Earth.

The priest made his offering, afraid that he might see the whole

Universe vanish. But he made his offer at the exact moment that the dying heart made its last contraction, sending a spray of blood directly into the eyes of the priest, burning them and temporarily blinding him. But still holding the heart tightly, he shook his head violently from side to side to clear them of blood, then collected all his physical strength and mental concentration into his voice, to say:

"Accept, we beseech thee, O Chicomecoatl, O Goddess of Corn Harvests, this sacrifice of a living heart, a heart that we offer in our gratitude for your provision of a bountiful harvest, a harvest that will keep our men strong and brave, our women strong and fertile, and our children strong and growing. We entrust to you completely our continued survival!"

After an interval of 500 years, and at an altitude five miles above where the ceremony to the Corn Goddess had taken place, the same drama was reenacted in the mind of a man that was a passenger in a commercial airliner preparing to land at the airport of present-day Mexico City.

The drama was terminated by the voice of a flight attendant who was speaking loudly and with a sense of urgency. "Mr. Christopher! Mr. Christopher! Wake up! Are you all right?"

The man, Mr. Christopher, answered. "Of course, I am all right! Why are you shaking me? Is something wrong?"

The flight attendant responded quickly. "I was called by the lady seated next to you. When I got here, you were shaking your head from side to side and both your arms were raised above your head, and you were shouting something in some language I didn't understand!" She quickly paused to gather her breath, then said quietly, "I was afraid that you were having a strong psychotic episode…but I'm glad to see you were only having a bad dream. You seem okay now. So please fasten your seatbelt. We're starting our descent into Mexico City. You were probably having had a bad dream—something that happens frequently on this red-eye flight from Boston. Let me bring you some coffee to help you wake up, and if there is anything else I can do for you, please call me."

"That is very nice of you," Mr. Christopher said in response. "But I am all right and quite awake now, so I really don't need coffee. Thank you, anyway."

Lucien Christopher's traveling companion, the attractive woman seated next to him who had called the flight attendant during Lucien's disturbance asked under her breath, "What was going on with you? You really scared me! I was sound asleep, warm and snuggling against you, when I was awakened by your fidgeting. I wasn't worried until you raised both your arms above your head as though you were trying hard to hold onto something, but then you shook your head from side to side and started shouting something in some strange language. I thought you were having either a nightmare or a seizure."

"I'm okay, Crystal; I'm sorry I caused a problem. I was having a very vivid experience that I was an Aztec priest conducting a human sacrifice. I was at the crucial part, when the God must decide whether to continue the existence of the Universe…a very important part of the ceremony. That must have been why I became so excited."

"What did the God decide to do?"

"I'm afraid I don't know, because I woke up just before that. But since the last Aztec sacrifice took place about five hundred years ago, and you and I still exist, I would say that the Universe *did* continue. However, since the Aztecs no longer exist as a separate nation, maybe the God only granted a part of the Universe? I still recall most of the dream, however, and it leaves me with a question that still concerns me."

"What question is that?"

"Before the Aztec priest began to perform the sacrifice, he had already started to doubt whether the sacrifice could have any effect on what decision the God would make. That question concerns me today, about whether God ever intervenes in human affairs."

"Lucien, you just verified my first opinion of you—that you are a very deep thinker, an intellectual always searching for answers to important questions. No wonder you were so respected among your peers. But you won't be able to get any help from me; I'm no philosopher, I am an art teacher. But at times, I have also wondered about that myself. Does that question concern you? I'm asking because these last few months I have noticed a certain restlessness in you that was not there when we first met."

"I compliment you on your perceptiveness, but I certainly don't consider myself an intellectual. We have grown closer to each other in the last few months, haven't we?"

"I certainly feel that way, especially when you asked me to come with you on this vacation. I have been afraid that your restlessness might lead you to decide not to return to teach at our little college next year, and I did not want our relationship to end abruptly. I am hoping that we can get to know each other better on this trip."

"I want that too, and I am enjoying this vacation with such a good-looking companion. But should any of our trustees have questions, we came so that I could introduce you to Mexican culture and religiosity, and you are here to teach me about Mexican art."

The woman paused and sat back in her chair, looking more relaxed now. "Of course. And I want to say that I am also enjoying this trip, since I am accompanied by a handsome rising star of academia. I think you have published more papers than other professors who have been there longer. Your reputation is outstanding, and you are very well liked by everyone, even freshmen girls, and that makes me a little jealous! But seriously, I would enjoy an immersion into Frida Kahlo's world. I would become a better teacher. But for the present time, let me say that I am relieved that you are still yourself. For a while there, I was afraid that I had lost my traveling companion. Those Aztecs must have had a very strong influence on you."

"True, Crystal. But in my brief studies of their religion and my knowledge of their presently existing descendants, I have learned that they were people much like us today, only they had to cope with the wild world of their time. They seemingly lived in a harsh world, but their feelings of peace and hope and love are identical with our own feelings now."

"Is that something that you really believe, Lucien?"

"Of course I do."

"Give me a good example and maybe I'll believe you."

Lucien remained silent for a time, pondering her question. Then the airplane made a turn to the left to make the approach to the Mexico City airport, and two snow-clad peaks became visible through Crystal's window. Lucien quickly pointed them out. "Crystal, can you see those two mountains with snow on their peaks? They are two extinct volcanoes that are important in Aztec mythology. The one on the left is called 'Popocatépetl,' and the one on the right is 'Iztaccíhuatl.'"

"I like the way you pronounced those names, Lucien. They sound much like the words that you were yelling about in your dream."

"Those names are in Nahuatl, the old Aztec language. Those peaks represent the Aztec version of *Romeo and Juliet*."

"Tell me more! You know that I love art, but I also love literature, especially Shakespeare, so I know all about *Romeo and Juliet*. I'm surprised to encounter *Romeo and Juliet* here. Is there any similarity between the Aztec and English versions?"

"The Aztec version preceded Shakespeare's version. But since there was no communication between Mexico and England in Shakespeare's time, they are completely independent. If I start to tell you the story, I hope that I will be able to finish it before we land."

"Before you start, please excuse me for a moment to freshen up before we land," Crystal exclaimed. "When I return, you will have my full attention, but I'll be right back."

She returned after brushing her long, soft black hair, which made her blue eyes even more noticeable by their contrast with the luster of her locks. When she crossed in front of him to reach her seat, a scent of peppermint reached Lucien, probably from her toothpaste.

She settled herself. "Okay, I'm ready for *Romeo and Juliet.*"

Directing her attention to the view, Lucien said to her, "Crystal, by using a little imagination, you will note that the mountain on the left has the shape of a woman reclining on her side. That mountain is named 'Iztaccíhuatl' in the Aztec language. Her name sounds like 'ecstasy,' does it not? I always associate ecstasy with women, so she is Juliet's counterpart. The mountain next to her that looks like an upright man standing watch over Iztaccíhuatl is called 'Popocatépetl,' who corresponds to Romeo."

"I have them correctly placed, Lucien, so please go on."

Lucien went on. "Iztaccíhuatl was a beautiful princess, the daughter of a king of a powerful tribe in Mexico at the time. Popocatépetl was a warrior, but was of a different tribe, one that was at war with the family of the princess. As you may guess, Iztaccíhuatl and Popocatépetl fell madly in love, and knew they were meant for each other. Popocatépetl was willing to do anything to make his beloved Iztaccíhuatl his bride, so he risked his life to enter into the enemy territory of Iztaccíhuatl's tribe in order to personally ask her father, the enemy king, for his permission to marry his daughter.

"But the king had other plans of his own for her, so he initially withheld his permission. After giving the matter more thought, he saw that his daughter was truly in love, and that Popocatépetl was sufficiently in love, and honorable enough to risk his life in order to appear before him and plead for his permission. So he took the matter into serious consideration and formed a solution: If Popocatépetl could conquer a third tribe with whom the king was also at war with, Popocatépetl could have Iztaccíhuatl as his bride upon his return. The task was difficult and dangerous, and the king did not really expect Popocatépetl to survive it. That would leave the king free to arrange another marriage for his daughter, which would be more to his political advantage.

"To the king's surprise, Popocatépetl accepted the dangerous challenge. After several years and many battles, he returned victoriously to claim his bride.

"But shortly before Popocatépetl could arrive, another suitor for Iztaccíhuatl's hand deceived her, and falsely told her that Popocatépetl had been killed in battle. Iztaccíhuatl was inconsolable, became ill, and soon died of a broken heart. When Popocatépetl finally arrived, Iztaccíhuatl had died only moments earlier, and he found her lifeless body still warm. In desperation, he lifted her up in his arms and carried her to the top of the nearby high mountain, in hopes that the cold air would revive her. When Popocatépetl finally accepted the fact that she was dead and would never revive, he laid his own body next to hers, and before long, he, too, had died of grief.

"The Gods knew of the tragedy, and were so moved that they covered both bodies with snow and united them for eternity, transforming them together into the two snow-clad peaks that you see out the window. So now, the two lovers are united forever, with Popocatépetl standing guard over Iztaccíhuatl, his true love."

Crystal said excitedly, "Lucien, that is amazing! The Aztec version is like Shakespeare's *Romeo and Juliet* in many important aspects, and the two tragedies are certainly equally touching!" She started to say more, but her voice was interrupted by an announcement over the plane's speakers instructing them to fasten their seatbelts and return seats to their upright position in preparation for landing in Mexico City.

They encountered a few minor problems going through customs, but they were both so enthralled to be in a strange country that they did not mind the brief delay.

"Lucien, thank you for inviting me to come on this trip with you!" said Crystal. "I know that we are going to enjoy ourselves. This is much more exciting than those boring faculty meetings, although I did enjoy them when you sat close to me. I want to learn more about Mexico and hear more stories like *Romeo and Juliet*."

"The story of Iztaccíhuatl and Popocatépetl is legendary, but I can tell you another story—one that is true—perhaps better than *Romeo and Juliet* because it affects Mexico even today, although it also began in the time of the Aztecs. I am referring to the appearance of the Virgin of Guadalupe who made her appearance in Mexico during the time of the initial conquest of Mexico. I consider it to be a good example of God's intervention in human affairs, but I am hesitant to tell you this story because it involves events that will seem quite miraculous."

"I don't believe in miracles. I was raised Protestant, and I don't believe in the Virgin Mary."

"I am not surprised to hear you say that, but I will not argue, because I know that a lot of people do not believe that the Virgin Mary has a place in Christianity and that most people do not believe in miracles. I will not try to change your beliefs, but I would like for you to hear her story, and you may accept it or reject it. Can we leave it that way for now? I certainly don't want to start an argument with you at the beginning of our vacation!"

"That sounds fair. I promise not to be too rigid or judgmental, and you will have my full attention."

"That's fine, but I don't want to begin that story now. Sometime later, perhaps."

"Don't forget, okay?"

After clearing customs, they cruised by taxi to the hotel where they had their reservations. Lucien stepped out of the taxicab and immediately felt that he was standing on sacred ground, because he knew that somewhere below him was the location of the main Aztec temple, where five centuries earlier, sacrificial rites had been practiced. He was also happy to be near to the Shrine of the Virgin of Guadalupe. In fact, he had chosen this hotel, El Prado, because of its proximity to the Shrine of the Virgin of Guadalupe.

The El Prado was an older hotel that aged gracefully over the years and was updated with modern conveniences. The rooms had twelve-foot ceilings, decorated with handmade fancy woodwork. It conveyed the solidity and stability of a fortress, having survived several severe earthquakes. Besides having modest prices, the hotel had stability, safety, comfort and a faded elegance.

The man who greeted them warmly at the front desk had carefully groomed white hair and a mustache. He was wearing a blue blazer jacket over a white shirt with a maroon tie. He spoke English fluently with only a slight Spanish accent. "Good morning, and welcome to El Prado. May I have your passports, please?"

He scanned their documentation briefly and noted that Lucien's surname was Christopher and Crystal's was Wilson. He then glanced at their unadorned ring fingers and commented, "Although you have reserved a single room with two beds, I am afraid that our hotel policy does not permit unmarried persons to share a single room. We are still a very traditional hotel."

He noted their look of disappointment, but quickly carried on. "However, I can give you two adjoining rooms. If you are planning to stay for a week, the weekly rate for two rooms will be only slightly more than one single room at the nightly rate. Would that be satisfactory?"

Lucien accepted. After completing their registration, the concierge had a slightly warmer tone with them. "My name is Alfredo Gutierrez, at your service. I am here to assist you with whatever will make your stay with us more comfortable." Then he handed Crystal her room key and another key to Lucien, saying, "I believe you will find this arrangement satisfactory."

They took the elevator to the tenth floor, and found their adjoining rooms separated by a common interior double door that could be locked or unlocked from either side. Lucien unlocked his side and took a warm bath in an old-fashioned bathtub six feet long. After his pleasant bath, he dressed and relaxed on his bed.

Crystal entered through the interior door a short time later, as if dressed for a special occasion. "Lucien, I came to invite you to join me for a bite to eat in the dining room."

"I'm glad to do that, but you look so beautiful that I must upgrade my appearance to be in the company of such a beautiful woman."

"Thank you, what a nice thing to say! If you continue to say such nice things, I will enjoy this trip very much. But if you are going to wear a jacket, I want to change to better match my handsome escort." She headed to her room, and when she returned, she had added a lime-green silk shawl that contrasted nicely with her form-fitting black dress that accented her long black hair. When they left their rooms, the connecting door remained unlocked from both sides.

In the dining room, they sat at a table near the windows, ordering tequila margaritas with premium spirits; Lucien's with salt, Crystal's without.

"Before we left the plane, I didn't thank you for the beautiful story about the Aztec *Romeo and Juliet*," Crystal replied as their drinks arrived at the table. "I want to thank you now, because I had not expected that such a touching, romantic story would come from the warlike culture that you first described. From the way you were describing them, I did not expect their culture to have the sensitivity required to produce such a beautiful legend. Lucien, why doesn't more of the world know the beautiful Aztec story?"

"Crystal, I am not sure that the world cares. Or they have a very vivid view of them that is locked into one thing. It is easy to think of everything from the perspective of one's own cultural heritage. But why do so few Americans know that Shakespeare's *Romeo and Juliet* is such a masterpiece?"

"I, for one, consider both the Aztec and Shakespeare versions to be masterpieces, and I would like for you to tell me more stories like that about Mexico."

"I am glad that you are interested, because I happen to have another story for you—the story about the Virgin of Guadalupe that I mentioned earlier. Would you like me to start now?"

"Yes, of course. One nice thing about being on vacation is having plenty of time and freedom. I'm ready, please proceed."

The Virgin of Guadalupe

"Crystal, I want you to know more about the Virgin of Guadalupe because she is an important, mysterious, miraculous part of Mexico's history. I chose this hotel because the Shrine of the Virgin of Guadalupe is within walking distance of where we are staying."

"A visit to her Shrine is the highlight of your trip. Am I right?"

"Yes, exactly right. But before we visit, I want to be sure that you have enough information to appreciate her effect on Mexico and the entire world."

Crystal took a sip of her drink. It was now getting late. "I am listening, Professor, but I don't believe in miracles."

"I don't want to argue about miracles at this point. There is a man sitting across the room who has his eyes on you, and I want him to think that we are on our honeymoon, so stop calling me 'Professor.' To continue only briefly with 'miracles,' let me say that at one time I did not believe in miracles, either, but I started to change when I realized that our minds are not fixed at birth—that they develop as we grow, and we have all grown up in the Scientific Age… An age that makes belief in miracles more difficult."

"I don't understand what you mean, Lucien."

"I mean to say that our minds are formed by our parents, friends and teachers, and the age in which they were born."

Crystal nodded, still with an apprehensive look on her face. "I agree that we live in a Scientific Age in which 'miracles' seem a thing of the past. Maybe I am just too scientific to believe in miracles."

"Okay," Lucien said with a smile, "maybe I am too unscientific; I'll try not to use the word 'miracle' and substitute it with something more acceptable to you instead, such as 'extraordinary.' Would you be more comfortable with that?"

"Thank you for being so understanding, Lucien."

"Then let me start with Michelangelo's statue of *David*. Would you agree that the statue was created by a miracle?"

"Of course not! It was created by a man—a human being—that used only a hammer and a chisel."

"I agree with you, but let's look at the creation of *David* in a different way. Do you remember the words of Jesus of Nazareth? 'Wherefore by their fruits you shall know them.'"

"Of course I do. Do you think that I would be here with you if I were unaware of the good works that you have done with your students, and the high esteem in which your peers hold you? Please go on."

"Thank you, Crystal. Let me go back to *David* before you inflate my ego. …Michelangelo proved the truth of 'Wherefore by their fruits you shall know them,' by achieving widespread fame through his work of art. He was able to look at a block of raw marble in a quarry, and see that a statue of a magnificent, well-proportioned, biblical young man was locked inside the block. By using his skills, Michelangelo produced a statue of such excellence that even after six hundred years, no man in the world has been able to produce a statue that matches the grandeur of *David*. People come from all over the world to Florence, Italy, to see this magnificent work of Michelangelo. Many people even say that the work is a miracle, but at least we can say that it is extraordinary.

"So when I tell you about the Virgin of Guadalupe, even if you disbelieve that she caused the conversion of nine million Aztecs to Christianity, you should be aware that twenty million people from all over the world come annually to see the beautiful and sacred Image that she, or someone, or something produced, that if not miraculous, is certainly extraordinary.

"So I will start by telling you about how the Image came into existence, and simply label its occurrence as a 'mystery,' and later you can decide for yourself whether or not it was a miracle. …The Virgin Mary first appeared on the cloak of a man named Juan Diego…"

"Wait a minute, Lucien. Do you expect me to believe that the Virgin Mary actually appeared to someone and left him an Image? I said that I don't believe in miracles."

"Thank you for straightening me out by reminding me that I am asking you to take too much for granted. But I don't want to start by having you think that I am totally gullible and uncritical. In fact, for quite some time I have wanted to learn if it would be possible to provide scientific poof of events contained in various religions. I may be even more cynical than you, so I will try to present the events as objectively as I can, and try my best to understand your point of view. Let's start by agreeing on the definition of a 'miracle.' The dictionary defines a 'miracle' as 'an event that appears unexplainable by the laws of nature and so is held to be supernatural in origin, or an act of God.' Can we at least agree on this definition?"

Crystal seemed rather unconvinced, but said that she agreed. "That sounds fair to me, Lucien. Please go on."

"…A little more than six hundred years ago, an image appeared on a cloak that belonged to an Indian named Juan Diego. The first remarkable thing about the Image is that somehow it was imprinted on a cloth made from fibers of a cactus plant. The normal life span of cactus fibers is only about twenty years, yet the cloth upon which still contains it is almost six hundred years old, and is currently in good condition, without showing any sign of age or degradation."

"Lucien, may I assume that strong efforts have been taken to preserve the Image as carefully as possible, as well as the cloth, correct?" Crystal asked politely.

"On the contrary. For most of the five hundred years, the Image has been exposed to the ambient atmosphere of Mexico City with its wild temperature swings, to cigarette smoke, to the touch of hands and kisses of thousands of visitors, without any preservation efforts at all. In fact, the Image was not even covered with glass until 1647, more than one hundred years after its first appearance. It has survived direct attempts to destroy it, such as when, in 1921, a bomb detonated directly beneath the Image with such force that it ruined the altar of the church, broke a heavy brass candelabra, bent a heavy brass crucifix, and shattered windows blocks away. Yet the Image, only inches away from the explosion, was unharmed. Not even the glass that covered the Image was broken. I know that seems hard to believe, but it is true!"

"Lucien, I won't concede that having survived those events is a miracle, but it is certainly difficult to explain."

"I will continue with my story about Juan Diego. The Image was imprinted on a cloth that was made from cactus fibers into an ordinary cloak that Juan Diego used daily to keep warm, and there is no reason to believe that it was any different from any other cloak of its time. No special efforts have been taken to preserve the cloak in any way, and although it has survived for more than five hundred years, no other cactus cloth of that time lasted beyond its normal life span of twenty years. How the cloth of Juan Diego's cloak has managed to survive is a continuing mystery. My personal belief, however, is that it's possible for God to intervene in human affairs when it suits a good purpose, and if we ever have that kind of discussion, I can back up that statement with some good authority."

"I believe you, but I don't wish to discuss that subject at this time. And I still do not feel that I have heard of anything miraculous so far."

"I understand. May I suggest that we move to that small table—the round one with the marble top that is close to the windows? Those people over there are going back upstairs." After a few words to their waiter, the couple shifted to get a better view of the fading sunset.

Lucien gestured out the window. "Crystal… As far as you can see, six hundred years ago in the time of Juan Diego, *this* was a city called Tenochtitlan. It was the religious and political capital of an extensive Aztec empire that included all of present-day Mexico and part of present-day Guatemala. Tenochtitlan was built on an island in the middle of a lake named Texcoco and was connected to the mainland by three causeways. It was a large, beautiful city that housed more than one hundred thousand people, with wide streets that were lined with marketplaces and flower stalls, and was larger than the city of London at the time. When the Spaniards first saw Tenochtitlan, they marveled at its beauty, but their real interest was gold, and they wanted to conquer the city only for the gold that they believed was stored there. Two years later, after some heavy fighting, the Spaniards were able to conquer the Aztecs."

Crystal interjected. "Lucien, how were the Spaniards able to conquer such a large territory with such a small number of soldiers, and without even being able to speak the language?"

"With a lot of luck and determination. One great stroke of such luck enabled someone to communicate with the Native inhabitants. Cortés happened to land on the Yucatán peninsula, where he picked up a former Spanish soldier who had been shipwrecked there seven years earlier and had learned to speak the Mayan language. After Cortés sailed northward, he found a woman named Malintzin, the daughter of an Aztec chieftain, who was captured earlier by the Mayans, and had learned to speak the Mayan language. Through these two people, Cortés was able to communicate with the Native inhabitants, and through his shrewdness and cunning ability, he was able to enlist the help of smaller Native tribes that resented the Aztec rule…

"Cortés was shrewd enough to exploit the shock value of his arrival. Because the Natives had never seen a horse, they thought that the Spanish soldiers on horseback were a new type of creature that they had never seen before. These strange creatures also had guns that enabled them to act like gods who could kill by using thunder and lightning, and were impossible to resist.

"Cortés was also helped by Moctezuma, the Aztec emperor. When Moctezuma first received reports of the presence of Cortés in his land, he believed Cortés to be the Aztec God Quetzalcoatl, who, in Aztec mythology, was expected to return to Mexico at some time to end the custom of human sacrifice. It was for this reason that Montezuma vacillated, and at times treated Cortés as a god, and offered the Spaniards food, shelter and gold, but at other times, Montezuma attacked the Spaniards as invading enemies. This was a significant cause of the Aztec defeat. The Spaniards were also helped by the terrible effect of smallpox that killed many Native people, since they had no natural immunity to the disease."

"Lucien, I have always wondered about that. May I make a suggestion? Let's sit on those more comfortable padded chairs over there. I am still suffering from the flight." Now onto dessert, they moved once more and ordered another round of margaritas, making small talk until Crystal continued their discussion by asking Lucien how long it had taken for Cortés to complete the conquest.

"It took two years," Lucien answered, "and it left the country in ruins. And the lives of the people had been turned upside down. The conquerors had not established their new way of life in the new country, and the old way of life had been taken away. The old religion had been abolished, but Christianity was having difficulty in establishing itself, the new civil government was dysfunctional, and the entire country was in turmoil. The new bishop that was sent to Mexico by Spain to convert the Natives to Christianity felt overwhelmed by the immensity of the task and the small number of priests available to him. He was also afraid that a new war would break out, and New Spain, as it became known, would again be drenched in blood.

"So what did the new bishop, Juan de Zumárraga, do? He did what he knew best, and prayed. He prayed for peace and the conversion of the Natives. When some time had passed with no improvement to the situation, the bishop became discouraged, and concluded that perhaps he was praying for too much and too soon. He decided to lower his expectations and pray to the Virgin Mary that he would receive only a sign that his prayers had been heard in heaven."

Lucien noted that Crystal was fidgeting and beginning to yawn. "Are you getting tired? Shall I stop talking?"

"I am tired, so would you mind if we went to bed early tonight? I had expected to hear about the Virgin of Guadalupe sooner, and not so much about the history of Mexico… But it has been interesting."

"Forgive me for getting carried away, and not noticing how tired you are. I had to make you aware of the state of Mexico before the appearance of the Virgin of Guadalupe, so that you can realize the extent of all the changes that she caused after she appeared. Only please let me add one more thing, because it is important, and I will make it very brief."

"Okay, if you promise to make it brief."

"I will. Before coming to Mexico, Bishop Zumárraga lived in Castile, an area of Spain that was known for its roses, and especially for a particular variety of Castilian Rose."

"I like roses myself, Lucien," Crystal expressed through sleepy eyes. "Normally I would be very interested, but I don't see any connection between roses in Spain and the Virgin of Guadalupe."

"The bishop himself could not have foreseen the important and prominent part that roses would play in his prayers, but you will see the importance of the roses when I finish my story. I am finished for tonight. I hope you rest well. I'm sorry if I overtired you."

They took the elevator to their floor, saying goodnight in the hallway in front of their respective rooms. Crystal was happy about being with Lucien in an exotic place and learning new things about the man with whom she felt more and more compatible with. Lucien went to bed feeling grateful to be in a place with so much history and mystery. After completing his unusual nightly prayer, he fell asleep like a contented little boy.

The following morning, after a good night's sleep, Crystal slipped through the inner door into Lucien's room, and they went together to the dining room for breakfast. The space was elegant and traditional, with white tablecloths on the round tables, set with china place settings and a bottle of bubbly water on each table. They both decided, upon Lucien's recommendation, on a typical Mexican breakfast of huevos rancheros that consisted of fried eggs and corn tortillas, covered with a hot sauce that was not excessively spicy, accenting the different flavors. Over breakfast they discussed the bright sunshine and the altitude of Mexico City and their restful sleep they had had.

After finishing their coffee, Lucien asked her how she would like to start the day.

"My original plan was to spend this day at the Palace of Fine Arts, but right now I would like to hear the rest of your story. I am sorry that I did not let you finish, but I suddenly felt tired. I would rather postpone the visit to the Fine Arts so that you can finish your story. … Lucien, this is not another legend like *Romeo and Juliet*, is it? I still don't believe in miracles.”

"I understand. Everything that I have told you, and what I am going to tell is a well-documented historical fact. The rest of the story may take a little more time than we should occupy this table, so why don't we go to the lounge to explore and sit in one of those nice chairs?”

When they were comfortably seated in the lounge on the second floor, Lucien took his cue from Crystal and gladly ushered into his story. "I left off after I told you about Bishop Zumárraga's prayers and his roses.”

Crystal was more wide-eyed this morning. The effects from the flight must have worn off and she was well dressed, taking in the sights and sounds of their new surroundings.

"Now, I must tell you about the other principal actor of this drama—an Aztec man who was one of the first to be baptized. This man was about fifty years old, and received the name of Juan Diego as his Christian name. His original name, however, was Cuauhtlatoatzin, that in the Aztec language means 'Eagle That Speaks.' This meaning has later significance, so you should take note of it, Crystal. Juan Diego took his new religion very seriously, so every Saturday and Sunday, he arose at dawn and walked nine miles from his Native village to receive religious instruction in a newly built Christian church. His usual route took him across the hill known as Tepeyac, a hill long sacred to the Aztecs, because it contained a shrine to Tonantzin—the strongest Aztec female deity. The symbol of Tonantzin was a serpent. This is another symbolism to keep in mind.

"On a Saturday morning, December 9th, 1531, something happened that changed the life of Juan Diego, as well as the lives of everyone living in Mexico at the time—and has since changed millions of lives throughout the entire world. This momentous event took place in the early morning as Juan Diego was crossing Tepeyac Hill on his way to church. In the morning mist, he heard the sound of beautiful music coming from the top of the hill, and stopped to listen.

"At this point, Crystal, I don't want to paraphrase anything. I want you to hear the exact words Juan Diego used to describe what he heard and saw, because they are so beautiful! I don't have the words memorized, but I did bring this text with me to finish the story! It is one of my favorite books, which I brought for this trip. It contains Juan Diego's words verbatim, and was written in 1548, during Juan Diego's lifetime." He started reading from a small publication that was held under his arm, entitled *Nican Mopohua*:

> "It was Saturday, not yet dawn, when he was coming in pursuit of God and his commandments. And as he drew near the little hill called Tepeyac, it was beginning to dawn. There he heard singing on the little hill, like the song of many precious birds. When their voices would stop, it was if the hill were answering them. Extremely soft and delightful, their songs exceeded those of the coyotl and the tzinitzcan and other precious songbirds.

> "Juan Diego stopped to look. He said to himself, 'By any chance am I worthy, have I deserved what I hear? Perhaps I am only dreaming it? Perhaps I'm only dozing? Where am I? Where do I find myself? Is it possible that I am in the place of our ancient ancestors our grandparents told us about, in the land of flowers, in the land of corn, of our flesh, of our sustenance, perhaps in the land of heaven?'

> "He was looking up toward the top of the hill, toward the direction from which the sun rises, where the precious heavenly song was coming from. And then, when the singing suddenly stopped, when it could no longer be

heard, he heard someone calling him from the top of the hill, someone saying to him, 'Juantzin, Juan Diegotzin.'"

"Lucien, I thought you told me that his name was Juan Diego."

"Well, Crystal, at least that tells me that you are paying attention! You are right, I did say earlier that his name was Juan Diego. But Juantzin and Diegotzin were spoken in the Nahuatl language. In Nahuatl, the diminutive is formed by adding 'tzin' to the nouns, so the Aztec diminutives for Juan and Diego become Juantzin and Diegotzin. You see, the woman's voice calling Juan Diego was using his native tongue to speak to him affectionately…

"Then he dared to go to where the voice was coming from, his heart was not disturbed and he felt extremely happy and contented, he started to climb to the top of the little hill to go see where they were calling him from. When he reached the top of the hill, he beheld a maiden standing there. She called to him to come close to her. And when he reached where she was, he was filled with admiration for the way her perfect grandeur exceeded all imagination: her clothing was shining like the sun, as if it were sending out waves of light. And the stones, the crag on which she stood, seemed to be giving out rays like precious jades, like jewels they gleamed. The Earth seemed to shine with the brilliance of a rainbow in the mist. And the mesquites, prickly pear and the other little plants that are generally there seemed like quetzal feathers. Their foliage looked like turquoise. And their trunks, their thorns, their prickles were shining like gold. She said to him, 'Listen, my son, my youngest son, Juantzin, where are you going?' And he answered her, 'My lady, my Queen, my little girl, I am going as far as your little house in Tlatelolco, to follow the things of God that are to us given, that are taught to us by our priests, those who are the images of the Lord, Our Lord.'"

Crystal interrupted, "Juantzin called the lady a 'little girl?' Wasn't that being disrespectful?"

"Not at all, Crystal. 'My little girl,' and 'My lady,' are typical signs of respect that were used by the Nahuatl speakers of the time. The use of the diminutive is really indication of the authenticity of the translation."

Crystal relaxed after hearing that.

"Then she spoke with him, she revealed her precious will; she said to him: 'Know, know for sure my dearest and youngest son, that I am truly the ever-perfect Holy Virgin who has the honor to be the Mother of the One True God for whom we all live, the Creator of people, the Lord of all around us and of what is close to us, the Lord of Heaven, the Lord of Earth. I want very much that they build my sacred little house here, in which I will show Him, I will exalt Him upon making Him manifest, I will give Him to all people in all my personal love, Him that is my compassionate gaze, Him that is my help, Him that is my salvation.

"'Because I am truly honored to be your compassionate mother, yours and that of all the people that live together in this land, and also of all the other various lineages of men; those who love me, those who cry to me, those who seek me, those who trust in me. …And to bring about what my compassionate and merciful gaze would achieve, go to the palace of the Bishop of Mexico, and tell how I have sent you, so that you may reveal to him how I very much want him to build me a house here, to erect my temple on the plain; tell him everything, all you seen and marveled at, and what you have heard.'

"Immediately, Juan Diego went straight to Mexico City, to the palace of the bishop, and told him everything that had happened to him. The bishop, of course, could not believe such a story that came from an uneducated 'savage,' or so he referred to him as, so he directed Juan Diego to come back later with stronger proof about what he had said. Juan Diego then returned to Tepeyac and met the Virgin in the same place as before. He told her of the bishop's reception.

"'He received me kindly and listened with attention, but from the way he answered me, it is as if his heart did not recognize it, he doesn't think it is true.

"'…So I beg you my Lady, my Queen, my little girl, to have one of the nobles, who are held in esteem…to have him carry your venerable word, so that he will be believed.'

"The perfect Virgin, worthy of honor and veneration, answered him: 'Listen, my youngest son, know for sure that I have no lack of servants, of messengers, to whom I can give the task of carrying out my breath, my word, so that they carry out my will, but it is necessary that you, personally, go and plead, that by your intercession, my wish, my will, become a reality. And I beg you, my youngest son, and I strictly order you, to go again tomorrow to see the bishop.'

"Juan Diego again returned to the bishop, and once again was disbelieved. According to the Bishop, something more—some other sign—was necessary if he was to believe that the Queen of Heaven was personally sending Juan Diego as a messenger. Juan Diego relayed this information to the Queen of Heaven, and she said to him:

> "'That's fine, my little son, you will come back here tomorrow so that you may take back to the bishop the sign that he has asked you for.'

"On the following day, Juan Diego's uncle was dying, so to avoid being delayed by the woman, Juan Diego took a different route instead of his normal route over Tepeyac. Nevertheless, the woman appeared to him, and asked:

> "'My youngest son, what is going on? Where are you headed?'

"Juan Diego responded, 'My uncle is very ill, and will surely die from it soon. I go quickly to call a priest to hear my uncle's confession and prepare him. Because in reality for this we were born, we who came to await the task of our death.'

"As soon as she heard Juan Diego's words, the Merciful Perfect Virgin answered him. 'Listen, put it into your heart, my youngest son, that what frightened you, what afflicted you is nothing; do not let it disturb your face, your heart. Do not fear this sickness or any other sickness, nor any sharp or hurtful thing. Am I not here, I who have the honor to be your mother? Are you not in my shadow and under my protection? Am I not the source of your joy? Are you not in the hollow of my mantle, in the crossing of my arms? Do you need anything more? Let nothing else worry you, disturb you.'

"At this time, Crystal, I want to emphasize that these last comforting words spoken by the Virgin have been taken to heart by all of Mexico, and much of the world. That is why the Virgin Mary is so revered! Diego himself was comforted by her words, and his comfort is confirmed by the *Nican Mopohua*:

> "When Juan Diego heard her words, he was greatly comforted…and begged her to send him immediately as a messenger with her sign to see the Governing Bishop, for the proof that the bishop demanded in order to believe.

> "But the Virgin Mary told Juan Diego that he was to carry her sign wrapped in the fold of his tilma, his cloak, but that he was not to open it to anyone until he was directly in front of the Bishop."

Crystal intervened, "What was the sign that she gave Juan Diego to take to the bishop?"

"If I continue reading from the *Nican Mopohua*, you would know the answer. But I don't want to give you the answer right now, because we are reaching the point where the ordinary and the miraculous intersect… and I want to be sure that you recognize that point. To separate them in your mind, I am going to ask you to think about the sign that Juan Diego was given to take to the bishop, to see if you can guess what it was. After you tell me your answer, I'll tell you if you are correct. Will you do that?"

"Lucien, I think that you haven't been on vacation long enough to have forgotten that you are an instructor who gives homework assignments. I know that this is important, and I would like for our relationship to grow on this trip, so yes, I will do my homework. Besides, I think we both need to get over the jet lag, so I plan to spend the rest of the day napping and sending postcards to my friends back home. And congratulations, Lucien! You have told me another wonderful story, even better than *Romeo and Juliet*! I would be very happy going through my life just listening to you tell me one beautiful story after another!"

"That is nice of you to say, Crystal, but this is not a legend. This is a true story!"

"Are you serious? Can somebody's cloak change the course of history?"

"I mean exactly that! One of the first accounts of the changes that took place after her appearance, is that nine million Aztecs were baptized into Christianity!"

"What made her Image so powerful? Can you tell me that much?"

"Yes, I could, but let's postpone the answer until after you have seen the Image directly, because when you first see it, you see only the figure of a woman praying. But after you have studied it, you begin to see many of the details that convey the power and mystery that was powerful enough to cause nine million pagans to become peace-loving Christians. This happened so quickly that the Spanish priests had great difficulty in performing all the baptisms that the Natives were demanding! But let's stop here for today. We're on vacation, and not pressed for time."

Lucien went to bed early that evening. Because of his tiredness, he had a vivid dream during the night. Although he could only recall some parts of it, he clearly remembered that he had carried Crystal in his arms across the threshold of some coffee shop as she told him, "I don't like this coffee shop, it's going out of business." He did not yet know the meaning of the dream.

When he awoke the following morning, after shaving and dressing, Lucien knocked on their adjoining door and asked Crystal to meet him in the dining room for the third time. The two of them had stayed at the hotel the previous day and were now getting ready to venture out. When she arrived about twenty minutes later, she ordered a continental breakfast with coffee and a croissant.

"Lucien, do you know that your homework kept me awake half the night? As tired as I was, I was trying to guess the sign that Juan Diego carried to the bishop. My first guess was that he was carrying money to build the temple she wanted. But then I realized that so much gold would be too difficult to carry, and you had said nothing about a heavy load. I must have gone through a dozen other theories until I settled on one that felt right. I finally concluded that Juan Diego had carried something of religious significance, and since the apparition had asked for a temple to be built to replace the shrine of Tonantzin, and since Tonantzin was represented by a serpent, I reasoned that when Juan Diego unfolded his tilma, a dead snake fell out! Maybe he was carrying a dead snake in his tilma as his message for the bishop? Was I right?"

"Crystal, you arrived at your conclusion by following a very well-reasoned and impressive thought process! You were correct in concluding that replacing Tonantzin was the Virgin's objective, so you had been listening carefully. But I am sorry to tell you that you were only partially correct, because your conclusion that Juan Diego was carrying a snake was wrong."

"I was wrong? I'm so sorry, I did want to impress you with my reasoning ability! I am tired of guessing, so please tell me the answer. What was he was carrying?"

"Remember that last night I told you that roses would be important? That the bishop cultivated roses in Spain?"

"Yes, I remember being peeved with your digression about roses, because I was very tired. So, Juan Diego was carrying roses in his tilma?"

"Yes, roses. When Juan Diego opened his tilma, some red roses fell at the bishop's feet! Their fragrance filled the room, as if they had been cut only a moment before. The bishop recognized the Castilian Roses that he had cultivated in Spain. He also knew that the Castilian Rose grew only in Spain and bloomed in May, yet this was Mexico in December! He was aware that the roses could not have been grown locally, and could not have remained so fresh and fragrant after a long sea voyage, had they been shipped from Spain. Finally, the Bishop came to the conclusion that the flowers before him had been sent as an answer to his prayer requesting a sign that his prayers had been heard in heaven.

"But there is more. When the bishop turned his gaze from the roses, he saw something very strange and incomprehensible! Imprinted on the tilma of Juan Diego, in full color, was a large image of a woman who was wearing a cloak with a hood that covered her head, in the style of women from Palestine in the time of Jesus of Nazareth! The woman's eyes conveyed a look of supernatural grace, kindness, compassion, lovingness and forgiveness, along with a trace of sadness. Under a long green mantle, the woman wore a full-length carnelian-colored dress with a white border on the collar and sleeves. The woman's features were neither entirely European nor Indian, but seemed a blend of both. Around her neck, she wore a tight necklace from which hung a small black cross. Most importantly, her figure was dramatically backlit by rays as if she were standing in front of the sun."

Crystal seemed dumbfounded.

"The bishop tried to rationalize what he was seeing. He thought that it somehow could have been possible to grow roses that looked and smelled like his Castilian Roses somewhere in the warmer parts of this land, that could have been brought by fast runners. The Image, however, was much more difficult to explain. He had recognized it instantly as a representation of the Virgin Mary, but unlike any version that he had ever seen. How and where could such a masterpiece have been produced in such a short time? How could it have been produced at all, since there were no artists in this land with the necessary skills? Gradually, after discarding rationalization after rationalization, the bishop came to the realization that a miracle must have occurred and was presented directly in front of his eyes. The bishop then recalled that he had asked for a sign that his prayer be heard in heaven, and now realized that there, before his eyes, was not only a response to his prayer, but a response more magnificent than he could have possibly imagined! Then the feeling came over him that he was unworthy of receiving such an incredible response. In complete humility, he fell upon his knees and prayed in silence for a long time."

At this point Lucien stopped speaking and remained motionless with his eyes closed, as if deep in prayer. Crystal said not a word for a long time, and even two Mexican men who had been conversing earlier at the bar had stopped chatting, possibly because they had been overhearing Lucien's conversation and they, too, had joined in on the silence. Even the bartender had continued polishing his glassware without saying a word.

Crystal was the one to break the silence when she said, in a subdued voice, "That is an incredible story, Lucien. If you had not told me that all you have said is factual and historically verified, I would have dismissed it as pure fiction, and poorly written fiction at that! What writer would have been willing to say that a heavenly creature had come into the world to bring, what? Some flowers and an image? Neither of those things have utilitarian value; why not bring something that had some intrinsic value or something more obviously connected to some religious value? But instead, the absurdity and improbability of the events that you have recounted are beyond my ability to rationally explain. I have to be honest with you, and I don't think that I am only being stubborn when I say that I still don't believe in miracles, but I totally admit that I can't give you a good naturalistic explanation. I admit, however, that you have brought me closer to the point of being able to believe in miracles, and I am ready to concede that the event is certainly extraordinary, particularly if you have more details for me stored somewhere in your mind or in your books. Wow, Lucien, how do you know so many details?"

Lucien's answer was somewhat oblique. He replied, "Though much is taken, much abides. I am a part of all that I have met, yet all experience is an arch wherethrough gleams that untraveled world whose margin fades forever when I move."

Crystal felt a rush of tenderness. She reacted quickly. "I know you are not a poet. You were quoting from Tennyson's *Ulysses*, weren't you?"

"Now it is my turn to be impressed. I thought art teachers were all oils, pastels and tempera, but you are obviously well versed in literature!"

Crystal smiled.

"But to give you a more direct answer, I happen to know more about the Virgin of Guadalupe than some of my other subjects, because for some time I have had an interest in events that seem incomprehensible through 'normal' thinking. I hope that sometime in the future, I will be able to learn more about those kinds of events. But I want to tell you that you are not the only person who has been unable to explain how the Image was formed. Even the highly respected historian of Mexican History, Henry B. Parkes, said, 'One may ascribe whatever origin one chooses to the picture of the Virgin of Guadalupe, but nobody has discovered any concrete evidence in support of a naturalistic interpretation,' and the first official inquiry conducted in 1666 by a group of art specialists and professional painters with much experience, examined the Image and ended their inquiry with the statement that, 'It is humanly impossible that any artist could paint or work something so beautiful, clean and well-formed on a fabric which is as rough as the tilma. There cannot be a painter as skillful as he may be, or as good as there has been, in this New Spain, who could succeed to imitate the color, nor determine if such a painting is in tempera or oil, because it appears to be both, but it is not what it appears, because only our God knows the secret of this painting.' Then a group of chemists examined the work, and concluded their report with, 'Our limited intelligence cannot account for it.'"

Lucien took a deep breath. Crystal was still more wide-eyed and energetic than before.

"Well, Crystal, I am done for this morning. Time passed very quickly and it is past Noon. All that's left is for you to see the actual Image, and we can walk from here to the Shrine. Maybe we can get a snack from one of those truck taco vendors. The fish tacos are surprisingly fresh."

"I am most anxious to see the Image now! But I have one more question for you. Why isn't the Virgin known as the Virgin of Tepeyac? Didn't she appear on Tepeyac?"

"You must have been paying attention to what I said, as she *did* appear on the Hill of Tepeyac. It is possible that the bishop may have misunderstood Juan Diego when he told the bishop her name. Some modern scholars of the Aztec language have raised that possibility. They think that the Virgin may have actually said 'Texquantaxapeuh,' which is pronounced 'Texquitalope.' *Texquitalope* sounds more like *Guadalupe*, doesn't it? And Texquitalope does have a meaning. In Nahuatl, it means, 'She who saves us from the Devourer.' Other scholars, however, think that the Virgin may have said that her name was 'Coatlaxopeuh,' which I personally believe is more likely to be the correct name. It sounds closer to Guadalupe, but more importantly, in Nahuatl it means, 'She who crushes the head of the Serpent!' And maybe it's only a coincidence, but remember that Juan Diego's name in Nahuatl means 'Eagle That Speaks.'"

Crystal cut Lucien short. "'Coatlaxopeuh' makes more sense if the purpose of the Virgin's appearance was to crush the head of the Serpent. That is, to crush the Goddess Tonantzin, whose symbol was a serpent!"

"She certainly accomplished that," Lucien agreed. "Almost everyone in Mexico today worships the Virgin of Guadalupe, and not the Serpent of Tonantzin. So, Crystal, when you concluded that Juan Diego had carried a dead snake in his tilma, the Image on his tilma symbolically said that 'the Serpent was dead.' So, in a sense, you were correct when you said Juan Diego was carrying a dead snake in his cloak!"

Crystal held a radiant, beaming smile.

"But other remarkable events took place after news of the appearance of the Virgin on Juan Diego's tilma became well known among the Native population," Lucien added. "The Aztecs interpreted the Image of the Virgin as a sign that their old religion of Tonantzin had been supplanted by a new, more powerful religion, and as a result, nine million Aztecs were converted to Christianity! The terrible war that the bishop feared did not happen, so his prayers were answered in the best way possible. We should learn to recognize the apparition of the Virgin through the good fruits that she has produced. If her works are not miraculous, I think you can at least agree that they are extraordinary!"

"Lucien, you're saying that for my benefit, aren't you?"

"Yes, but I understand your skepticism. To be told of an apparition that speaks Nahuatl, that conjured roses from Castile, that produced an image on a cactus cloth that has survived almost six hundred years and normally lasts twenty years, and converted nine million Natives to Christianity, is certainly enough to raise doubts in anyone's mind. But all that I have said is true; all are well-documented historical facts. You may decide to reserve your opinion until you see the Image yourself, in person."

"Lucien, I am so anxious to see it that I would like to go by taxi, because we can get there sooner than walking."

A Visit to the Shrine

The taxi took them to the Basilica of Our Lady of Guadalupe. When they arrived, the huge pavilion was populated by visitors from all parts of the world.

"Why so many people?" Crystal wondered.

"Because this is the world's third most visited sacred shrine. The most visited Catholic shrine in the Americas!"

They followed the crowd toward a circular building with so many entrances and exits that made it look more like a basketball stadium than a religious shrine.

"This building doesn't look very old to me."

"It isn't. It was only built about thirty or forty years ago, when the building that housed the Image—the building that you see over there—was damaged by an earthquake. Even at that time it could not accommodate all the visitors."

"Is that the original building?"

"No, not the original one, but it did house the Image from the 1700s into the 1960s."

"The older church is much closer to what I expected to see."

Lucien and Crystal became separated by the press of the large crowd. When they reunited, Crystal came close to Lucien. "Why don't you walk behind me, and put your hands on my waist so we will not get separated again?"

Lucien placed his hands at the narrow part of her waist, where her body flared into the curve of her hips, and Lucien could feel the motion of her hips as she walked. When the crowd would jostle him against her backside, he was not at all disturbed by the feeling, and sometimes found himself losing concentration on the purpose of their visit to the Shrine.

Once, when he was distracted by a bump on his right side, he looked down to see a sixty- or seventy-year-old woman walking alongside him. The woman's face was parched and as dry as a desert, her hair was in two long salt and pepper braids, and her eyes were brimming with tears. Other people were also staring at her because she was walking on her knees, and they were both bloody and torn. Lucien could tell by her expression that the tears were not from sorrow, but ones of joy and gratitude. She was holding her hands together in prayer, and that caused a little wobble that left the print of a bloody knee with each step. As the woman passed, Crystal placed her loving hand on her shoulder, as she looked up and gave Crystal a very tender look.

The pair finally reached a circular walkway that provided a clear view of the Image, which was situated above and behind the main altar of the church.

Lucien and Crystal remained motionless and silent, staring in awe. The Image showed a standing woman with numerous golden rays emanating behind her, obscuring the source of light as if she stood in front of the sun. She was wearing a pink tunic from her neck to her feet, and over the robe was a cerulean-colored mantle emblazoned with eight-pointed gold stars. The left side of her mantle was folded inside her left arm, and around her neck she wore a cloth necklace from which a small black cross was suspended. The most striking feature of the Image was the woman's face, which expressed an extreme serenity that projected understanding, compassion and love.

The entire crowd, which earlier had been chattering in every language of the world, was now reduced to total silence. Lucien again saw the woman who had been walking on her knees, and although tears still streamed down her face and neck, she now expressed the same serene look on the face of the Virgin.

Lucien and Crystal remained silent and unmoving until Crystal took Lucien's hand to signal her desire to leave. They did not speak during the entire taxi ride back to their hotel, not even when they passed close to the excavation in progress of the ancient Aztec Pyramid of the Sun.

When they arrived back at their hotel, Crystal was flushed from the day's activities. "Let's eat dinner again here in the hotel tonight. I want some time to reflect upon what I have seen. In some ways, I was as disturbed by the woman with the bloody knees as by the Virgin of Guadalupe. Both aroused very deep feelings in me."

Back in the dining room, Crystal spoke first. "I was afraid when I promised to show you all the art here in Mexico City; that upholding my end of the bargain would be much too easy. There is so much art that I could show you. I know that you would enjoy seeing the works of Tamayo and Camarena, and of course the works of Diego Rivera and Frida Kahlo. But I confess that I had no idea that I would be so moved by seeing the Virgin of Guadalupe. Now I feel that whatever I could show you would not come anywhere close to giving you the overwhelming experience that you have shown me."

"I am glad you enjoyed the Shrine, Crystal."

"I'm not sure that 'enjoyed' is the right word, especially after seeing that woman walking on her bloody knees. But as an artist, I was certainly impressed with the Image itself. Did you notice how some things about the Image are not normal?"

"Like what?"

"Did you notice how the Image looked larger than when we first looked at it, when we were farther away? That is not normal. Did you notice how it looked sharper from a distance instead of becoming sharper when we were close up? How the Image changed colors, depending upon how far away we were? How her robe appeared to be a greenish-blue from a distance, but later appeared to be a darker shade of blue when we were close up? And how her face and hands looked olive-colored from a distance, but up close they appeared grayish-white? How could the colors have remained so fresh, after more than five hundred years? Has the Image been restored or cleaned recently?"

"Not that I know of," answered Lucien. "For a long time it was not protected in any way, not even with a plain glass cover, much less bulletproof glass. The Image has been exposed, without even minimal protection, to centuries of dust, humidity, incense, perfumes, corrosive hydrocarbons from votive candles, as well as direct touching and kissing. Despite all these dangers, the Image remains unharmed. In fact, that is one of its major mysteries—how it has survived all this time without deterioration."

It was hard to tell the expression on Crystal's face as she took in Lucien's words.

"Crystal, I know that you told me earlier that you do not believe in miracles, but perhaps now you can see why the very existence of the Image is a miracle to me. Not only was its creation a miracle, but also how it has managed to survive all these years under conditions that long ago would have destroyed any other work of art. But before I get carried away talking about miracles…I would like to hear more of your artistic observations, because I lack your insights into the artistic subtleties that you saw. But I can share with you a few scientific studies about the

Image, but the studies raise more questions than they answer, and none of them explain how the Image was formed, or how it has managed to survive."

"Can you give me some examples, Lucien?"

"Yes, I can share with you some of the observations noted by serious experts. Some studies have shown that there is no paint penetration into the fibers, so the Image has definitely not been painted on the cloth. Even that first inquiry in 1666 noted that the front of the cactus cloth is silky and smooth, whereas the back surface is rough and irregular, like all cactus cloth. More recently, an ophthalmologist studied the Virgin's eyes and found that a single image in her eye is formed in three different places."

"You have lost me, Lucien; I know only a little when it comes to human anatomy, but nothing about the interior of the eye."

"I will try, but I am certainly not an eye doctor. Let's say that you look at me. When you do that, an image of me is reflected on the outer surface of your cornea, and a second image is formed on the inner surface of your cornea. Then a third image of me is formed on the surface of the lens of your eye, which is behind the iris of your eye. This is known as the Purkinje-Sanson effect that was not discovered until the 1800s."

"Nice try, Lucien, but it really has not helped me. Why are three images significant?"

"Because that means that the eyes of the Virgin represented on the tilma act exactly like a living human eye!"

"How would somebody be able to paint that?"

"I don't think they can. The Purkinje-Sanson effect was not discovered until the 1800s, so how could it have been produced in the eye of the Virgin of Guadalupe more than three centuries before this characteristic trait of the human eye was even known? As I said before, some scientific tests raise more questions than answers."

"Lucien, I hate to admit it, but you are closer to convincing me that there is something supernatural about the Image!"

"I am glad to hear you say 'supernatural,' although I would have been happier if you had said 'miraculous.' But we have both become aware of some things that are quite unexplainable."

"I hate to admit it, but I agree with you. But even if the Image is or is not miraculous, its effect on people cannot be discounted. I saw so many expressions of awe and humility in the crowd, and I have never seen such devotion anywhere! Seeing those expressions made it easier for me to believe that the Virgin *did* convert nine million Natives, although I still wonder how she managed to do that."

"Crystal, at least a partial explanation is that she managed to convert the ancient Aztecs through the symbolism contained in the Image. To the Aztecs, the rays that are shown emanating from behind her figure symbolized the rays of the sun, and because the Virgin blocked out the sun, that meant that the Virgin was more powerful than their Sun God, the most powerful God of the Aztecs. And did you see that she wore a small black cross on her necklace? The Aztecs associated the cross with the Spanish priests and the new religion they were introducing. The priests also pointed out that the features of the Virgin were a blend of European and Aztec features, which was an indication that the Virgin wanted to create a new people at peace, and not two different people at war with each other." Lucien stopped to pull out his favorite book. "She also spoke to Juan Diego, an Aztec man, in a consoling manner that was more like a blessing. Do you remember how she spoke to Juan Diego?

> "'Know for certain that I am the perfect and perpetual Virgin Mary, mother of the True God. What frightens you is nothing, do not fear any sickness nor any sharp or hurtful thing. Am I not here, I who have the honor to be your mother? Are you not in my shadow and under my

protection? Am I not the source of your joy? Are you not in the hollow of my mantle, in the crossing of my arms? Do you need anything more?'"

"Such comforting words, Lucien!" Crystal exclaimed with her eyes wide open. "Merely looking at her face made me feel like a baby cuddled in my mother's arms. No wonder that the woman walking on her knees had such a look of loving gratitude! I don't feel that it matters one bit whether the Virgin can really work miracles, or whether they are an illusion. What does it really matter as long as the woman feels better? But what about you, Lucien? Do you believe that the Virgin can cause miracles to happen?"

"To be honest with you, Crystal, I am struggling to answer that question along with the larger mystery about whether God ever intervenes in human affairs. For me, that is such an important examination that I have been thinking of not returning to teach next year, but instead taking a sabbatical to try to answer that for myself. I would really like to know whether there is a scientific basis for so-called 'miracles,' or must we rely only on faith? But I don't know where to begin right now to look for the answers."

"Do you know what I think? I think it's time that we turn in for the night. This has been an exhausting day for both of us."

"I agree. Let's get to bed early, and sleep late in the morning."

Lucien retired to his room feeling exhausted, but sleep did not come right away. His mind was troubled, wondering whether God ever interfered in human affairs; whether He allowed miracles to occur, even if they contravened the known laws of nature.

His thoughts were fixated upon the Virgin of Guadalupe, then appearances at Lourdes in France, and Fátima in Portugal—locations where many miracles are said to have occurred. He also thought about the words of Jesus, "that unless we became like children, we would not enter into the kingdom of heaven." Did that mean that we should accept His teachings with the faith of little children and not look for logical proof? He thought about the greatest miracle of all: the resurrection of Jesus of Nazareth. What greater miracle could there be than Jesus coming back from the dead? If we believe in the greatest miracle of all, then it should be easier to accept the truth of lesser miracles, such as the appearance of the Virgin and her Image, shouldn't it?

Before he fell asleep, he thought that tomorrow he would ask Crystal if she was a Christian, and if she believed in the resurrection of Jesus. If she answered "Yes," then he would point out to her that therefore she must necessarily believe in miracles. He had dreams throughout the night, and in one dream, he was walking through a field of lavender. The aroma was so real that it woke him up, and when became more fully lucid, he realized that he was not dreaming, but was actually smelling a real woman's expensive perfume. When he had turned to adjust his position, he had brushed against the magic mound of a real woman's breast. He sat up and saw Crystal's face close to his, with her naked body that was radiating the warmth of her recent shower. He took a deep breath to inhale the exciting perfume that awakened him. He pulled her face close, and as their lips touched, hers parted, and the mysterious ancient dance had begun. Mutual proclivities swelled into mutual passion. Mister Yang bowed stiffly when he was introduced into Miss Ying, who responded in a fluid curtsy. Protrusions located profundities, breaths came in quick gasps, undulating frictionless friction foamed and floundered in secret passages until passion flowed freely, and transported them gently into a peaceful, contented sleep.

When the sun rose, they slept late but awoke ill at ease with each other, having found themselves together in the same bed. Crystal quickly returned to her room, and later, when they met for breakfast, they tried to act as if nothing had had happened, albeit unsuccessfully.

Without talking about their feelings, they felt a change in their relationship, each in their own different way. After breakfast was finished, Crystal returned to her quarters to write letters until near the end of the day, when she knocked on Lucien's door to ask, "Could we go out for an early dinner tonight away from the hotel? I would like to eat some place with authentic Mexican food, and where we can hear authentic Mexican music. We could use a break from so much religious stuff, don't you think?"

Lucien agreed, and went to the front desk. He asked Alfredo, the concierge, to recommend a place that would meet Crystal's requirements.

Alfredo nodded. "Yes, I can recommend a place that has good food and good music called El Torito. It's not too far away in the Zona Rosa."

"Isn't that the Red Light District?"

"No, not the shady-type Red Light District that you might have in mind. The Zona Rosa that I am referring to is a fashionable area with many fine shops and restaurants. A place there called 'El Torito' has everything you want and there won't be any problems there." He thought for a moment before he added, "Then again…maybe there could be something to worry about. They serve a specialty drink called 'El Torito' and if you drink more than two—you might pass out and wake up later to find yourself sprawled out on the hood of some car somewhere. So be careful, but should you need any help, just call the desk and I will see to it that you make it back safely. But don't say that I didn't warn you!"

The Witch

A taxicab took them to El Torito, in a neighborhood where well-dressed people were strolling and looking into shop windows that were stocked with the latest fashions from New York, Paris and Milan.

El Torito was easy to find because of the large herd of young people standing by to enter. Crystal worked her way through the crowd and placed her name on a waiting list. She was told to wait about one hour. She returned to ask Lucien whether they should do so or leave.

Lucien inquired at the desk about the wait, but before he asked, he extended a handshake with a twenty-dollar bill in his hand. The man thanked Lucien, directed them to stand outside, and that he would call them as soon as a table became available.

Lucien discovered that Crystal had moved closer to a stairway with a sign that had a small sign reading, "ADIVINACIONES" followed by a black arrow that pointed up a set of stairs. Lucien's eyes followed the arrow, and at the top of the stairs he saw a very attractive woman with long black hair and large black eyes in her late 20s or early 30s enter her studio, moving with the lithe grace of an athlete or a dancer. Lucien thought that anyone doing divinations must be something of a witch, but he had always associated witches with ugly old hags with a warty nose, stringy gray hair and menacing gleaming eyes. But this witch looked nothing at all like that. Before she entered her studio, the woman had stared at Lucien, and her large, almond shaped eyes had transfixed him, even at that distance.

Lucien heard Crystal gleam excitedly, "She is a fortune-teller! Would you be upset if I have her tell my fortune while we're waiting for our table?"

"Crystal, why would you want to do that? You'll be wasting your money. Why do you think it is possible that a complete stranger could tell you anything meaningful? Don't you know that in Spanish, 'adivinaciones' also means 'to guess'?"

When she was halfway up the stairs she threw Lucien a winning response: "Yes, but doesn't 'adivinaciones' also have something 'divine' in it?"

Crystal slipped into the studio and did not return until shortly before they were called to their seats. Soon they entered a dining room with rustic round wooden tables covered with yellow tablecloths imprinted with an Aztec design.

Entertainment was provided by five musicians dressed in white cotton pants, loose white pullover shirts, and large brimmed white hats— the typical male dress of the state of Veracruz. They chanted solos or in harmony, accompanying themselves with four guitars and a harp. They sang from table to table, serenading the occupants with songs in two renditions. The first version was sung in its original lyrics, but their second performance was sung with lyrics that they improvised to make teasing comments tailored to the occupants of each table.

At a nearby chair, a man who sat with both hands joined was teased for holding his hands "like a homosexual." At another table, a young woman was singled out as being "the blonde with the hungry eyes." In this way the musicians interacted with their audience members and kept everyone in good spirits. That is, everyone except for Crystal, who had returned from the fortune-teller quiet and pensive. When the musicians came to their seats, they focused their attention on her. They sang the first verse of a traditional song in the correct version about a young bull, but in the improvised version, they directed a phrase to her that said, "that little bull which you have brought from a distance, lasso him or he will get away."

Instead of making Crystal laugh, the words from the song seemed to make her even more unhappy and tears even came into her eyes. As soon as the ballad was finished, she stood up and said that she wanted to leave.

The couple rode back to their hotel in silence. Crystal entered her room appearing quite agitated with Lucien following closely behind her. She turned to him quickly and in a confrontational tone of voice she blurted out, "Lucien, are you planning to marry me?"

"Of course I am! I told you so last night!"

"Last night doesn't count! After the way I threw myself at you, you would have said whatever I wanted you to say!"

Lucien hesitated unintentionally but briefly, which gave Crystal enough time for her next move. "Right now, at this moment, are you uncertain about marrying me? Are you having any doubts?"

Lucien stammered, "Crystal, you really go for the jugular. What brought this on so suddenly?"

"I'm upset, but much more upset with myself than I am with you," she started. "I feel I've made a horrible mistake in jumping to the conclusion that you had asked me to join you on this trip because you intended to propose to me. I'm beginning to see that I came to that idea on my own. I can see now that my thinking was very one-sided and wrong, because I must have been projecting my own desires on you."

Lucien shifted uncomfortably for a moment, and said nothing.

"I know we agreed to come on this trip to exchange knowledge about art and Mexican culture, but we can't deny that we've had a desire to be together in a romantic place. That must have been where I got carried away with the idea that before this trip was over, you'd propose to me. I even imagined that we might marry before we returned from Mexico! I must have been wanting to move my dream along when I jumped into bed with you. True, you did ask me to marry you, and your proposal did carry me away last night… I thank you for making me feel so special and making my dream come true, even if it only lasted for a brief moment."

Lucien could do little except listen.

"But this morning when I awoke, in the light of day, I began to see that I may have made a mistake. That the thought of marrying you was only my own, but I helped that idea become implanted in your mind. Since then I've been trying to determine whether the marriage idea would have come from you if I had not been so forward, and had let things develop naturally, on their own. Forgive me if I seem jumbled and confused, but that was my state of mind when I woke up this morning, and I'm still uncertain. When I get into this state of confusion, I try to find the answer by listening to what the Universe tells me—and I think I've gotten answers from the fortune-teller as well as the musicians—but they were not the answers I wanted to hear. That is why I am so upset, but I am really more upset with myself than with you."

"What did that witch tell you?"

"Please don't call her a witch, because that lovely woman—even without my asking or telling her anything about me or what I was thinking—without informing her about anything, she answered the exact question that was on my mind. As soon as I walked in her door, she immediately told me that the man I was with would never be my husband!"

"Are you going to believe the word of someone that you have never met before? Someone who knows nothing about you? She probably only guessed what your question might be, and when it was apparent that she had made a lucky guess, she played more things back to you, guessing at what you might want to hear! Fortune-tellers are the same everywhere; they are all con artists!"

"You are wrong, Lucien. She did not ask me anything about myself. She started talking as soon as I entered her door—and did not stop talking until I left. She told me other things about my life that I have never shared with anyone—things that I thought no one else knew. But I don't want you to ask me about those specifics, because I won't tell you. But the 'witch' as you call her, gave me a note before I left, and asked me to give it to you. I don't know what it says, I haven't read it." She quickly handed Lucien a small, folded paper.

Lucien glanced at it and remarked, "This note makes no sense to me. It doesn't say anything about either of us, so why don't you tell me exactly what she said about me that made you so upset?"

"She said that my future life did not include you, because you were not going to marry me, that you had other things to do with your life—things in which there was no place for me."

"Did she say anything specific?"

"She did not say what those things were, or if she did, I didn't pay much attention after she told me that you were not going to marry me." At this point, Crystal started to cry, so Lucien moved to console her, but she swiftly pushed him away.

"Crystal, how can you place so much faith in what a stranger has told you? She has never seen me except at a distance. How could she know anything about me?"

"I don't know the answer to that, Lucien, but she is not the only thing that has bothered me. Do you remember the musicians who sang to us before we left the restaurant?"

"Yes, I remember. What about them?"

"Their song said, 'Lasso that little bull you brought from afar, because he is getting away from you.' That's exactly what the fortune-teller told me, although not in the same words. Did you pay the musicians to sing that song to me?"

"Of course not! Now you are being even more ridiculous, letting musicians direct your life!"

"You are wrong! You gave me the same answer when I asked you a moment ago whether you wanted to marry me. You hesitated, and there would have been no hesitation had you been certain. So, I am making my final decision based on your actions, and not what anybody else has done or said. The fortune-teller and the musicians only prepared me for your answer, one that makes me very sad. For me, our vacation is ruined, so I am not staying and I will be going home tomorrow. Don't feel that you have to return with me or even take me to the airport. I can take care of myself. I am sorry to end things this way, Lucien, but I think it's for the best. Sometimes I feel that I am not in control of my own life, and that the Universe, or Fate or God, whatever you want to call it, decides what happens to me, and there is no use fighting the decision. If God wants it, maybe we will end up together, who knows?"

Crystal was trying to hold back her tears and control herself, and she could only motion to ask Lucien to leave. She locked her door on her side after he left.

Lucien awoke the next morning to discover a new note that Crystal had slipped under his door. In her handwriting the note said goodbye, that she was leaving on an early flight back to Boston, and that she was extremely sorry that things had not worked out.

After reading her message, Lucien sat on his bed for a long time thinking about what their future together might have been and how he could have handled things in a more considerate way.

After some time, Lucien had to accept that Crystal was gone;

that she was not coming back, and that he was alone. That forced him to think about what to do next.

Lucien took the small piece of folded paper that the fortune-teller had given to Crystal to give to him, and read it more carefully:

NOTA BENE

Forces roil and swirl

Past and Present realign where they meet

Myrrh emerges emboldened, Frankincense flows forever

Through the portal of the Future, Gold glistens eternally.

Boldness beckons, Integrity Intensifies, Persistence is prized

Where the sun sets vermillion in a land of little rain

A clear river gets its name, a hostile domain once nourished by fallow fields

Near great treasure now long gone, will your destination yield.

Where the Cross from the Crescent did once flee, there persistent you must be

Awake to Love and Trust and Reason in your mind

And glistening Gold your final find.

Lucien read and re-read the note several times, but could make no sense of it except that the meaning of "nota bene" was "note well" in Latin. At the same time, he thought it also sounded rather forceful and somewhat pressing. However, it did remind him of the witch, and he felt his anger rising, because he was reminded of the intrusion into their personal affairs.

Lucien felt that the woman was responsible for Crystal's departure. The more he thought about it, the angrier he became, until he decided to confront the witch in person. Face-to face, he would make her aware that her "divinations" affected other people's lives, as she had so badly affected his own. He planned to throw the note directly at her face and accuse her harshly of spreading meaningless gibberish.

At Noon, Lucien reached El Torito, and the stairs that led up to "Adivinaciones." The woman was at the top of the steps, and when she saw Lucien climb them two at a time, she quickly entered her studio. Lucien barged in without knocking and faced the woman.

Although Lucien had rehearsed the angry words he planned to use, the woman did not give him a chance to say a single one of them. She had preempted him by saying, as soon as he had walked through the door, "You are not going to become a priest!"

Lucien thought that she must have learned his personal secret intention from Crystal, but then remembered that he had never shared that thought with Crystal or anyone else.

He was momentarily dumbfounded and could not think of anything to say. The woman continued, "I said that to make you realize that I am not a 'con artist,' as you think I am. Also, I did not meddle into your girlfriend's affairs. In those instances when I can foresee something of a future, I only say what I see with the purpose of helping those who come to me for assistance. I tell them what I see, but I give no advice about what they can do afterwards, and I make it very clear that whatever decisions they make are their own responsibility. In your case…"

Lucien interrupted. "I am very impressed that you seem to know the secret thoughts of people. My notions of becoming a priest are very recent, and I have never shared that with anyone, not even Crystal. Somehow you have learned my secret thoughts without having seen me ever, or ever having talked to me. I must apologize for the things that I have said and thought about you."

"Like calling me a witch and a con artist?"

"You know that also, without ever having talked to me?"

"I saw you when you first came, at the bottom of the stairs."

"You were not even close to me!" Lucien pushed. He took a

moment to restrain himself against the edge of the door he found himself standing next to, then calmed down. "I told Crystal that you probably only listened to your clients and then repeated back to them things they wanted to hear," he continued gently with a quieter tone, "but now I believe that you must truly have some strange ability." He paused. "Please accept my sincerest apology."

"I know you are sincere. I accept your apology. Now, what may I do for you?"

"May I ask you a question?" he rushed. "You gave Crystal a note for me. Since you composed it, please tell me what it means."

"I did not 'compose' the note. I wrote the words exactly as they came through to me."

"How did you know that the message was for me?"

"That was not very difficult. That took no special powers."

"…Can you tell me what the note means?"

"That I cannot do. For very good reasons. …But I sense that you are a good man, very troubled right now, wondering what you should do with your life. Did you bring the note with you?"

Lucien's face turned red as he handed it to her. "It is all crumpled up because I had intended to throw it in your face. I apologize again."

She ignored him, taking the letter. "…Do you remember how the note was folded when your girlfriend gave it to you?"

"Yes. Vaguely. First it was folded once lengthwise, then once crosswise."

"Like the form of a cross?"

Lucien hesitated. "Yes, is that important?"

"It could be because the cross is very symbolic."

"Well… Does it have a meaning in this case?"

"That," she handed him back the slip of paper, "I cannot tell you. Because sometimes things that I say may change or distort what happens in the future. I will not be responsible for that."

"But what about the words?" Lucien pressed. "Can you tell me what the words refer to?"

"No, for that very same reason. But a much stronger reason why I cannot tell you what the words mean is because I don't even know what the note says."

"I don't understand," Lucien shook his head. "Isn't this your handwriting?"

"Yes. That's my handwriting, but I simply write things down as I hear them often without knowing or understanding what was written. I simply channel what I receive; the information comes and goes through me, but I don't retain anything."

"I don't understand how that is possible," Lucien began to have compassion for the woman, for that "witch." "Would you do me the favor of reading the note, and if you can make any comment whatsoever, that would be a big help to me. I am troubled, I feel lost at this time and I don't know what to do with my life. I am trying to decide whether I should continue to teach or whether I should be looking for something else. It would be a great help to me if you could give me even the slightest sense of direction."

"Let me see the note."

The woman read the note silently, yet said nothing. Then she looked up and stared into Lucien's eyes. Lucien looked directly into those large, dark, almond-shaped orbs, and he could see that they did no blinking. Her eyes were not focused on him, but seemed to be seeing through him, and were directed at another place or some other time. Then he witnessed tears start to form.

In a panic, Lucien asked her, "What do you see? Is it something bad? Am I *dying*?"

Lucien's voice startled her, and she shook her head as though she was returning back to the present. Immediately and in a very commanding voice, she said, "Don't dare say a word! Don't ask me a single question!" Then she paused as if trying to decide something important.

She hesitated slightly, then unbuttoned the top of her blouse and had started to reach for something between her breasts. Then, realizing what she was doing, she stopped and asked Lucien to face away from her, and after a brief moment, she asked him to turn toward her again. Lucien saw in her hands an oblong ivory pendant on a silver chain.

She handed him the pendant and chain, and spoke very firmly. "Take this pendant! Keep it always next to your skin, under your shirt. Never take it off!"

Lucien took the pendant from her that was still warm and perfumed with the natural scent from her body, which smelled of orange blossoms. When Lucien started to say something, she quickly stopped him.

"You must not say anything! You must leave this instant, before I say more than I should! Take my card, now get out of here instantly! May God bless you!" She pushed him out the door and locked it behind him.

Lucien paused outside for a moment, scared and confused. He was still unnerved when he reached the bottom of the steps, and entered El Torito to get himself a drink. He ordered their specialty, needing something quick-acting and strong. When he drank it, it immediately warmed his stomach, and his fears began to subside. He stopped thinking of the woman as a witch, but thought of her more as a prophetess or a divining woman.

His mind was full about what had happened. He felt that she would have warned him if he was in immediate danger—and had asked him to leave because she did not want to affect the future. If that was the case, maybe the future was not too bad. On the other hand, if there was nothing bad in his future, why would she have given him her pendant? Was that for his protection? Protection against what?

He decided to order another drink and consider what to do next. His first option was the easiest: stay in Mexico City and salvage what he could of his planned vacation. But without Crystal, that option didn't seem very exciting.

His next option was to return to his former teaching job—something that had even less appeal.

He even considered embarking on a treasure hunt that the Nota Bene seemed to suggest. He read the entire note again, and although it seemed less cryptic than before, it still made no sense to him.

The first stanza appeared to be a generic opening script for fortune-tellers that needed some sort of a prompt to get them started, while the next lines suggested a travelogue to ill-defined locations, ending in a treasure hunt for gold. *How ridiculous*, he scoffed. *Certainly the note had no X to mark the spot where treasure might be found!*

Enough time had passed for his second drink to take effect. He had enough good sense to realize that he was not in any condition to make proper choices. Immediately he called for a cab and arrived safely back in his room in his hotel, but fell into bed fully dressed.

As morning light fell through the window, it became clearer to Lucien that he did not want to stay any longer in Mexico City. He definitely did not want to return to teaching. While thinking about his future, he was able to recall a letter before leaving Boston—a letter that he had not yet taken the time to fully contemplate.

He opened his leather briefcase full of texts and notes. Inside was an envelope that contained a letter printed on high-quality paper, with a fancy letterhead of a company called UNITA.

The letter said that he was being considered as the recipient of a one-year fellowship, at a good salary and paid living expenses, in exchange for one year of research on any subject of his choosing. If he was interested, there was an invitation attached for an all-expenses paid personal interview in San Fransisco with George Mason, the director.

Before leaving Boston, Lucien had left the letter tucked in-between a few significant stacks of papers for safekeeping. He had not felt a strong need to make any changes in his life then. But now, re-reading the letter he had not yet replied to, he felt an excitement take charge.

Why not find out if this was a serious offer, even if it seemed too good to be true? Perhaps not replying would seriously be a mistake. *What do I have to lose?* He came to an immediate decision.

"Good morning, Mr. Gutierrez," Lucien practically flew to the front desk. "If you're not too busy, would you please help me book a flight to San Francisco?"

"Are you going to meet Ms. Wilson there? I thought that she was going back to Boston. I presume that from San Francisco you will want to go to Boston to meet her—"

"I'm afraid not, Mr. Gutierrez. We had a misunderstanding, so I have no plans after San Francisco. No flight to Boston will be necessary."

"What a shame; you two seemed a good match for each other. I hope that we did not cause her to leave because we did something wrong."

"Nothing like that happened, Mr. Gutierrez."

He nodded. "I'm glad to hear you say that. Life can be unpredictable, but you both have a lot of life ahead of you. I will be glad to help you with your flight arrangements. If you ever return to Mexico City, I hope you will stay with us again."

UNITA

When Lucien disembarked at the San Francisco airport, he followed the signs to the baggage claim for his luggage and public transportation into downtown San Francisco. As he approached the conveyor belt, he could see a tall, expensively dressed, attractive-looking woman holding a placard directed towards arriving passengers that read "L. CHRISTOPHER."

He saw two men ahead approach the woman, but she had only smiled at them and shook her head. When Lucien neared her, he confirmed, "I am Christopher."

With a smile, she looked at him and replied, "You are the fourth man claiming to be Christopher. If you're truly the man I'm looking for, tell me why you're here in San Francisco."

"I am here for an interview with Mr. Mason in an organization called UNITA."

"Congratulations, Mr. Christopher! I'm Peg Ledbetter, Mr. Mason's administrative assistant. I'm here to escort you to our office. Please claim your luggage while I call our driver."

They left the terminal in a chauffeur-driven limousine. Lucien enjoyed the trip into the city, absorbed in watching the rolling green hills and the ships and boats sailing in San Francisco Bay. When they entered the city itself, Lucien saw a movie poster advertising *Braveheart.* He pointed to a high building with the shape of a tapered cone.

Noticing where his attention was going, Ms. Ledbetter interjected his thoughts. "That's the Transamerica Pyramid, in the Financial District. Our office is near there."

"Ms. Ledbetter, what does UNITA stand for, exactly, and what kind of an organization is it?"

She answered in a teasing tone of voice. "Mr. Christopher, do you mean to tell me that you came all the way to San Francisco without knowing about who you were expecting to see?"

"I made an effort, but I couldn't find anything about your company other than its name."

"Don't feel bad. You wouldn't have been able to find much more than that on your own. We are a private, closely held company, and we don't make our finances or our business known to the public. The only Latin I know is 'E Pluribus Unum,' so I know I don't pronounce it correctly, but UNITA stands for something like 'Unum Novum Institutus Teleologicus Americanus.' If you know Latin, you'll probably know the meaning, but if you don't, Mr. Mason will tell you what you need to know."

Their limo stopped in front of a small, older building that was flanked by two newer skyscrapers. They entered the lobby, and Ms. Ledbetter went directly to a small elevator with a door she opened by placing her right thumb on a small piece of glass that looked like a camera lens. Once inside, she pushed a button to start it, but the lift had no floor level markings.

When the elevator stopped, Ms. Ledbetter crossed the hallway to another small aperture and pressed her right eye to it. That door opened, and a tall slim man dressed in an Italian silk suit was standing there. His face had the somber look of a serious businessman or a sympathetic undertaker. Ms. Ledbetter formally introduced them. "Mr. Mason, this is Mr. Christopher."

"Welcome," Mr. Mason uttered with a deep undertone, and extended his hand. He escorted Lucien into a large office with views of both Alcatraz Island and the Golden Gate Bridge. During the introductory formalities, Mr. Mason asked Lucien what he had enjoyed most about Mexico City. When Lucien responded that he had enjoyed seeing the Virgin of Guadalupe, Lucien saw a brief expression of disapproval, but it vanished quickly.

After more general conversation, the subject turned serious, and Mr. Mason asked, "So, Mr. Christopher, are you ready for a change from your teaching career?"

"Yes, sir. I have been teaching long enough to know all my lectures by heart."

"Do you have any specific research projects in mind, should you accept our offer?"

"To be honest, Mr. Mason, I don't have any specific project at this moment, and that is something that I would like to discuss further. Your letter said that you were not looking for specific research projects, yet were willing to finance a one-year study program on any subject of my own choosing. Do I understand your terms correctly?"

"Yes, you are correct. I know that an offer like that is quite rare and almost sounds too good to be true. Of course, we don't make that kind of offer to just anyone, and we have specific criteria that must be met. Frankly, we know quite a bit about you already, Mr. Christopher. You first came to our attention through your publications, and we have a copy of them all. You are a prolific researcher and are highly respected in your field. You live modestly and have a personal reputation that is beyond reproach. You are an independent thinker, the type of mind that we favor. For that reason, we believe that you are a good candidate for our program. One of the courses that you currently teach, 'Philosophy and Religion in Modern Civilization,' fits quite well with the objectives of our organization, and it impressed me, as did, 'The Enlightenment and the Founding Fathers.' You have a broad range of interests and you like to be challenged, so I understand why you might begin to feel bored, but we are confident that you have the capability to produce serious, original research. We are interested in you for that reason."

Lucien clenched his fists around the edge of the armrests of his smooth, white leather chair and stared at the man sitting in front of him. Ms. Ledbetter was standing in the corner, and was nothing more than a shadow.

"Mr. Mason…when you recited the title of my papers, I was reminded of a more compelling reason why I am looking for a change. I am being very honest with you: When I say that to some extent, I feel that I have lost my faith, and that makes me feel like a hypocrite when I teach religious subjects. I get the feeling that I am not being fair to my students. It is possible that I need some time for self-reflection, time to examine how I can relate to the world, to my life, and to God. I am being completely transparent with you, but I am worried that you will know my confused state of mind and have no further interest in me."

"You have nothing to worry about, Mr. Christopher. We welcome someone in your state of mind. That is a transitional stage that has already produced some of our best and most original work. Please understand that UNITA is a totally free think tank that does not restrict its scholars to any particular point of view or subject. Neither are you restricted geographically, so you may do research anywhere in the world. We want your mind to be completely free, which is why we don't require a synopsis of your proposed field of study or its objectives. We want your mind to be free of any and all constraints. To make it easier in that regard, we provide you with credit cards and cash draws as necessary for your expenses. We are aware of your history of modest ways—that is our assurance that you will not abuse the privileges we offer."

"Mr. Mason, I would be an idiot should I deprive myself of this opportunity. But what if I should fail to produce anything useful for you?"

"Mr. Christopher, I appreciate your frankness. You have been on our watch list for several years now, and we are not beginners at this, so we are confident that you are very capable and good for our organization. But why should you express a fear of failure? Has a difficult research project just entered your mind?"

"I have already confessed to you that I have lost faith in some of my religious beliefs," Lucien disclosed sincerely, "and I know that many other people feel that way also. Which does not surprise me, given the times in which we live. But if I should be able to strengthen their beliefs by providing them with a rational, scientific basis, wouldn't that make their faith stronger, and my own? If they lived with stronger faith, wouldn't that make this world a better place to live? I am not sounding too quixotic, am I?"

Mr. Mason smiled. "Let me put you at ease, Mr. Christopher." He pushed a button on his desk, which caused a section of the mahogany panels behind him to open, revealing a collection of several volumes bound in leather.

"What you see behind me, Mr. Christopher, is only part of our research papers on the same subject you mentioned—because it happens to be one of our most popular topics. So you may conclude that your contribution would be a welcome addition to our collection. I urge you to accept the offer we are extending to you, and I sincerely hope you will."

"But Mr. Mason, you obviously have a lot of information on the same topic. What if I duplicate what you already have? I would be wasting your time and money."

"Please don't let the topic of money concern you. With such a broad topic and with your exceptional capabilities, I am certain that you will make a useful contribution."

"In that case, may I have some access to the material that you already have?"

"I am afraid that I cannot grant you that request, Mr. Christopher. All research done for us becomes our property after we receive it. Because we want your work to be totally original and uninfluenced by work that has already been done, I cannot share this material with you."

Lucien was a bit stunned and uncomfortable. His desire for change and a new frame of mind was overriding his sense of discernment.

"I believe that we have now covered everything. I am ready to make a firm offer to you. If you accept, be assured that we gladly welcome you."

Lucien found his mouth moving quicker than his mind could fully rationalize. "Of course. I accept." After hesitation, he added, "I have only dreamed of such an opportunity, one that would give me the chance to expand my mind, that would give me time to ponder books like the *Meditations* of Descartes that I see on your desk."

"Mr. Christopher, this copy is from my personal library. As an expression of my confidence in you, please accept it with compliments and good wishes. It is yours, whether or not you decide to accept UNITA's offer, which I hereby tender to you."

"I accept right now, Mr. Mason."

"I understand your enthusiasm, but we don't want to rush you into a quick decision. Here is the written agreement which must be signed to accept our offer of employment. I prefer that you give the matter a little thought. Take this contract with you tonight, and we will meet tomorrow morning to finalize everything. Shall we say, nine o'clock? You are already acquainted with Ms. Ledbetter, who will be your primary point of contact with UNITA." He swiveled to his associate. "Ms. Ledbetter, are you available to spend some time this evening with Mr. Christopher? He may have questions that you can answer."

"It would be my pleasure to entertain Mr. Christopher," Ms.

Ledbetter moved out of the shadows and took him into her office that adjoined Mr. Mason's. Her space was smaller, but still quite ample. Her desk was delicately crafted, and the matching chairs were more elegant than Mr. Mason's solid furniture next door. A good reproduction of Monet's *Garden* was the visual centerpiece, and the color of the walls and smaller decorations complemented Monet's colors. There was a hint of lavender in the room.

She addressed Mr. Christopher directly. "Mr. Christopher, it will be my pleasure to entertain you. I regret that I can't do more than invite you to supper. I still have some work that I must submit by tomorrow morning, and I intend to use the remainder of my day to finish it. I would like to see you settle into your hotel and meet you for dinner at about eight o'clock. Will that be all right?"

"I haven't made any reservations in San Francisco. Is there any hotel that you would recommend?"

"I have taken care of that for you. I made reservations for tonight at the Ritz-Carlton, with an open departure date in case you decide to stay longer in San Francisco, if that is agreeable."

The Ritz-Carlton was a five-star hotel that lived up to its rating starting at the front door, ending with the quality of his room. In a daze, the first thing Lucien did after his luggage was delivered to his space was unpack to see whether the other business suits he brought along his journey would be presentable enough to dine in these surroundings with his new dinner date.

At 7:55, Lucien was dressed and ready in the lobby when Ms. Ledbetter made her impressive entrance, not in an austere business suit, but in an eveningwear royal blue dress, set off by a pearl necklace and matching earrings. She was very gracious and welcoming, and instantly set the mood for the evening.

"Thank you for your visit, Mr. Christopher, and for making this part of my job so pleasurable. Where would you like to dine? Do you have a preference for any of the fine restaurants in San Francisco?"

"No, I am afraid I am unfamiliar with San Francisco."

"Then I suggest that we should eat here in this hotel and keep things simple. The food is very good, and this is one of my favorites. In fact—I went ahead and made reservations for us, assuming that you would not be familiar with S.F."

The restaurant Ms. Ledbetter had chosen was expensive, furnished with white tablecloths on a small number of tables, in keeping with the fine quality of the hotel. There was a sign hanging somewhere near the entrance that reminded him of a road they'd crossed while heading to the office earlier that day, called Maiden Lane. He wondered if that street had been named to honor the maidens remaining in San Francisco.

The restaurant staff was comprised of formally dressed male waiters, and the place settings contained enough silverware and stemware sufficient for a small village. Lucien's initial worry about the cost of their meal ended when Ms. Ledbetter said that the expense of the evening was paid for by UNITA, and suggested that they start with a bottle of French champagne.

Their meal was leisurely and relaxed after they had gotten past their beginning distant, formal feelings. As they neared the end of sharing their entrees, a delicious Chateaubriand five-course meal, each plate accompanied by a varietal wine recommended by the sommelier, they began to treat each other more like old friends.

"Peg, I am very glad that you are going to be my liaison with UNITA."

It had been rather dark inside their vehicle—or perhaps it was because he was attentive to his own mind that evening—yet he could not fail to notice the way her strapless royal blue dress displayed her marvelous shoulders and bosom.

"Lucien, I have a confession to make. Part of my job is to develop a list of scholars into a list of potential candidates for a fellowship. I must confess that for some reason, I took special note of you some time ago, and I am glad that you are here in person as a candidate. If you accept, we will have to meet periodically, and I would find that enjoyable."

"Peg, that may turn out to be the best part of this fellowship, as far as I'm concerned."

"Does that mean that you are going to accept our offer?"

"I will be there in the morning, with my signed contract in hand." They were now both enjoying Napoleon Cognac. "…But I *also* have a confession to make. I know that it is getting close to eleven o'clock, and I am still on Mexico City time, so please don't think me rude if I say that I am beginning to feel tired and sleepy. May I take you home?"

"Of course. I understand. My apartment is not far away, on Telegraph Hill. The chauffeur is waiting for me, so there's no need for you to escort me. Here's my private number, so call me in the morning when you're ready to leave for your meeting at my office, so I can take you to Mr. Mason."

Lucien walked her outside to her limo, where they embraced warmly. He returned to his room with the intent of reading the contract, but tiredness overcame him upon seeing his bed. He decided to postpone the reading until morning. But the next day came too early—earlier than expected.

Lucien, slightly rumpled from not enough sleep, met with Ms. Ledbetter in the lobby of the UNITA building, where she nodded curtly and guided him to Mr. Mason's office.

Lucien looked at Mr. Mason through a haze of blurred eyes. His figure appeared out of focus. The man wasted no time but came directly to the point. "Mr. Christopher, was everything agreeable? Is there anything to discuss?"

"Everything was just fine," Lucien agreed, handing him the signed contract, which he had read on the way to the UNITA building only by skimming the printed pages.

"Glad to have you as our newest scholar, Mr. Christopher! If you'll excuse me, Ms. Ledbetter will assist you with the financial arrangements."

With a formal manner that contained nothing of the intimacy of their previous evening, Ms. Ledbetter led Lucien into her office. She handed him credit cards, a cash advance, and a peculiar closed leather box about the size of a shoebox.

"This is an international phone that you can use to call me from anywhere in the world that you might happen to be. Another part of my job is to keep track of all our scholars—so you must keep me informed periodically of your whereabouts." She piled more papers into his arms. "All your expenses should be paid with this credit card. You must call to keep me regularly informed, because if you don't call, I will have to call you." Her business-like manner did not change, even when she wished him goodbye. When she escorted him out of the UNITA building, they departed with a handshake, not an embrace.

The cold treatment from Ms. Ledbetter disturbed Lucien, and he wanted to get away from San Francisco as quickly as he could. He was left wondering whether her change of manner had been caused by his abrupt ending of their dinner; if it had something to do with his disregard of her statement that her apartment was close by, or whether there could be some other reason for the notable change in the reception he had received before and after signing the contract.

To give this question more thought, he decided to walk back to the Ritz-Carlton instead of using the UNITA limo, and to get a better impression of San Francisco. He saw that this city was complex; that it included successful, well-to-do people, many foreign visitors, but also had an underlayer of homeless and down-and-out people that looked lost.

Before he checked out of the Ritz-Carlton, he went to ask the concierge for directions to a car rental office. Instead, the clerk mentioned that he could have any type of car delivered to him, as per instructions from UNITA. "Would you like a Mercedes or a BMW?" Lucien asked for a Toyota Camry that was delivered to him at the front door, complete with road maps tucked in the glove compartment and written answers to the questions that Lucien had asked at the front desk.

For whatever reason, Lucien had no desire to remain any longer in San Francisco, and so he drove out of town heading eastward into the natural beauty of the High Sierras. He did not stop until he reached a place called Kyburz, where he quieted down for the night in a motel with a facade designed as a Swiss chalet.

Crossroads

As the sun rose above the horizon, Lucien took a walk through the pine trees that surrounded the motel. He inhaled, loving their clean scent, enjoying the whisper of the wind in the pines amid the contrast of the coming blue sky and the few remaining patches of white snow.

He felt the sense of freedom that he had been missing during his years of teaching. He basked in his happiness and felt a joy in facing the prospect of a year without lectures or classes.

He was grateful for the opportunity from UNITA and resolved to do everything necessary to fulfill his contract. At this stage, the fact that he had no particular research project in mind did not bother him, knowing that he had plenty of time to get organized. For the moment, he was enjoying his sense of liberation while surrounded by the beauty of nature.

After a time, thoughts in the background of his mind interrupted his experiences and brought back a fear that he had not felt since being pushed out of the woman's studio in Mexico City: What had the prophetess seen that she could not share? Why had she given him her pendant and told him to always wear it?

To make certain that he was still following her instructions, he took the amulet from inside his shirt and looked at it closely. The pendant was oblong, with carved figures on both of its sides. The front contained a part of the frontal figure of a naked reclining man. The reverse showed a partial posterior figure of the same man whose figure was incomplete because the pendant appeared to have been broken in half. Lucien only had the part that showed the upper portion of the man's body. The edge of the amulet near the man's head had been rounded to a smooth point, but the other end that was broken off was blunt with an irregular surface that had been worn smooth by the woman who had previously worn it.

Between the top of the man's head and the point of the pendant, there was a figure of a shield enclosing a coat of arms. Lucien did not recognize any of the symbols.

Looking for a possible connection between this strange object and the note, Lucien took the Nota Bene out of his shirt pocket and re-read it. Although he reviewed it several times, that did not help him to understand either item. He then tried analyzing the description line by line, but it was not until he reached the stanza, "Where the sun sets vermillion in a land of little rain," that something clicked for the first time.

In the deep recesses of his memory, he recalled a book by Mary Austin entitled *The Land of Little Rain*. Its setting was the country on the eastern side of the Sierra Nevada mountain range. All the moisture from the Pacific Ocean side fell entirely on the western face of the Sierras, leaving virtually no dampness on the east side of the mountains.

Lucien returned to his modest room and studied a map that he had retrieved from his rental. He soon learned that the eastern side of the Sierras—*the land of little rain*—was now called Owens Valley, which was not very far away.

Quickly recovering his sense of freedom, he checked out of his motel rather suddenly and drove eastwards on Highway 50 until he reached a smaller Highway 89. This narrower road branched off southwards to the right, and descended through the pine forests into Owens Valley.

As he dropped in elevation, he could feel his nostrils become drier, and could see the pine trees drying out and becoming less tall and more stressed. After some time, the trees finally gave way to small shrubs of dull-green sagebrush. After that, Lucien drove only through flat, dry desert, and his senses soon tired of the drab landscape. His mind soon formed the blasphemous thought that God must have exhausted his pallet of bright red, green and yellow colors, and had been forced to paint "the land of little rain" with the only remaining colors: dull grays, the faded browns, and washed-out greens. Lucien promised himself that if he ever returned to New England, with its forests of bright colors, he would appreciate them even more.

He continued driving for hours, it seemed, until he developed an urge to stop. Not necessarily in any order, he needed to relieve himself, eat breakfast, and add gasoline to his car. He checked his map and saw that there was an intersection of two highways only about twenty miles ahead. When he arrived, he was pleased to find a gas station and a restaurant appropriately named the Crossroads Café. He first filled up his car, used the men's room, washed his hands meticulously, then entered the café.

While he waited for a table he remained standing to stretch himself. He bought a pair of sunglasses to spare his eyes from the glare, and another map that hopefully covered the local area. Soon he was escorted to a seat by a woman with long red hair tied in a ponytail that swished back and forth when she walked ahead of him. She said, "Welcome to the Crossroads Café! I'm Julie and I'll be your server today. You're not from around here, are you?"

"No, I am just another person passing through."

"I had a feeling you weren't local."

Lucien responded, "I don't think there are many redheads like you around here."

She smiled. "I'm not local either; I'm originally from Canada. Are you ready for me to take your order? You should try some of our biscuits and gravy. They're our specialty." Lucien ordered ham and eggs with her recommended dish.

While he waited for his order, Lucien spread out his new map on the table. He became disappointed when he found that the map had not only very little local information, but also informed him that "the land of little rain" was actually a huge area that included parts of California, Nevada, Arizona, Colorado, Oklahoma, and sections of Texas.

He decided that if the note could not provide him with more specific information other than simply "a land of little rain," then it was useless, and perhaps he should have thrown it away in Mexico City.

When Julie returned with his meal, she saw the map spread out before Lucien. She set his loaded plate in front of him, glanced at the map, reached over Lucien and placed her finger on a particular spot on the paper and said, "You're right here!"

Lucien smiled at Julie. "Julie, I appreciate your helpfulness, but you would help me even more if you could direct me to something with lots of color, like fields of flowers or forests of bright green trees."

Julie smirked. "I know what you're feeling—you don't like the desert and you're tired of seeing so much sameness. When my husband and I get tired of all the dull colors around here, as we often do, we have to get away for a little while to feast our eyes on anything that's bright and colorful."

"Where do you go?"

She contemplated for a moment. "Our favorite spot is Yosemite Valley, particularly in the fall when the colors are simply glorious!"

"I don't want to go back to California," Lucien stated. "Is there any other place that you could recommend?"

"Well… Last month we went hiking in Utah and Arizona and

saw great colors there."

"Is that only in the fall?"

"No, silly! The colors are not in trees, the colors are in the ground! You have never seen so much color!"

"That sounds exactly like the place where I want to be right now. How far is it?"

"It's the closest place, but it'll take you about a day to get there."

"Is that the closest place with color?"

"Yeah, I'm afraid so—unless you like the colored neon signs in Las Vegas!"

"No thanks. Would you please point out the place with color that you talked about? Not Las Vegas."

Julie had been laughing slightly, and then calmed down to collect herself. "Of course. I'll be glad to do that. …The place is called the Vermillion Cliffs. To get there, drive east on that road over there."

Lucien recalled the phrase in the note that read, "Where the sun sets vermillion in a land of little rain." He told Julie that he did not want to continue south on the road to Los Angeles, nor did he want to drive westwards toward California. So when he finished his hearty meal, he drove eastward, following her directions toward the Vermillion Cliffs.

He drove past Las Vegas into Arizona on Highway 89. When he reached the Vermillion Cliffs, the drab desert had turned into a riot of color. Around him, he could see rock formations and canyons with striations of colors that ranged from deep violet to delicate pink to a scarlet red, all delighting his sense of color. Lucien silently thanked Julie for her help.

As sunset approached, the shadows grew longer. Lucien stopped the car and got out to better appreciate the vista before him. He happened to look back in the direction from which he came and saw the setting sun. The sunset was the color of vermillion.

He realized that he was standing "Where the sun sets vermillion in a land of little rain." However, he did not consider that to be very significant, because the next line referred to a "clear river" and looking around, he could not expect to see any rivers in this dry country. So he continued to drive as the sun faded and darkness fell.

For the next several hours he passed nothing of any significance until he reached a long, lighted bridge. He crossed it and continued in darkness, until there was a brightly lit commercial area called the Cameron Trading Post. All the shops were closed, but a restaurant and a motel were still open. He ate his dinner in the restaurant and stayed in the motel for the night.

After a restful night's sleep and a refreshing shower, Lucien returned to the restaurant for his breakfast. He seated himself at a table served by a lean, athletic man with strong facial features that were tanned brown by the desert sun. The man told him that he was a member of the Navajo Nation. He carried himself proudly, like a warrior.

Lucien enjoyed his meal respectfully, and while he was finishing his coffee, his thoughts started to wander to the note: "Where the sun sets vermillion in a land of little rain." The poem was already something of a treasure hunt, so he wanted to engage his server in conversation to find out more. Lucien, before thinking, very innocently but carelessly asked his server if he knew whether there was any gold in the vicinity.

The man's face was instantly converted from quiet resignation to a fiery look of contempt and anger that made it very clear to Lucien that he had made a very stupid mistake. Blood rushed to the man's face, and his voice exploded with sparks of flint and steel. "Mister, what kind of an idiotic question is that? If this barren wasteland had any gold anywhere in it, do you think your government would have settled us in it? You can be absolutely certain that if there were any poorer land, any more useless land than what we have, that is exactly where we would be! That is where your government would have forced us to live! You would be the biggest, most stupid damn fool in the world if you really expected to find gold anywhere near this place!"

Lucien made a sincere effort to apologize for his insensitive remark, but did not succeed, so he left the restaurant after leaving an overly generous tip to make himself feel better, which probably made the waiter even more angry.

He tried to calm down by walking to the end of the parking lot, onto an old bridge that ran parallel to the highway—a bridge that had once been the main vehicle crossing, but now remained only as a pedestrian walkway across the Little Colorado River Gorge. After he managed to shake himself free of his flustered feeling, he looked down at the flowing water.

The stream was bright red in color. His eye followed the water upstream, and saw that the Little Colorado River had flowed through miles of red sandstone formations, causing its waters to stain red.

Lucien knew that the word "red" in Spanish was "colorado"—and that it must have been how the Colorado River got its name.

Lucien realized that his aimless wanderings, without any conscious direction, had led him to the succession of places described by the Nota Bene. His heart jumped to think that perhaps the note was something more than meaningless gibberish. And he also realized that he could be "in a hostile domain," but where in this hostile domain could he expect to find "a hostile domain once nourished by fallow fields"? He felt that the only thing for him to do was continue driving into Phoenix, where he would try to find a more solid course for his future.

He passed through Flagstaff, Arizona, and on its south side, he saw a highway sign that indicated a scenic route to Phoenix through "Scenic Oak Creek Canyon: Sedona," twenty-five miles away. Since he was in no hurry, Lucien chose the scenic route, and drove through miles of beautiful pine forests until he reached a viewpoint that overlooked the gorge of Oak Creek Canyon. He parked his car and walked onto an edge where he could see Oak Creek deep in the canyon below him, the crisp flowing water appearing to be a white ribbon that wound its way through the deep grooves of the Earth.

The roadway dropped two thousand feet down in altitude, through a series of winding switchbacks, and he quickly arrived at the bottom of the canyon, driving along the banks of the white water rushing through rapids, making the air cool and fresh.

Refreshed by the delightful canyon, Lucien left behind the unpleasantness of the restaurant incident. But he was soon reminded of it again when he drove past a faded, barely legible, hand-painted wooden sign with the words, "Indian Gardens." The sign was at the end of a small orchard of dead apple trees that had been planted in a random pattern, not in orderly rows.

Lucien continued past the orchard until he reached Sedona, located where Oak Creek Canyon flared into a broad valley. Sedona was a small town surrounded by red sandstone cliffs, sculpted into unusual shapes, forms and patterns, by wind and rain over centuries of time.

Lucien drove through Sedona's Main Street, which had a definite western flair. He stopped at a business named the Cowboy Bar and went inside.

The pub had a timber floor with a wooden bar that ran the length of the room. He was the only customer in the place, and he sat in the middle of the bar. The only other person in the room was the bartender, who was standing at the end of the bar that was farthest from the door.

The bartender was a stocky, weather-beaten man, like someone who had spent a lot of time in the sun. His brown face contrasted sharply with the white apron that he wore, and he was stroking a large moustache turned up at the edges. He asked Lucien for his order without leaving his spot.

In a loud voice, Lucien answered, "Whiskey," because in every western movie that he had ever seen, the cowboys always ordered whiskey.

"Would you care to be more specific?" the bartender asked, moving closer and pointing to a large collection of whiskey bottles behind him.

"I'll have some of that Irish whiskey," Lucien replied, pointing to a particular bottle.

When the bartender returned, he had brought with him a bottle of Irish whiskey and two shot glasses. "This is my private whiskey, but occasionally someone that I believe has good taste comes in and orders it. Would you mind if I had a drink of it with you?" He filled both glasses. "It's a quiet night, and I know you're not a local. May I ask what brings you to Sedona?"

Lucien answered with the first thought that came into his head. "I am looking for treasure."

The bartender laughed out loud. "You are looking in the wrong place, my friend. The only treasure we have are the gorgeous views of the red rocks around here. We should be a national park so we could preserve and share them with the rest of this country!"

Lucien smiled along with the bartender and told him, "I am coming here directly from the Vermillion Cliffs, and I have already seen plenty of red rocks."

"There is no comparison, friend. The Vermillion Cliffs are a work in progress, and it is just getting started. In Sedona, God has already finished his work, and we have rock formations in the shape of cathedrals, coffee pots, drunken sailors, and just about everything else you can imagine. We even have pornographic rocks!"

"I don't believe you; that must be some trick that you play on tourists. How can rocks be pornographic?"

"I'm willing to make a bet with you that they can be. …If I can convince you that some rocks are pornographic, you buy the next round. If I don't convince you, your drink is on the house. Since I own this joint,

I'm not stealing from anyone. Are you willing to make a bet?"

"Sure, see if you can convince me."

"What direction did you come into Sedona?"

"From Flagstaff through Oak Creek Canyon."

"You probably got here too late to see it, but if you'd come in earlier, you would have seen a rock about two miles away on the left side—off to the left side of the road—that shows the silhouette of a group of people. One of them is a woman on her knees, and a male shape is standing in front of her. The woman rock has two prominent protrusions on her chest like breasts! And the man rock has a cylindrical rock that sticks out below his waist, pointed directly at the woman's head! The other four men are standing around—either looking at the couple or waiting for their turn. Is that pornographic enough for you?"

Lucien took a sip of his whiskey. "Strictly speaking, what you have described are only some inanimate rocks, and you have given your particular interpretation of them. But that interpretation is not intrinsic to the rocks. Therefore, I could argue with you that only your interpretation is pornographic, but that the rocks are not themselves intrinsically pornographic, so I should win the bet. But I know that our minds go through a process called 'intellection' that is able to turn a neutral description into something pornographic. Because I can agree that your interpretation is pornographic, you should win the bet. But why don't we say that we both won, and simply buy each other a drink?"

"That's fine with me! You sound like you must be a professor or something. What're you doing in Sedona?"

"You are correct that I was formerly a professor, but now I am only doing some traveling, enjoying the sights, and playing at being a treasure hunter. Your conversation tells me that you know this area quite well, so maybe you can help me. When I drove through Oak Creek Canyon, I saw an old sign that said 'Indian Gardens' in an orchard of some dead apple trees. Can you tell me anything about them?"

"Sure, I know the place! My grandfather was one of the first settlers around here. When he moved in, there was a patch of squash and corn and wild apple trees cultivated by the Indians, so my grandfather named it 'Indian Gardens.' The Indians that tended the place went somewhere else after he moved in. Most of the trees died, so it's somewhat fallow now, but there are a few that still yield a few good-tasting apples. Is that of any help to you?"

Lucien was mildly shocked when he realized that the bartender had fulfilled another checkpoint that described "a hostile domain once nourished by fallow fields." This made Lucien think again that perhaps the Nota Bene was more than just random words strung together to create a coincidence. Since only one step remained for him to learn his destination, he said to the bartender: "Friend, I am very glad that I stopped into your place tonight, because I have enjoyed talking to you. I have another question to ask. Is there any place around here that you would personally consider once having a great treasure?"

The bartender spoke very warmly. "I enjoyed the evening too, my friend. …You made a slow night worthwhile. Be glad to help you if I can. The only place around here where there was a great treasure is a place up the road called Jerome, Arizona. I guess you could say there was a treasure of copper there that was probably worth billions of dollars, but that's all gone now. A couple of mining men named Clark and Douglas beat you to it, a century ago. They only left a bunch of run-down buildings, but it's an interesting place. Jerome is only about a half hour's drive from here."

Lucien put his now empty glass of whiskey down and began to settle up for the night. "Thanks for the information. I think I will stay in Sedona for the night, and visit Jerome tomorrow, since it is so close."

"Thanks for your visit. Come back anytime, I will buy you a drink."

Lucien left for Jerome the following morning. He continued driving out of Sedona. Only fifteen minutes later, Lucien could vaguely see a cluster of houses on the other side of the valley, built on the edge of a mountain with steeply sloping sides. A large white "J" was painted on the rocky mountainside above the houses.

The "J" must stand for "Jerome," he thought, and continued driving until he reached a sign that read, "Jerome, founded 1886, elevation 5000 feet."

After rounding another hairpin curve, he could see a number of small, single level, well-aged residential wooden houses and a few commercial buildings. Every structure in Jerome seemed to be having difficulty trying to remain stable on the steep slopes of the barren mountain. The buildings must have been keeping themselves from sliding down the thirty-degree angle by digging their nails into the surface and hanging on for dear life. Some houses that had already lost the battle had left empty spots in the rows of houses still standing, and had slid down the side of the mountain, scattering their bleached bones down the mountainside.

While driving into what was left of the town, Lucien saw only two living inhabitants: two old women wearing plain cotton dresses that reached to their ankles, walking, carrying a tin pail in each hand—their pails contained something wrapped in corn husks. All the stores on Main Street were closed, except for one saloon named Paul and Jerry's, but he did not stop because he did not want to waste such a beautiful morning sitting in a bar.

There was no place to park except for on Main Street, and Lucien could see that no provision had been made for parking cars anywhere except there, because flat ground was at a premium. The miners must have needed to build their houses close enough to the mine entrance to be able to walk to it.

Lucien found parking in front of a two-story brick building named the Connor Hotel, which had been built in 1898. To his surprise, it was still open for business, and he entered and rang a bell on the counter.

A door opened behind the hotel's front desk and flooded the lobby with cooking odors. The clerk said there would be no problem in booking a room, so Lucien told him that he would return as soon as he had a chance to look over the town, and then exited back out onto the street.

Lucien saw some stairs leading up to the road at the next higher level on the hill, and curiously climbed them. From there he could view another building with a sign that read "Holy Family Church." The edifice was made of bricks that had once been red, but were now a faded pink.

When Lucien walked to the front door of the church, he saw someone sitting on the steps at the entrance. It was a man who was dressed entirely in black clothing, including shoes made of black goat leather. Lucien recognized them as the same type of shoe worn by his grandfather, who always said that those shoes were the only kind that did not hurt his feet. The only other piece of clothing that was not black was a white Roman collar, so Lucien knew the man was a priest.

The man was about thirty-five or forty years old, with facial features that were almost too delicate for a person. He was wearing round, old-fashioned glasses with a thin silver rim. His hair was light brown, straight and thin, parted on his right side, and combed straight across his head. The man looked as if he had only moments before stepped out of an old-fashioned, wooden-framed, sepia-toned photograph.

Lucien started to walk past him into the church, but the priest quickly stopped him. "Are you a tourist? If you are, it will cost you five cents to see the inside of the church."

"I am not exactly a tourist. I like to call myself, 'a hunter of treasures.'"

"Oh, what a coincidence! I, too, can say that I am looking for treasure! What kind of treasure are you looking for?"

"I am not exactly sure. I came to Jerome only because a man—" Lucien did not want to say "a bartender"—"in Sedona told me that there was a lot of treasure here at one time, but everything is all gone now. Is that true?"

"Yes, that is true, but sad. At one time, Jerome had one of the richest and largest known copper deposits in the world… Billions of tons of copper, and millions of ounces of gold and silver. Many miners lived and worked and died here, but now the mines are completely worked out, and the only thing left is this poor old town that you see. Perhaps you are here prospecting for some new precious metal, and planning to reopen the mines?"

"No, I am not here for that! I am not even sure what I am looking for!"

"If you don't know what you're looking for, how do you expect to find anything?"

Lucien looked around. "I know that it sounds crazy, but I came here because I was directed here to look for treasure where treasure once was found, but is now long gone. Jerome fits that description, and so I think that I am where I am supposed to be, but that is all I know. That doesn't make much sense, does it?"

"You are right, you make no sense at all!"

"But, sir, you told me that you are also looking for treasure. What do you look for? Where do you look?"

"To be honest with you, I have almost lost hope of finding anything here in Jerome. I am afraid that my time is past, and lost time is irretrievable. But if I could find someone that would continue my work, that would give me hope that I could return to Spain, to Seville."

Lucien asked, "Why Seville?"

"In a way, Seville is like Jerome. All the gold and silver that was taken out of the New World passed through Seville but very little stayed there. If I could return there, perhaps I could finish my work, something that I have always wanted to do."

As he was speaking, his hands started to shake, and soon his whole body followed suit. He made an effort to calm himself and dropped his gaze, the excitement in his voice fading into one laden with sadness. "If only I had been given more time! You see, when I was young like you, I had bigger aspirations than being merely a backwater priest. That is all that I am, and all that I will ever be. But if I look back on my life, I can plainly see that my aspirations were much too grandiose, and without a doubt, I was constantly committing the sin of pride. That must have been why God denied my aspirations. You see, my goal was to prove that the Gospels that concern the life of Jesus of Nazareth are true; that Jesus truly existed and died; that He was truly divine; that He truly resurrected. I wanted to develop a proof strong enough to make it easy for everyone to believe in Him. I wanted to do that, not by faith alone, but by using the strength of logic and reason. You can see what grandiose ideas I had when I was young!"

"Well…you certainly did not choose to do anything easy! I hope that you will not give up, and I wish you all the luck in the world!"

The priest continued in the same sad voice, "I am afraid that luck will not help me, because I have not been granted more time. I cannot finish the work to be done, so the only hope I have is to find someone to help me. There is still so much work to be done, and I am only at the beginning." As he was talking he picked up a leatherbound book lying beside him, as if to leave.

Lucien could see the book's title: *Gramática Hebrea*, meaning "Hebrew Grammar." At almost the same time, Lucien reached for the book to look at it more closely. The priest reached for it first and pulled it back abruptly. Then the priest, moving his face closer to Lucien's, stared directly into Lucien's eyes. Lucien could also see directly into the eyes of the priest, where he recognized that same faraway, unfocused look that he had observed in the eyes of the divining woman in Mexico City, when she had given him her pendant.

The priest blurted out, "I have no experience at this, but I will do what I can to help you. I can see now that you are no ordinary tourist. You may go into the church without paying."

"I am nothing special; I am only a regular person, but I thank you for the compliment, and for letting me go into the church. It is a pleasure for me to attend Mass when I can, and I would like to attend your Sunday Mass if you have it tomorrow. What time would your Mass be?"

Without thinking, the priest responded automatically. "Sunday Masses are at eight o'clock, nine-fifteen and ten-thirty." His Spanish accent had become more apparent, so his answer sounded more like "eight o'clock, nine-fisteen and ten-tharty."

Lucien walked into the church wondering why a small, deserted town would need three Masses on Sunday. Inside, he saw the beautiful, old-fashioned pews, with a statue above the altar of the child Jesus, standing alongside His mother and father. Lesser saints and angels were arrayed below them. The church was completely empty. Lucien knelt and said a few prayers, then returned outside. The priest was no longer there, although the book of Hebrew grammar still lay on the steps. Lucien opened it and saw inscribed inside the front cover, in neat old-fashioned handwriting, "Property of Fr. Juan Atucha." The book had been printed in Seville in 1922, and having an intact cover of fine leather in excellent condition, Lucien thought the book to be of value. He decided to take it for safekeeping, and return it to Fr. Atucha after the Sunday Mass.

When he returned to the Connor Hotel that night, the clerk asked whether Lucien preferred a room above the bar, or something quieter. Lucien opted for a quiet room, but even so, he did not get a good night's sleep, because there were loud noises that persisted throughout the night in the hallway.

Lucien settled into his room, spartan and austere, but not quite as bare as a room in a monastery. It had a brass bed frame, a wooden bedside table, and a wooden chest of drawers, and everything was clean. Satisfied with the room, Lucien returned to his car to retrieve his suitcase—the smaller Samsonite one that contained his toiletries and personal care items. He felt that his larger suitcase with the bulk of his clothes would be safe overnight in his trunk while staying in this small town. Back in his room, he opened it to transfer his belongings into the rickety drawers, even though he did not expect to stay long in Jerome. He removed all his socks packed in tight rolls in one corner and put them together at the edge of the chest. In another corner he placed his folded underwear, and over them, one crisp pair of pants and a neatly folded shirt. He quickly stored his separate leather bag of toiletries in the bathroom.

Soon after he laid down on the bed, propping himself up with a pillow to sift through Fr. Atucha's book.

The text was in Spanish with two columns on each page. The left-hand column was in Biblical Aramaic, and the right-hand column contained the corresponding Spanish translation. In a list of conjugated Aramaic verbs in the Appendix, Lucien found a loose paper with some handwriting. The cursive matched the inscription on the inside of the front cover, so Lucien knew that the writing belonged to Fr. Atucha.

The loose sheet at the back was also written in an organized fashion, with the same two columns. The left-hand side was in Aramaic, and on the right-hand side was the Lord's Prayer in Spanish. Below the prayer, Fr. Atucha had written:

Greetings, my brother!

Open the door, enter and close it. My soul has long been sojourning, and

I may never see your face again. Amen.

…and that other disciple did outrun Peter and came first to the sepulcher.

And when he stooped down, he saw the linen <u>cloths</u> lying: yet he went not

in. Then cometh Simon Peter, following him, and went into the sepulcher:

and saw the linen clothes lying. John. And the <u>napkin</u> that had been about

his head, not lying with the linen <u>cloths</u>, but apart, wrapped up into one

place. John 20:4-7.

Then that other disciple also went in, who came first to the sepulcher, and

he saw and believed. John 20:8

Near the bottom of the page, the priest had written the word "napkin" in English, and next to it, its Spanish translation, "SER̶VILLE̶T̶Ā̶" in capital letters; the letters R, T, and A had been crossed out with a line drawn through each of them. The remaining word spelled: "SEVILLE."

From his prior studies, Lucien knew well that the biblical citations were references to the third day after the Crucifixion of Jesus of Nazareth, when the disciples Peter and John had gone to the tomb of Jesus and found it empty. He also knew that one "linen cloth" referred to the cloth that Joseph of Arimathea had provided as the burial shroud of Jesus. But Lucien did wonder why the words "cloths" had been underlined. Was the priest trying to emphasize that "cloths" were plural, thus more than one burial cloth?

The word "napkin" was also underlined. Was that designed to give special emphasis to the napkin? That made Lucien wonder why he had never placed any importance on the word "napkin" before, but now he noted that the "napkin" had been "about the head" of Jesus. Was the napkin the reason why the words "cloths" were always underlined in the plural form? Was "napkin" mentioned elsewhere in the Bible?

From his previous studies, Lucien understood that the burial shroud of Jesus had been known at various times and various places as the "Sindone of Edessa" and the "Mandylion of Edessa," and was presently known as the "Shroud of Turin." But why did the priest underline the word "napkin"? Did it still exist? If it no longer existed, what happened to it?

Lucien could not answer the questions he was posing to himself, so he decided that he would ask the priest for answers after he would see him the next day.

Lucien awoke earlier than usual because his sleep had been so disturbed during the night. He decided to attend the first Mass at eight o'clock, instead of the later one at ten-thirty.

He arrived at the church a few minutes before the sermon was set to begin, but found only an empty church, empty of parishioners, without a priest.

Still expecting Fr. Atucha to arrive, Lucien waited outside on the church steps.

A few minutes later, an old model black Chevrolet drove past the front of the church and parked nearby. Three older men left the car and started towards the church entrance. One of them said, "Can you believe that it's been another year?"

Another man answered, "Every year seems to go by faster, doesn't it?"

A third man asked, "How many years has it been now, Andy?"

"About twenty years by my count," Andy replied.

When the men were close, Lucien asked them if they knew Fr. Atucha.

Andy answered, "We should know him! All of us have served him as altar boys for a combined total of thirty years! We still get together once a year to pay him a visit, and we're on our way now to see him after we say a few prayers."

Lucien first assumed that these men were the first parishioners to arrive for the Mass, but they stayed inside the church for only a short time. They started to pass Lucien by completely, but the last person—the one named Andy—said, "Are you still here? Are you waiting for someone?"

"I would like to see Fr. Atucha."

"Well, you're wasting your time here because he's not comin' back. We're on our way now to see him in Clarkdale at the bottom of the hill. Do you have a car?"

"Yes, I do."

"You can drive yourself, I'm sure, but you might have difficulty if you don't know the roads around here really well and you don't know where to find him. If you'd like you can come join us—and we'll bring you back here when we're all finished. We have to come back this way anyway, so there's no problem. You can ride in the back seat with me. We have plenty of room."

Lucien realized that he could have been mistaken by realizing that he had assumed, without thinking, that the Mass was going to be in this church. Apparently it was being held in some other church. He accepted Andy's offer and sat in the back seat with him.

They headed down the mountain. Andy asked Lucien how well he knew Fr. Atucha, and Lucien told him that he had only met him once. After that, the men ignored Lucien and started to reminisce among themselves about their time as altar servers. From their conversation, Lucien learned that Fr. Atucha was a scholarly priest that knew the Bible in Latin, Greek and Aramaic, and that he was a good teacher, but also a strict disciplinarian that did not tolerate mistakes or half-hearted efforts.

During a temporary lull in the conversation, Andy filled it by asking, "Have I ever told you guys my favorite story about Fr. Atucha?"

The other two men immediately responded rather in unison, "Yes, Andy, about a thousand times!"

He continued anyway. "…Well, you're going to hear it again, because our new friend here has never heard it. You two just be quiet while I tell him." And Andy began to tell his story.

"…One year when the weather was very cold, Fr. Atucha staged a Christmas play for the church. He was the narrator of the play, speaking from the altar behind a lectern. The church was packed for the occasion. At one point in the play—for dramatic effect—the lights of the church were turned off, and the only light in the church was a small penlight that Fr. Atucha was using to see the script that he was reading for the congregation. I played the part of an angel, and waited in a small room next to the altar. I was supposed to enter with a lit candle in my hands at the time that I heard Fr. Atucha say, '…and the angel illuminated the night!' Everything had gone well, up to the point that I first heard Fr. Atucha say, '…and the angel illuminated the night.' But I did not enter. Then Fr. Atucha repeated the words a little louder, but I still did not appear. He repeated the line a third time, in a much louder voice. I could hear a touch of anger in his voice, and I panicked and entered the altar space with a candle in my hands, but it was unlit, and the church remained dark. Then I blurted out the truth: '…AND THE CAT PEED ON THE MATCHES!'"

All the men in the car, including Lucien, burst out laughing, even though the others had heard the story before. When the laughter died down Andy added, "It took a long time for the congregation to stop laughing, too, and I've never been able to live that down! But I told the truth; what else could I have said?"

As Andy was finishing his story, Lucien noticed that their car was turning into a cemetery. He did not think anything was amiss, assuming that perhaps due to some emergency, Fr. Atucha had been called to perform a graveside ceremony. He looked around, trying to locate a group of people around an open grave, but could see nothing of the kind. Then the car stopped and all the men got out, gathering around a particular grave with an upright granite headstone. Lucien moved forward and read the inscription on the tombstone:

Fr. Juan Atucha: Born Seville, Spain, November 23, 1901;
Died, December 15, 1979.

Above the inscription, set into the stone, was an oval photograph showing a man dressed in black with a Roman collar, wearing round glasses. The facial features were unmistakably those of the man that Lucien had been speaking to only the day before.

Lucien was shocked to learn that Fr. Atucha had been dead for almost twenty years! He was taken aback by the fact that only yesterday must he have been speaking to a ghost; an apparition!

Because he did not want anyone to think he was crazy, he said absolutely nothing to the altar boys about having spoken to Fr. Atucha the day before. He also said nothing about the book he was carrying. He remained very somber and quiet on their trip back to Jerome. He thanked the men and shook hands with them when they left him at the Connor Hotel.

Lucien slipped up to his room in an emotional and mental turmoil. He had to make some sense of his experience. *Were ghosts real? Could they communicate? What is reality? What is illusory? How to distinguish between ghosts and real people?*

To retain his mental equilibrium, Lucien applied himself to making a list of concrete facts and using them to make decisions. He began with the fact that he was in Jerome, Arizona.

Question: *How did I get here?*

He answered himself: *I got here because I followed a note that somehow laid out a path that brought me here.*

Question: *Who laid out the path in the note?*

Answer: *A divining woman.*

Question: *How did the divining woman predict your path? Was your path predetermined?*

Answer: *I don't know.*

Question: *Do you believe in predestination?*

Answer: *I haven't made up my mind on this question, but in one of the last books I read,* Gandhi's Truth, *Ghandi said that "it would not be improper to say that 'the Spirit' had directed the greatest steps in his life."*

Question: *Did you really follow the note?*

Answer: *No, I was wandering aimlessly.*

Question: *If you were wandering aimlessly, what brought you to Jerome?*

Answer: *I don't know.*

Question: *Could it have been predestination that brought you to Jerome?*

Answer: *I don't know.*

Question: *What was the note's purpose in bringing you to Jerome?*

Answer: *To learn my destination.*

Question: *Have you learned your destination?*

Answer: *Yes; Seville.*

Question: *How did you learn your destination?*

Answer: *From a book I took from a ghost.*

Question: *Do you believe in ghosts?*

Answer: *I don't know if I do or not. This is my first ghost.*

Question: *Was the ghost real?*

Answer: *I don't know. The man* looked *real.*

Question: *Is the book real?*

Answer: *Yes, it is there on the table.*

Question: *Are you going to Seville?*

Answer: *I don't know.*

More questions without answers kept swirling in Lucien's mind, so he gave up trying to answer them all, and attempted to fall asleep.

As was his custom, he said a few prayers at bedtime before settling into bed. He recited a prayer by Thomas Merton that he knew by heart, that he had personalized for himself:

"My Lord God, I have no idea where I am going; I
cannot see the road ahead of me, I cannot know for
certain where it will end. Nor do I really know myself,
and the fact that I think that I am following your will does
not mean that I am actually doing so. But I believe that
the desire to do your will does in fact please you. I hope
I have that desire in all that I am doing. I hope that I will
never do anything apart from that desire. And I know that
if I do this, you will lead me down the right road though I
may know nothing about it. Therefore, I will always trust
you, and though I may seem lost and in the valley of the
shadow of death, I will not fear, for you are ever with me
and will never leave me to face my perils alone."

Another one of his usual bedtime prayers was the Lord's Prayer, which he normally recited to himself in English, but tonight he chose to say the prayer in Latin. He stopped himself when he came to the words "… fiat voluntas tua…" and for the first time in his life, he achieved a clearer understanding of the meaning of the phrase, "Thy will be done." Lucien had always interpreted the line as "God will be done," but the Latin had made the English meaning of the line very clear: The meaning was not "God will be done," but instead it was "God's will" that was to be done.

His understanding of that line made things clearer for Lucien.

God's will was unchangeable, but the course of worldly events was not predestined, because Lucien had been given a choice: the choice of whether or not to act with the desire to do God's will. The degree of his desire to conform with God's will was an important factor in the determination of the course of events in his life.

The turmoil in Lucien's mind ceased immediately after he reconciled the prayers of Thomas Merton and Saint Francis. He knew that his life was at a crossroads, but nevertheless, he decided to proceed to Seville. When he firmly made the decision, he had no difficulty falling asleep in spite of the persistent loud noises in the hallway.

Lucien checked out of the hotel. He told the clerk that he was surprised that the hotel was so busy last night.

With a puzzled look, the clerk made a comment. "Mr. Christopher, you were our only guest here last night."

"…Are you telling me that there are ghosts in this hotel?"

"We don't publicize it, but there are ghosts everywhere in this town. We don't think it's necessary to warn anyone, because not everyone can see or hear them."

"Well…I heard voices and footsteps last night, and I saw a ghost yesterday at the old Catholic church."

"What did he look like?"

When Lucien described the priest, the clerk said with conviction, "That's Fr. Atucha. He died an unhappy man because he felt that he had not fulfilled his life's work. But before he died, he was searching for someone to help him accomplish something he was trying to do. But he wasn't able to find anyone."

Later, Lucien went back to the church and said a prayer for Fr. Atucha, and his words, "I can see that you are no ordinary tourist," stayed with him, as well as the strange look in the eyes of the priest—the same look within the eyes of the divining woman in Mexico City.

Juan Belmonte

Lucien arrived in Seville mid-morning and checked into a small hotel in the El Arenal section of the city.

The hotel he chose was old and matched its surrounding neighborhood, on a street that had once been one of the principal avenues in the days when Seville was the main port for receiving all the treasures coming from Mexico and Latin America.

His room was small but adequate; quiet, but comfortable and reasonable. The light was limited yet sufficient, and came through a window connected to an inside central shaft. There were several small restaurants with outdoor eating areas within walking distance that filled with families clear into the late evening, which informed Lucien that he was in a safe neighborhood.

He laid himself on the bed only to test the mattress, but that test resulted in a two-hour nap, although that was no bother to him because he was not on any schedule. He had learned to trust and relax more, because he had the feeling that he need not search; that sooner or later, if something was supposed to happen, it would.

He awoke from his nap feeling refreshed, and decided to explore Seville as a tourist.

Downstairs, he picked up several brochures of the "Must See

in Seville" type. He noticed that the bullring—the "Maestranza"—was considered an important attraction in all the pamphlets. Although Lucien had no special interest in bullfighting and knew that this was not the season for it, he chose the Maestranza as his first introduction to Seville and Spain. He inquired at the front desk and was told that the bullring was within walking distance, and that the best way to learn about the bullring and bullfighting was to hire a tour guide at the ring.

Lucien had no problem finding the bullring for it was a large, circular Baroque structure painted yellow and ochre, large enough to seat more than twelve thousand people. He bought a ticket and inquired about hiring a tour guide, and was told that he should make direct arrangements with one of the numerous tour guides inside.

The outside corridor of the ring enclosed an inner ring where the actual bullfighting took place. In the passageway between the rings, Lucien met a female tour guide surrounded by a group of about twenty people whose different clothing and languages identified them as tourists from different countries. This tour guide was a good-looking woman who wore a black jacket that matched tight-fitting black pants. Lucien moved to join her group, but she had already started on her prepared lecture by saying, "This is the world-famous bullring of Seville, known as the 'Maestranza.' Its construction started in 1761 and was completed in 1765. It is the finest and most famous bullrings in the world." She said this first in English, then repeated her phrases in German, French and Spanish. When she noticed Lucien, she told him to wait for the next tour, because that one was already filled to the limit.

Lucien found a place to sit down. On a long stone bench that ran along the inner wall of the corridor, he noticed that the corridor was cool and restful; although the lighting was somewhat dim, because the ambient light came from small windows placed high on the wall.

An older man came walking down the corridor. He sat down near Lucien at a reasonable distance, close enough to speak comfortably.

At first glance the man appeared to be well dressed, but when Lucien looked more closely, he picked out various details that did not seem quite right.

The man wore a vest, but no one wore a vest these days. His coat lapels were too wide, the collars of his shirt were too long, and the color of his pants was a shade off.

The man started an impromptu conversation, saying, "That would never happen in my time," with an arm gesture that indicated the multilingual woman tour guide.

Not wanting to be rude, as the man was clearly talking somewhat purposefully in his direction, Lucien responded in Spanish, "What do you mean, sir?"

The man had been waiting to speak. At first, he spoke heavily in Spanish until he heard Lucien's accent, whereupon he switched quickly to English. "I mean, the tour guide. A young, good-looking woman wearing pants like a man, showing her ass to the world. That would have never happened in my time. In those days, there were no women tour guides, and certainly no women dressed as shamelessly as that!"

"Are you a tour guide, sir?"

"Not exactly. But if I were, I would be one of the best! I specialize in communication, and I knew many bullfighters in the time when they were truly brave, not just flashy performers playing at being bullfighters."

"…Sir, I came to see this ring not expecting to see anything other than an empty arena. …But what you say interests me. Do you mean that bullfighters have changed since your time?"

The strange man spoke loudly. "Don Gabriel, sir," he introduced himself and stuck out a hand to shake Lucien's, whereupon they exchanged a firm handshake. "If you wish to understand what these guides can teach you about this ring, then wait for the next tour. But I'm afraid you will learn nothing much about bullfighting. That would be like trying to learn something about women in general by listening to a female tour guide!"

Lucien hesitated. "How did you learn about bullfighting? Were you a bullfighter yourself?" After this question, the man shifted close enough to Lucien that he could make out his eyes and facial features. His overall appearance held a kind aspect about him. His eyes were a darker shade; Lucien could not categorize them as exactly black or brown, only that they gave him the impression that they saw everything.

Lucien's new acquaintance waited until the now oncoming crowd of tourists rounded the bend of the circular ring, leaving the two of them alone. A distant murmur of the cluster of people could be heard off in the distance.

"Good question!" the gentleman continued with a smile and raised voice. "I was never a bullfighter myself, but my specialty is communication, so I was very much in demand around a good number of bullfighters, and I became friends with some. As for a few others, I got to know them quite well. One of my best friends was arguably the greatest bullfighter who ever lived. His name was Juan Belmonte. Have you ever heard of him?"

"No, I am afraid not."

"That's understandable," he quipped, "because he lived before your time. But no matter how many generations have passed or will pass, there will never be another like him. I was able to know him well because he was the kind of man that was closest to God while he was fighting. —You said that you wanted to learn something about bullfighting. Well, let me tell you about Juan Belmonte, then, and the qualities that a bullfighter must have to succeed. Those qualities are what Belmonte developed to a higher degree than anyone."

"Mr. Gabriel," Lucien began to say, then quickly corrected himself. "Don Gabriel," he said, "I am very aware that I could never be a bullfighter. But I am interested in what you have to say because bullfighting is so closely associated with Spain. In addition to that, I am even more interested in what you said about Juan Belmonte—that he was closest to God when he was fighting. I would have expected you to say that he was closest to death when he was fighting. I would be honored to hear what you have to say."

"Thank you; I'm glad to find someone who's truly interested, so I would be happy to share what I know," and without any hesitation, he continued freely, much to Lucien's interest. "There are two qualities that a good bullfighter must have: perseverance and courage. By courage I mean fearlessness—and by fearlessness, I mean having no fear of death; having no fear of your own death. To tell you about Juan Belmonte I have to start with his life as a child, as he was forced to develop the qualities of a bullfighter quite early. Do you have the time and inclination to hear more of what I have to say?"

Lucien, out of habit, reflexively looked at his wrist to mark the time, but quickly recalled that he wasn't on any particular schedule, so he could spend whatever time he wanted to listen to Don Gabriel. The stone bench felt cool, and he was very comfortable in the quiet surroundings. "I have whatever time you need, Don Gabriel, but before you continue, please allow me to introduce myself to you, too. My name is Lucien Christopher."

The man smiled and leaned in so the two of them could shake hands once more. "I am Don Gabriel De Los Arcos. My surname translates as 'Of the Arches,' or 'Of the Arcs.'"

"Do you mean like in Joan of Arc?"

"*Preciso*; exactly! But I think a surname that has three characters is a bit pretentious, so just call me Don Gabriel." By the way he was emphasizing "Don," Lucien knew that he was accustomed to being treated with respect and courtesy.

After some more courtesies the man asked Lucien, "Do I know you? You look somewhat familiar. Have we met before?"

"No, I don't think so. This is my first time in Spain, and I arrived only yesterday. My full name is Lucien Christopher, but please call me Lucien. I am a teacher."

The man's dark eyes lit up. "In one sense, I, too, consider myself a teacher, Lucien, but because I only pass on information, I think of myself as more of a communicator. I can't teach you how to become a good bullfighter, but when it comes to those good qualities a bullfighter must have to succeed, I really can't give you a better example than Juan Belmonte."

"Please forgive me, Don Gabriel; I am sorry to interrupt you, but I must ask you to treat me as your beginner pupil. If you could give me a little background information on him, I think that I would learn better. What made you hold him in such high esteem?"

"For two reasons, Mr. Christopher. The first reason is that in his time—that is, in the nineteen-twenties of this century—he was the best bullfighter in Spain, and that made him the best in the world. The more important reason is that he achieved all his accomplishments in spite of the physical handicaps that would have made his choice of profession extremely difficult, if not impossible. No reasonable person would have advised him to try bullfighting!"

"Did Juan Belmonte fight in this ring? Did he die in this ring?"

"No, he didn't die in this ring; but here, he was closer to death in his art of bullfighting without dying than any bullfighter before him… and possibly any bullfighter after him!"

"As a good teacher, Don Gabriel, you have certainly aroused my interest, and so you have my complete attention. So please, continue."

At this point, another crowd of tourists surrounded them, so Don Gabriel took Lucien from the inner corridor into the actual arena. He seemed to have some sort of backdoor access, and Lucien was enthralled to follow him for what felt like a rather secret tour. This was not the bullfighting season, so when they stepped out into the bright sunlight, the stadium was empty of spectators and the sand of the ring was undisturbed. They did not stay long, and they spent it mostly in silence. As they returned to the corridor, Lucien saw Don Gabriel wipe a tear from his eye.

When they reclaimed their previous spot, Don Gabriel continued where he left off. "…Juan Belmonte was born a cripple, and could not even walk until he was four years old. He was not even able to run until after he was six. And even after that, his run was always very awkward. His mobility problem remained throughout his life, including during the prime of his career as the world's best bullfighter. Because he did not have the mobility to avoid the bull's charge, he was forced to develop a new style of bullfighting and learned to plant his feet and body fixed in one spot, without moving, even when the bull charged. He was able to avoid the bull's deadly charge only by using the graceful and artistic movements of his cape, without moving his feet. Although that may seem like a simple thing, it's anything but that. Think of trying to avoid a wild animal that weighs more than one thousand pounds, that can come rushing directly at you faster that a horse, that is trying to impale you with horns as sharp as daggers that are controlled by neck muscles strong enough to lift a horse and its rider. Think of confronting this beast while being physically unable to move out of harm's way, your only hope of survival being your ability to control a piece of cloth in such a way that its movement would be enough to distract the bull for only the fraction of time necessary to make the horns miss your body—close enough to spare you, but close enough to tear the cloth of your jacket. That is the stuff of nightmares, isn't it? Yet this must be done with your mind completely focused, and the movements of your body and your cape must be accomplished with grace and flair. Above all, you must show no fear. This type of confrontation you must endure, not only one time, but repeatedly during the course of a single fight. Can you imagine the persistence of Juan Belmonte? It took him years to learn his craft; to learn how to develop the courage necessary to keep his fear at the highest possible level of complete control."

Much time had passed in their conversation, and more and more people were wandering through the corridor. With the acceptance of his newfound friend, Lucien took a mild break and stopped at a vendor nearby who was selling lemonade and juices, and within the sounds and echoes of the noisy crowd, Lucien bought a drink for himself and Don Gabriel.

"I hope I'm not overtiring you!" Don Gabriel smiled. As he accepted the drink gratefully, his joy was shown clearly on his face.

"Please go on, Don Gabriel. Your insight is tremendous!"

Don Gabriel beamed. "Undoubtedly, development of the persistence and courage that Juan Belmonte possessed can prove useful in many ways, not only in bullfighting. But Belmonte had other qualities that are difficult to explain and understand. All I can tell you is that Juan Belmonte's faith was strong enough that he believed in miracles; the works of God. His victories, which all involved close confrontations with death, Juan labeled as 'miracles' because he could never explain how he had survived them. As an example, think about the most critical part of a bullfight known as 'The Moment of Truth.' That is the moment when both the bullfighter and the bull are closest to Death. That is the moment when the entire arena, holding twenty thousand people, is so quiet that you can hear a hat drop. At that moment, Juan Belmonte's body was exposed during the time that the horns were passing under him; the time that was his only opportunity to thrust his sword directly between the bull's shoulder blades into the bull's heart. At that point, Juan's death was as close as a twitch of the bull's neck muscles, that would drive the razor-sharp horn into Juan's abdomen or femoral artery. At this critical point, who or what determined the outcome? Juan himself could never explain why it was that he survived and it was the bull that had died. This was the miracle that he could never explain."

Don Gabriel's use of the word "miracle" set off a chain reaction in Lucien's consciousness. It allowed him to recall his previous concerns and doubts about whether miracles did sometimes happen, and whether God ever intervened in the world. He remembered his dream about the Aztec priest performing a human sacrifice, all the way through to the appearance of the Image of Mary on the cloak of Juan Diego. Could it be possible that God did intervene in not only human affairs, but also individual instances within people's lives, and major human affairs?

Don Gabriel must have noticed Lucien's mental distraction and paused for a moment before carrying on. "I personally observed that when he had finished his prayers in the chapel to the Virgin of La Macarena and left to enter the bullring, he was totally composed. I believe that he could only achieve that level of composure because he could accept that whether he lived or died was a matter that was completely in God's hands. His faith and belief were so complete and so strong that although he had, at that moment, already surrendered himself to his death, he also felt that whatever should happen would be God's choice. He was able to look at me with a very composed expression on his face and say very calmly, to me and to himself, 'Será suficiente.'"

Lucien was at first puzzled by Don Gabriel's words, but then felt comforted by them.

"Lucien, you know the translation of those words, don't you? 'It will be sufficient.' Those words are something else with a meaning you may have to decide about for yourself, because I never asked Belmonte exactly what he meant by them. There you have it, Mr. Christopher; I've told you about the necessary qualities of a good bullfighter, which are the necessary qualities to face whatever fate may bring to you. But I would like to give you some parting advice. The best bullfighters and flamenco dancers in all of Spain's history have, for some reason, come from the Triana District of Seville, so I recommend that you visit it."

The two men rose from their seats. Lucien started to extend his right hand for another handshake, but Don Gabriel gave him a warm embrace instead. Lucien added, "I have enjoyed spending time with you."

"It was a pleasure for me, also. But I must leave you now, to go on with my work. I am certain we will meet again." Soon after, the man disappeared as he was swallowed into another group of tourists.

Lucien exited the Maestranza and ventured back to his hotel, intrigued by what he had discovered about Juan Belmonte. He knew that he had learned something more important than Belmonte's courage and persistence in facing bulls—he had learned something about confronting Death.

The following morning, waking with the desire to learn more about Juan Belmonte, Lucien traveled to the University of Seville, which was a short walk away, in the old Royal Tobacco Factory that had been the setting of Bizet's opera, *Carmen*. At the library's desk he asked for information about Juan Belmonte.

"Are you an enrolled student?" the librarian asked, raising her head from looking down at some texts in front of her. She asked the question in English, with a charming Spanish accent. "If you are not, you cannot check out any material."

"I am not a student; I am a professor from a university in the United States. I only want to review what you have, but I won't take anything out of the library."

After a brief time, the woman returned with one manila folder entitled *Juan Belmonte and D.T. Suzuki*. She handed the enclosed stack of weighted papers to Lucien. "Normally we have twenty files about Juan Belmonte. But they are all checked out except for this one, so some class must be requiring an assignment on Belmonte. If this does not help you, sir, come back in a week or two, and we will have much more information for you."

The folder contained an old magazine and several yellow pages of handwritten notes copied from the works of D. T. Suzuki. The papers had either been left in the file by mistake, or were forgotten by someone who had seen a connection between bullfighting and Japanese swordsmanship.

Lucien was pleasantly surprised to uncover a connection between Juan Belmonte and D. T. Suzuki, a highly respected Japanese scholar with expert knowledge of Mahayana Buddhism, Zen, and Sanskrit literature.

Lucien asked himself: *What could a bullfighter and a Japanese swordsman have in common?* His question was rapidly answered by the first page of the handwritten notes, which began with a quotation from Suzuki: "Bullfighting is evidently very much like the Japanese art of swordplay." That line was followed by a comparison of Belmonte's state of mind during a bullfight, and the mindset of one of the greatest Japanese swordsmen of all time. Lucien had never considered such a connection and was highly intrigued, so continued to search the file.

There was an article taken from the *Atlantic Monthly* entitled "The Making of a Bullfighter" that contained a description, in Juan Belmonte's own words, of his own mental state during a particular fight that had established him as the foremost bullfighter of his time:

As soon as my bull came out, I went up to it, and at the third pass I heard the howl of the multitude rising to their feet. What had I done? All at once I forgot the public, the other bullfighters, myself, and even the bull. I began to fight as I had fought so often by myself, at night in the corrals and pastures, as precisely as if I had been drawing a design on a blackboard.

They say that my passes with the cape and the muleta that afternoon were a revelation of the art of bullfighting. I don't know, and I am not competent to judge. I simply fought as I believed one ought to fight, without a thought outside my own faith in what I was doing.

With the last bull, I succeeded for the first time in my life in delivering myself body and soul to the pure joy of fighting without being consciously aware of an audience. When I was playing with bulls alone in the country, I used to talk to them; and that afternoon I held a long conversation with the bull, all the time that my muleta was tracing the arabesques of the faena [a series of passes with the cape]. When I didn't know what else to do with the bull, I knelt down under its horns and brought my face close to its muzzle. "Come on little bull," I whispered, "Catch me!" I was executing the ideal faena, the faena that I had seen so often in my dreams, that every line of it was drawn in my brain with mathematical exactness. The faena of my dreams always ended disastrously, because when I went in for the kill, the bull invariably caught me in the leg. Nevertheless, I went on realizing my ideal faena, placing myself right between the horns of the bull and hearing the acclamation of the crowd only as a distant murmur; until at last, exactly as I had dreamed it, the bull did catch me and wounded me in the thigh. I was so intoxicated, so outside myself, that I scarcely noticed it.

Then Suzuki compared Belmonte's state of mind with the mindset of Takuan, one of the greatest Japanese swordsmen of all time. Suzuki concluded that, "If the Spanish hero had had Buddhist training, he would have an insight into Prajna Immovable."

Another yellow paper contained Suzuki's definition of the "Prajna Immovable: …the mind must be kept free from selfish aspects and intellectual calculations, so that original intuition is ready to work at its best, a state of 'no-mindedness.' No-mindedness is the personal experiential grasp as it faces the problem of life and death in the form of a threatening sword in the hands of an opponent."

Or facing the threatening horns of a bull, Lucien thought.

"…But the swordsman's problem is far more urgent and ominous and allows no time for reflection and erudition," the words on the yellow paper read. "He has to decide with no delay; his 'courage' is not something he can muster up after much deliberation. In such cases you cease to be your own conscious master, but become an instrument in the hands of the unknown."

That note also contained an epigram that was frequently used to train samurai swordsmen:

> No thinking, no reflecting,
> Perfect emptiness:
> Yet therein something moves,
> Following its own course.

The article concluded with Belmonte's words:

> Bullfighting is not a sport, and you cannot compare it with one. Whether you like it or not, it is an art, like painting or music, and you can only judge it as an art. Its emotion is spiritual and it touches depths which can only be compared with the depths that are touched in a man who knows and understands and loves music by a symphony orchestra under a great conductor.

Lucien wondered about who the "great conductor of the orchestra" was.

Although in the article Belmonte had not answered Lucien's most recent question, Lucien knew from Don Gabriel's description of him that Belmonte meant that the "Great Orchestra Director" and GOD were one and the same.

Lucien was forced to think about the events that brought him to Seville. Were the events described in the Nota Bene the result of his own free will, or were they the result of the actions of a "Great Conductor"? Had God led him to Seville? For what reason, for what purpose?

Lucien had previously considered the difficult question of free will and predestination, and though he had studied the Western approach based on logical discourse and the Eastern approach based on intuition, he had not believed that the Eastern approach was very practical, because it involved "enlightenment" that required a long period of rigorous self-discipline that he was unwilling to endure. Now, Lucien knew that rigorous self-discipline was also required in bullfighting.

Looking more thoroughly through the Suzuki material, he found a section labeled "Haiku." This was where Suzuki affirmed that "the Oriental mind was stronger at understanding the most fundamental things in life, like religion, art, and metaphysics." Suzuki also said that "when art presents those mysteries in a profound and creative manner, they move us to the depths of our being and become something that approaches the work of God."

Lucien left the library late in the day and returned to his room, eager to absorb what he had learned. He accepted what he had been suspecting for some time: that his presence in Spain was not accidental. He had been warned that some time, he would face Death, but Lucien did not take the warning as an immediate danger, because after all, everybody dies sooner or later.

But still, the woman in Mexico City may have foreseen something serious. Lucien thought that he should act with caution, and then realized that advance precautions were never possible. He decided he would live his life as close as possible according to the Prayer of Saint Francis and The Prayer of Trust and Confidence by Thomas Merton, and when the confrontation with Death would come, he hoped that he could face it with the faith of Juan Belmonte: "*Será suficiente*; it will be sufficient."

The Woman at the Bridge

Lucien walked to the Isabel Segunda Bridge the following morning. It was the bridge that spanned the Guadalquivir River and connected greater Seville with the Triana District, its oldest part.

Besides having produced Juan Belmonte and some of the best flamenco dancers of all time, the Triana District also contained the old Jewish District, the Juderia, where in times long past, the Spanish Inquisition held its proceedings. When a hearing was concluded, the Inquisitors would walk back to Seville across the bridge, still wearing black robes and hoods.

When he had walked halfway across the bridge, Lucien paused to look at the water flowing towards Sanlúcar de Barrameda, now Seville's port city. A fresh breeze blowing across the river brought the scent of orange blossoms from the Triana side. He also heard the sound of men's voices and the click of a woman's high heels on pavement. Looking up, he noticed a woman in a black pantsuit and hat with a wide, round brim, walking towards him. Her walk was so graceful that she seemed to be dancing.

The woman was being followed and taunted by four young men following closely behind her. One of them was trying to imitate the graceful sway of her walk and could only produce something that made the others laugh; the parody was so awkward. Lucien could also hear them directing lewd remarks to her.

The woman looked up, saw Lucien standing at the railing, and quickened her pace toward him. When she reached his side, she deftly placed Lucien between herself and the young men and stood close.

Lucien felt very glad to be standing so close to the beautiful stranger. The woman looked up at him with an expression so incredibly real and so full of love that the men could not fail to see it. Then she placed her hand on Lucien's arm and said to him in a sweet, melodic voice, "Mi amor, I hope that I have not kept you waiting too long!"

Lucien looked carefully at the woman, and although at first glance she initially looked familiar—which made him wonder where he had possibly seen her before—he understood that she was a total stranger. Her plea for help was obvious to him, so he tried to respond as naturally as he could. He placed his arm protectively around her shoulder and replied to her question, "Time away from you is an eternity, my love, but when I am with you, time seems to pass so quickly!"

Her whisper followed in a low, soft voice, "Very well said and done! I am very grateful to you."

After the men and danger had passed them, Lucien began to feel uneasy having his arm around this unknown woman. He removed his embrace and fully expected her to walk away without another word. Instead, she turned toward the railing and stood silently while pensively looking down at the river. After a moment of silence, she said, as if speaking to herself, "The treasures of this world are ever Sister to Sorrow. I love this Guadalquivir."

Lucien wondered which country could have produced such a beautiful woman, a woman exquisite down to her bones. Lucien thought she had the same nose, eyes, lips, and body as any other woman, but in her, all the ovals and curves and shapes had come together in the perfect combination to form the most beautiful woman he had ever seen. When she had pronounced the word "Guadalquivir," it had sounded like "Wad-al-quivir," the original Arabic name of the river. With that, Lucien knew that she was a native of Spain.

When she turned back again to face Lucien, their eye beams crossed and locked in a full embrace. When Lucien was looking into her eyes, he felt that he was looking into her soul, and was transported into a land of enchantment where blacks and grays became brilliant colors; where men and women were alike yet different, where they spoke the same language and understood each other completely without guile.

Her soul began to speak to him, saying, "I am a woman of deepest love and compassion. I am the tear that contains the ocean, I am the winged joy that flies. I would like to share with you all that I am, if you can assure me that for you, I am a treasure in heaven. You cannot buy me or take me by force, because my treasure would instantly turn to dust. You can earn my love, if you will value me more than life itself. A lesser commitment is not acceptable, so you must be absolutely certain of your love. If you are uncertain, if you have doubts, you should continue on your way."

Lucien turned his eyes away to relieve the intense emotion that he was feeling. For a moment he was in a fog, but heard her say, "Thank you for helping me. I could have taken care of myself, but I hate violence." As she was speaking, Lucien saw her right arm move extremely rapidly—so quickly that he caught only the briefest glimpse of what appeared to be a small, deadly looking knife. The image had appeared and disappeared so fast that Lucien doubted whether he had actually seen anything. He dismissed the doubt by thinking that if, in fact, he had seen a knife, then it was reasonable for such a beautiful woman to need some means of protecting herself.

Lucien peered inwardly into his own soul, and there was no doubt about his own feelings. He immediately wanted to say to her, "I want you in my life forever. I will love you and cherish you; I will give you everything of me, all that I am now or ever will be. I freely and joyfully want and accept your love on your terms. In return, I gladly give you everything of my love."

But Lucien said nothing, afraid that if he told her how he truly felt about her at their first meeting, then she would not think that he was a serious man, and would think him to be shallow and insincere. Instead, he asked, "Would you grant me the honor of joining me for a glass of manzanilla?"

Once more, she nailed his soul with her eyes, and with a hint of a smile, she placed her arm through his, and together they walked in silence to the Triana District.

In the old Jewish Quarter, the streets were paved with cobblestones, did not intersect at right angles, and were much more narrow. At one point it became necessary for them to stop walking side-by-side and press themselves against the wall in order to allow a car to pass. The driver needed to stop and fold both side-view mirrors to make sufficient passing room.

The woman led them to a business that had no sign at the entrance. The room they entered was not very large and was furnished with a bar and a dozen wooden tables. It was dimly lit and noisy, and the patrons were all men.

When they entered, the noise and chatter stopped momentarily, as if on command. When he saw the woman, the head waiter greeted them at first with a look of both recognition and surprise, yet regained his control before he spoke with the deference of one addressing royalty. "Señorita, follow me, please."

He led them into a larger room separate from the bar. As the woman passed, every man in the place feasted his eyes upon her, but as Lucien passed, he saw their eyes harden. They were led to a table in the back room, near the back wall, where the waiter seated the woman with a graceful flourish.

Lucien asked for manzanilla, confident that the waiter would bring him their best sherry without being asked. The waiter returned with a bottle, two glasses, and three plates of tapas, courtesy of the house.

The label on the bottle said "La Gitana" in bold red letters above a cameo of a beautiful Gypsy woman in red. Lucien noted that the figure on the label could have been a distant relative of his companion. Judging by all the courtesies she was receiving, Lucien believed his companion to be some important person, perhaps connected to production of this exquisite sherry, a well-known actress, or a member of royalty.

Lucien maintained his center. "I am honored to be in the company of a woman who commands such courtesy and attention. Who are you? Are you some famous actress or poet?"

"Why do you ask if I am a poet?"

"Because at the bridge, I heard you say, 'The treasures of this world are ever Sister to Sorrow.' Those words struck me as full of sadness, but beautiful and poetic."

She dropped her gaze and was silent for a moment. "Before I answer, may I ask if you are a poet yourself, since you were so impressed by mere words?"

"You speak with more than 'mere words,' señorita. But to answer you; no, I am not a poet."

"Neither am I a poet. I am only a woman much in touch with her feelings that I try to express frequently."

"You express yourself very well."

"Who are you? You haven't introduced yourself to me yet."

"My name is Lucien Christopher. How may I address you?"

"I am known as Liliana La Gitana. Liliana the Gypsy."

"Don't tell me you are a Gypsy fortune-teller?"

"No, I am not a fortune-teller. Do you not like fortune-tellers or

Gypsies?"

"Not at all! As a matter of fact, I am in Seville because of a fortune-teller I met in Mexico City. I don't know if she was a Gypsy, but she has thus far given me a good reason to believe that she was a good fortune-teller."

"That's very interesting. I would like to hear more."

"Certainly. A fortune-teller who I met for the first time gave me a strange poem that contained obscure directions. Without me trying, I followed them, and they have brought me here. That may sound foolish, but that is the true reason why I am in Seville."

"At least I know that you don't dislike fortune-tellers, and you must have some trust in them, since you came all the way from Mexico City, all based on what a fortune-teller told you."

"Perhaps I'm naïve, but that is why I am here, and I would like to say that I am very glad to be here."

People in the bar had come and gone during their conversation, and the noise level returned to its usual hum of talk and clinking glasses.

"How do you spend your time in Seville? Are you here as a tourist, or on business?"

Lucien watched her as she spoke, and he liked the way she pursed her lips when she sipped her drink, as if each sip was a kiss. She savored each bite of her tapas as though she gave each morsel her full attention.

"…I arrived only a few days ago and have done only tourist-type things. My business is research on a grant project that I have not yet started; I haven't even decided on a subject."

"That sounds like a nice position to be in. Does the grant support you and your family?"

"I don't have a family. I am here alone."

"Are you planning to stay in Seville?"

"Probably. I like Seville more and more every day, especially after meeting you. Right now, I do not have plans to go anywhere else."

Lucien noticed that she became a little more restless as she searched through her purse briefly. She returned her attention to the table and looked directly at Lucien before speaking once more. "You are an interesting man, Lucien. I wish I had more time to spend with you, but I am late for an appointment, and I must leave in a few minutes. Before I leave, I want to thank you and tell you that I am most grateful for your help. I was quite impressed by the way you handled my intrusion, so quick and natural that it took me by surprise. I am truly grateful, and you have my sincere thanks."

"I consider myself lucky to have been there to help. Things could have happened very differently and we could have passed each other without speaking. If that had happened, I would not have met you, and I would not be sitting here having a drink with you, and learning that you are Liliana La Gitana, a woman admired by everyone that sees her, and I would like very much to see you again. But if you say 'No,' I will spend every day of an entire year in Seville walking back and forth on the Isabel Segunda Bridge in hopes of seeing you again."

With a musical laugh, she said, "That won't be necessary, Mr. Christopher. If you wish, we can meet here tomorrow evening. Is eleven too late for you?"

"No, I will be here. May I escort you somewhere else this afternoon?"

"No, thank you; I will be fine by myself, I will be here tomorrow." Then she turned and left.

As she departed, Lucien was left in a tumbling emotional state. On one hand, he was very happy to have met Liliana in such a chance meeting; happy to have been able to spend some time with her. And then he was sorry that their time together had not been longer; sorry that she needed to leave abruptly. Overall he felt very happy with the expectation of meeting her sometime in the future, and nurturing a heartfelt hope that they would meet again.

Liliana La Gitana

From the moment he woke up and throughout the day, Lucien wanted time to pass quickly, so that he would be able to meet again with Liliana. To occupy his time, he searched for lodgings more suitable for an extended stay. He found a small place in the Arenales District where he felt comfortable, most likely because it was nearer to the place where he was to meet Liliana, and he felt a desire to be close to her.

When evening finally came, Lucien returned to the same bar. He arrived at ten o'clock to be certain that he would not keep Liliana waiting. The bar in the front room was again filled with men, and being alone, Lucien did not attract special attention. He was seated in the back room, at a table set at a distance from a low wooden stage that had been set up near the far wall. This adjoining room was densely filled with both men and women.

After Lucien had been seated properly and another bottle of La Gitana manzanilla was delivered to his table, he looked around the room. When his eyes became accustomed to the dim lighting, he noticed a man who had been sitting at a nearby table raise up from his seat and cross the room on unsteady legs. The man walked straight to open a door set into the back wall that opened onto the stage.

Not long after, Lucien observed a very handsome man, who was seated at a table closest to the stage, make a slight movement with his hand. He was in his mid-thirties, with a full head of dark hair that was starting to turn shades of gray, and was dressed casually like a professional at his leisure. Immediately, two bouncers appeared and stopped the unsteady patron from opening the door, and escorted him gently outside without making a fuss.

The stage was a square wooden platform raised about two feet above the floor, large enough to accommodate three men, with some room to spare. A triad of musicians was playing flamenco music with their guitars—songs Lucien could not identify. However, the audience was composed of people that knew the music well, for they were able to clap their hands in perfect beat with the complex rhythms.

At eleven o'clock the music stopped. The lights were dimmed further, leaving the room nearly dark. Since he entered, Lucien had been waiting anxiously to see Liliana come into the room—but eleven o'clock came and went, and she still had not appeared. He began to have doubts about whether she would appear at all.

Suddenly, a bright spotlight turned on, and he saw Liliana standing on the stage. She was motionless, one arm on her hip, and the other raised above her head. She was wearing a flaming red dress imprinted with lots of flowers, which had a tight bodice that flared at her narrow waist, curving and flaring out more below her knees, with a hemline that extended nearly to the floor. Two slits along the sides of the dress gave her more freedom of movement and, at the same time, displayed her beautiful, shapely legs. When they saw her, the audience enthusiastically cheered with loud whistles and numerous shouts of "Ole!"

Liliana remained motionless until she stamped her right foot hard on the wooden floor, whereupon the room filled with an explosion of sound and a flurry of movement on stage. The staccato sound of her heels hitting the wooden floor, the rhythm of the guitars, the hand claps, and the vocal sounds of a rasping, high-pitched voice of one of the male singers were all done in perfect coordination.

Liliana moved with the grace and fluidity of someone floating on air, and the sound of her heels seemed to be her only connection to Earth. She interpreted the intensity of the music and the changes of tempo with supple, lithe, flowing feminine movements. Her full skirt complemented the movements of her body, emphasizing her grace and beauty. Her entire body, including her fingers and arms, was in constant motion. The expressions on her face changed constantly, reflecting the mood of the music, so at various times she conveyed anger, sorrow, regret and joy. She portrayed a proud, confident, self-assured, self-possessed woman.

After her first dance ended, another chair was placed on the stage, allowing Liliana to sit while she sang. Her voice was very pleasing, with strong vibrato throughout the wide range of her voice. Lucien could not understand all the lyrics, because the words came fast and strung together in long phrases that matched the phrasing and rhythm of the guitars.

The expressions on Liliana's face also changed with the emotional content of the song. Lucien tried to guess the lyrics by watching the expressions on her face. She sang of loves, hates, laments, sorrows, successes, failures, pleasures and pains. Her songs also conveyed Andalusian history that included Gypsy caravans crossing lonely deserts, painful pogroms, and loves won and lost. Liliana showed that she was truly feeling the griefs and sorrows of her songs, because at times Lucien saw tears that were whirled away with an abrupt movement of her head.

She had the rare ability to make the audience feel her pains, the pains of a woman suffering the agonies and heartbreaks of passing love and fleeting ecstasies, of love stored in the secret abodes of her heart, of a woman engulfed in pain. The women in the audience were dabbing their eyes with tiny handkerchiefs, while men tried to hide their emotions by maintaining fixed facial expressions.

Her performance concluded, and Liliana bowed to her audience with genuine humility; the crowd responded by filling the room with even louder applause each time until she left the stage.

As she was exiting, Lucien saw her smile at the handsome man that was seated near the stage.

Lucien's mood sank when he saw the exchange of smiles and the dreadful thought came to mind that the handsome man must be Liliana's husband. All day he had been in a warm glow, feeling blessed by the chance meeting with Liliana on the bridge. Now that glow had vanished when he thought that Liliana might already be married, and that had changed his whole world.

He recalled the Nota Bene saying he should be persistent. But surely that did not include interfering in someone's marriage! He felt jealousy toward the handsome man arise and become stronger. Lost in that emotion, he was unaware that the noise of the room had stopped, and Liliana was standing at his table asking, "May I join you?"

Lucien recovered quickly and said, "Of course! Again, I am truly honored! If I seem flustered, it's only because I had been thinking that our meeting had only been a stroke of luck, and was something that would never happen again!" He stood up, offered her a seat, and she sat at his table. The previous hush of the room ended, and now the noise resumed even louder than before.

The rapid emotional change from despair to joy had been difficult and had made Lucien nervous. He managed to say, "Liliana, you are the best thing that has ever happened in my life! What an incredible artist you are! If I had wandered into this place alone and watched you perform, I could not have imagined that you would come off the stage and come to sit with me. That would be like seeing an angel descending from heaven and touch the Earth near me! So when I tell you that I am honored by your presence, I really mean it!"

Without guile, she answered, "Thank you for those nice compliments, but I don't feel I deserve them."

Lucien was planning to order a drink for her, then saw the head waiter already approaching them with another bottle of La Gitana and two glasses.

Lucien looked past Liliana towards Mr. Handsome, expecting to see a look of disapproval, but Mr. Handsome was quite unconcerned, talking to someone else. Liliana raised her glass, proposing a toast, and said, "I thank you for your help on the bridge, and for coming to see me tonight."

"The way you perform, I want to come every night to see you! I am lucky that I met you!"

"Maybe it was neither luck, nor an accident. Did you like my performance?"

"What can I say? You are magnificent! No wonder you command that much attention wherever you go! I have never seen anyone convey such emotion! How did you ever get so good?"

For a moment, Liliana's face became passive as her thoughts looked into herself. She must have explored her past with her mind before she answered, "To fully answer your question, I would need to tell you a lot about my life and a lot about other things, like the history of Spain, the Jewish people, the Moors and the Gypsies. All that is part of me, but that is a long story. Perhaps at some time I may tell you, but tonight I will only say that ability is not something that a performer 'gets,' it is something that is already within the performer. The real difficulty is the ability to bring that out, to express it, but it always comes at a price that must be paid. For example, the American actor Marlon Brando was tremendously capable of bringing out his emotions, but he must have paid a terrible price for that ability. He must have done a lot of suffering in his life."

"But how can you feel all those emotions? How can you be touch with all that grief and sorrow?"

"If you knew me well enough, you would be able to answer that question for yourself," she replied with her voice carrying some of the sadness that she conveyed in her songs. That made Lucien feel a strong rush of sympathy, and he reached over to place his hand on hers. As he leaned over, the pendant that he wore came out from under his shirt.

Liliana saw it and immediately made a quick motion with her left hand and grasped it. She looked closely at the amulet and turned it over to examine the reverse side. With her eyes wide open in amazement, she placed one hand on her mouth and gasped—a loud gasp that was heard by everyone in the room. Then with another quick movement, she slapped Lucien hard across the face, turned and walked hurriedly away.

Lucien was stunned and briefly paralyzed, then tried to follow Liliana, wanting to ask her about the cause of her outburst, but he was quickly surrounded by a group of angry men, pushing and shoving him. All were shouting, some were striking him with closed fists. There were yells: "Have you no decency! How can you insult a woman in public like that? Who do you think you are? Get the hell out of here!"

Lucien was struck in the face several times before three men intervened, two bouncers and Mr. Handsome. Mr. Handsome evidently had the respect of the men, because they stopped immediately at his command. Mr. Handsome then said to Lucien in a firm, controlled voice, "Leave right now and don't come back." He escorted Lucien outside and stood in the doorway to prevent others from following him. But Mr. Handsome had not considered the fact that some men had left the place before Lucien.

The Doctor

A few minutes after Lucien left, Mr. Handsome exited the club. At the first corner he found Lucien lying on his back on the cobblestone street, with a vacant look in his eyes that were wide open, with a pool of blood spreading concentrically around his head. Lucien was still partially conscious and tried to speak, but he could produce no sounds. Before he lost complete consciousness, he heard someone say, "He is still conscious, but he needs medical attention right away!"

Sometime later, when Lucien regained his senses, he realized that he was lying in a hospital room and that his head was wrapped tightly with bandages. He felt weak, and if he tried to turn his head, the pain forced him to remain as still as possible, with his gaze on the ceiling.

When a nurse entered the room, he did not look at her or try to speak. Then he heard another person enter, and by using indirect gaze, he saw a well-dressed man, good-looking, standing at his bedside, staring intently at him. Lucien reacted instinctively and made a movement to sit up and assume a more protective posture, but pain and the man gently restrained him.

The man said softly, "Take it easy. You're not ready for that yet; no one is going to hurt you. You are not in any danger, so lie back and remain still." In an even more gentle voice, he asked, "How are you feeling?"

"…Like I have the worst hangover that I have ever had. How did I get here?"

"You're in a hospital and you were brought here in an ambulance called for by me. You are injured, but not seriously, so your recovery time will be short. With your permission I would like to ask you a few questions to help me assess the extent of your injuries."

"Am I required to answer your questions? Am I under arrest?"

"No, you are not under arrest, and you do not have to answer my questions. All you need to do is tell me that you choose not to answer. Are you okay with that?"

"Yes, go ahead and ask your questions."

"Do you remember anything before today?"

"…I remember getting slapped by a woman. Then I was surrounded by men and was thrown out of a bar. I am not very clear about what happened before or after I got slapped, but I have a vague memory of having seen you before somewhere."

"Fine, you have retained a least a portion of your memory. You are doing well, but for now, keep yourself still. Now, slowly, try to move your extremities, and your arms and legs, one at a time. Can you feel them?"

Lucien complied before asking, "Why should I not be able to move them? Of course I can!"

"You took a hard blow to your head that could have caused you more serious injuries. The blow may have been from someone striking the back of your head with a hard object, or the injury could have been from your body falling backwards and causing your head to strike the cobblestones. Consider yourself lucky, because your injuries could have been quite severe; I am of the opinion that your recovery will be quick and you will soon start to feel better."

"When can I take these bandages off and get out of here? Are you my doctor?"

"My name is Pablo Penafiel. I am a doctor, but I am not your attending physician. You are suffering from a fracture, and you were fortunate that it did not penetrate the brain cavity. The bandages are on your head primarily to act as a temporary cast, and your attending physician will decide when to remove them. Since I am not your attending physician, you should ask your doctor when you will be released. But I am sure that he will want you to relax and rest as much as you can. If your pain becomes more severe, you should ring for the nurse immediately."

Then the man removed Lucien's chart from the receptacle at the foot of the bed and sat down in a chair close to the window. He remained in silence, studying the medical chart.

Meanwhile, Lucien could do nothing but keep still and helpless in his bed. One good thing he knew was that he was not a prisoner, because moving his arms and legs told him that he was not handcuffed to the bed. But he understood that he was in a precarious predicament, one that somehow related to the man sitting near the window.

He focused his attention on the man at the window and to the time that his face had been slapped, and more of his memory returned. He remembered then that it was Liliana that had slapped him, and the man who was now at the window was the one he believed was "Mr. Handsome," Liliana's husband!

The full realization of his plight came upon him suddenly. He found himself completely at the mercy of Liliana's husband.

The height of Lucien's fear peaked at the same time that the doctor started to walk from his chair and head directly toward his bed.

Lucien's panic remained escalated while the doctor crossed the room and stood at his bedside. Hiding his fear as much as possible, Lucien could see the doctor's eyes, and was puzzled as well as relieved that there was no visible anger or fire in them. Instead, the eyes were as calm as the doctor's voice. Sounding as if he were asking a favor, he commented, "This is somewhat of a personal matter, but one of importance to me."

Lucien thought to himself, *Of course the matter is personal and important. How could it be otherwise?*

The doctor continued, "I would very much like to know the answers to a few questions about matters that may well be personal to you, so I want to make it clear that you have no obligation to answer them if you don't want to."

Feeling his tension drop, Lucien conceded, "That is fine with me. Ask me whatever you wish."

"My first question is: Have you ever seen me before?"

Lucien paused to think, and then spoke. "When I first saw you, you looked somewhat familiar to me. But at the time I could not definitely place you. Now I remember that you were in the bar where I was slapped. You were sitting alone at a table near the stage."

"Good, you are recovering more of your memory! Yes, I was there, and I saw you get slapped. The slapping may involve some matters that are personal to me, and that is why I would like to ask you some questions about them. The questions are not related to your medical condition, so they are entirely personal; you don't have to answer if you choose not to. The question that I am most curious about is to know *why* you were slapped."

Lucien, still under the belief that Mr. Handsome was Liliana's husband, thought it entirely reasonable that a husband would want to know why his wife had found it necessary to slap another man, so he answered, "Doctor, I would be glad to answer your question if I knew the answer, because I, too, would like to know why that happened. But I assure you that I did nothing or say anything that was disrespectful to Liliana. Getting slapped by her was a total surprise to me! I have no idea what caused her to do it!"

"She slapped you after she took a look at some pendant that you wore around your neck. Do you remember that?"

"Yes, that is something that I will never forget."

"Was the pendant obscene, pornographic, sacrilegious or offensive in any way?"

"Of course not! Here, see the pendant for yourself." He reached into his gown, and then said excitedly, "I don't have it, I must have lost it! Where could that have happened?"

The man stared unblinkingly in response.

After a brief pause, Lucien blurted, "Maybe it was taken off when I was admitted to the hospital? Could it be with my other belongings? Doctor, would you please look in that drawer? See if it is there with my other belongings!"

In the drawer the doctor found the pendant along with Lucien's passport, wallet and keys. He took the necklace in his hands and examined the amulet closely, in silence and deep thought. "I think I know something about this pendant, but before I say more, I would like to show it to my sister. Would you trust me enough that I may take it and show it to her? I promise to return it. I think that this pendant is one that is very important to me as well as my sister, but I want to confirm it with her before I say anything more. May I have your permission to take it for approximately one hour, and then return it directly to you?"

Lucien's brain was a bit slow to react. "Doctor, I wouldn't be able to stop you even if I *didn't* want you to take it. However, I have been very curious about what the figures on the pendant mean ever since I received it."

"I can tell you something about it, since you have been kind enough to let me take it for a while. I believe that what you have been wearing is only one half of a pendant that has been broken into two pieces. The unbroken original of this amulet is on display at the Musée de Cluny in Paris. The front and back figures of the man are good copies of the man shown on the Shroud of Turin. The coat of arms belongs to a French Crusader knight named Geoffroi de Charny, who may have brought the Shroud of Turin back to France from Constantinople. The pendant was found in the River Seine upriver from Paris, and is an important piece of history because it is an indication that the Shroud of Turin could have been in France in the year 1357."

Lucien was slowly beginning to realize what was happening. He attempted to sit up once again, but to no avail. His reactions to the incoming information, however, were quite immediate. "…You told me you were a doctor, so I thought that you were a *medical* doctor, not a doctor of French history!"

"I *am* a medical doctor, but I became interested in the history of the pendant because your replica may have a strong relationship to my own family. That is what I need to verify through my sister. But before I leave, there is one more question that I need to ask you. How did you get this pendant?"

In response, Lucien gave the doctor an abbreviated account of how he had received the necklace. "It was given to me by a female fortune-teller in New Mexico. Before she gave it to me, she had given me a very cryptic note that seemed to be a travel adventure, but it turned out to be partially responsible for my arrival to Seville. When I asked her to decipher the note for me, she stared into my eyes, got a strange look that overcame her, abruptly reached into her blouse and gave me the pendant that belonged to her, told me never to take it off but to wear it always, then she quickly pushed me out of her office. That is the entire story, Doctor!"

Lucien's answer caused even more excitement in the man. "Was she young? Was she attractive? Was she happy?" He asked the last question, if not with a tear in his eyes, at least with some loss of composure. "Now I'm even more anxious to talk to my sister." He left hurriedly and took the pendant with him, saying, "I will return as quickly as I can!"

Lucien began to relax after the doctor left the room, feeling relieved that he had not been accused of any misconduct. A short time later, another medical practitioner entered and introduced himself as Dr. Serrano, and said that he was Lucien's attending physician.

He addressed Lucien in a formal manner, but with a warmness in his words. "Mr. Christopher, I have good news for you. The X-rays show no intrusion into the brain cavity, so you can be discharged into outpatient status. You will need to have your bandages replaced, and your pain level monitored, but Dr. Penafiel can take care of that. I have already discussed your status with him and he is willing to help. I am glad that we were able to take care of you with such good results. You were a good patient, and I wish you a complete and speedy recovery." With that, he left.

Lucien, alone in the silent room, fell asleep before long, but was awakened by the sound of excited voices in his room and near his bed. He opened his eyes, and for a moment he thought he was in Mexico City, looking at the face of the woman who had given him the pendant, but then quickly realized that in fact it was Liliana standing near him, with Dr. Penafiel standing next to her. Dr. Penafiel was smiling and happy, but Liliana was looking at him through eyes that were not only overflowing with tears, but also full of tenderness and love.

She stroked Lucien's cheek and between sobs, she expressed, "Lucien, I'm so very sorry that I slapped you. When I finish my show, all my emotions remain raw and close to the surface, so my reactions can react as quickly as a cat's. When I saw the pendant, I immediately recognized it, and the first thought that came into my mind was that you had somehow been involved with my sister before me, and that is what made me instantly furious! But now my brother has told me how you came to have the pendant, and since then I have been ecstatic over the incredible news that you have brought to us… That my long-lost sister is alive and well in Mexico City! It has been so long since we separated that I have thought for a long time that she must be dead!"

Lucien finally registered the news that Dr. Penafiel was Liliana's brother. "Did you say that Dr. Penafiel is your brother and not you husband? All morning I have lain here, fearful and feeling completely defenseless, because I thought that your brother was your husband, and that he would be angry thinking that you had slapped me because I had insulted or offended you!"

Dr. Penafiel, in a tender voice, using Lucien's given name instead of calling him "Mr.Christopher," said, "I am sorry for causing you that fear. I thought you knew that when I referred to 'my sister,' that I meant Liliana! I'm certainly glad that we have cleared that up!"

"You can't be as happy as I am, Doctor!"

"Please call me Pablo, Lucien. I am as grateful as Liliana!"

"What have I done to receive all this gratitude?"

Liliana turned to Pablo, "He is correct; he needs to know why we are so grateful and joyful." She asked her brother for Lucien's pendant. Then, with her free hand, she reached under her shirt and brought out another amulet almost identical to Lucien's.

Liliana placed the ragged edges of each pendant next to each other, and they matched as precisely as adjoining pieces of a puzzle.

In a voice as excited as a child's, she exclaimed, "See how they match exactly!"

"How does this prove that the woman in Mexico City is your sister?" Lucien asked with a quizzical look on his face.

"Lucien, before I answer, let me ask you one more question. Did the woman who gave you this pendant look like me?"

"…When I opened my eyes and saw you standing near my bed, I thought at first that I was still in Mexico City and looking at the woman who gave me the necklace! Then I realized that I was in Seville and that it was you who was standing in front of me. Before that, I had not realized that you and your sister look very similar!"

"Now I am completely convinced that the woman who gave you this amulet is my sister. If you wish, I could tell you about how we were separated, but it is a long story."

At this point, Dr. Penafiel interrupted her compassionately. "Liliana, I know that it is a long story. I suggest that you answer it later at my apartment, to where I want to move Lucien to make his recuperation more pleasant. I have already talked to Dr. Serrano, and he has agreed that Lucien can recuperate under my care. You can help me if you wish. Would that be agreeable to you, Lucien?"

Lucien's body finally relaxed. "Yes. Of course. I still don't know why I deserve all your help. But I gladly accept your offer if it is not too much trouble for you. I would like to know more about your family history, because for whatever reason, we seem to have become connected. I want you both to know that I am very grateful for your kindness."

Dr. Penafiel took charge of the arrangements necessary for Lucien to be discharged from the hospital into his care.

Dr. Penafiel's apartment was farther from the hospital than Lucien had expected, but it was in a nice building not far from the river. It was neat and orderly, and its walls were lined with books, mostly medical treatises. Several texts lay open in various places around the room. There were small pieces of religious art scattered across the space, and the main focus of attention in the living room was a large painting of Jesus on the cross, with the cross at a forty-five-degree angle, being raised to a vertical position. Lucien was absorbed in the painting until Dr. Penafiel led him into one of the bedrooms.

"This is your room for as long as you wish. It is comfortable enough; it catches the afternoon sun and looks toward the river. I will not be here all the time, because I must go to my office occasionally. While I'm gone, my housekeeper and Liliana will see that you have all you need."

"Doctor, you are being too nice to me. You have no responsibility for what has happened."

"Lucien, this is not a matter of responsibility. No one could have foreseen everything that happened, but you have made it possible for us to find our long-lost sister! Before you came, we had no idea what had happened to her, or whether she was alive or dead. We have been separated for a long time, but because of you, there is a possibility that we can be together as a family once more! How could we be anything but grateful to you?"

"You are most kind, but I can't take any credit," Lucien uttered as he steadied against the bed, still feeling woozy, but a bit sturdier than even a few hours ago. "I did not know that the woman in Mexico City was your sister. I did not know then that you existed, and I had no plans to come to Seville at that time, so I should not take any credit for reuniting your family. I am interested, however, in getting to know you and Liliana better. I have never known such fine and caring people."

The doctor nodded respectfully in response. "I prefer to leave that to Liliana to tell you about my family. I know she would like to tell you herself, so I hope that you don't mind waiting until she gets here. In the meantime, I hope that you feel as welcome as if you were in your own home. While we wait, shall we have some tea?"

Pablo soon returned from the downstairs kitchen with a silver tea set. "After my sister arrives, I will have to leave you for a short time."

Lucien was now lying on the bed, feeling newly at ease in his comfortable surroundings. The walls of the bedroom were a soft eggshell blue, and there was enough light streaming in through the window to give him energy instead of a headache. "I hope that I am not causing you too much trouble," he replied, "because you must have other patients to attend to."

"Other patients are not a problem because I am a specialist and do not have the patient load of a general practitioner. My specialty is forensic medicine."

"Do you work on cadavers to determine how they died?"

Pablo set the tea tray down in front of Lucien, on the bed. "That is the general type of work done by ordinary pathologists, but I have been working on only one case for the last fifteen years, as part of a team of specialists that is based in Spain and Italy, all working on the same case. I consider myself more a scientist than a pathologist."

"It must be an important case, if you have been working on it for fifteen years! Is it some famous murder case that I may have heard about?"

"The case is undoubtedly famous, but it is a very different kind of case. It is not known primarily as a murder case, although there was a death. And we are not concerned with the cause of death—asphyxiation—nor are we concerned about whether it should be classified as a murder or not."

"That sounds to me like you have already determined all the important features of the case. What is left?"

Pablo had to give his answer some thought before he could speak. "Your question is difficult to answer—but I would have to say that what we are trying to do is reconcile the physical evidence of the death with the historical accounts of that death."

"I don't mean to be disrespectful, but if some questions remain to be answered, and you have been working on the case for fifteen years, then it must be very complicated and anything but simple."

"Yes, you are absolutely correct. This case is so complicated that besides me, sometimes there are as many as eighty scientists working on it at one time. For example, there are specialists in many disciplines besides medicine—disciplines such as chemistry, physics, computer simulations, entomology, history, geography and theology. Even with all those scientists working on this for more than a decade, we're still not able to answer all the questions this case presents."

"If your case is that important and complex, surely I should know something about it."

"Without a doubt, you and the whole world know the name of my victim. In order to avoid distracting religious controversies among the scientists when we discuss the case, we simply refer to the victim by his initials, 'I.N.'"

Lucien had many more questions to ask but was interrupted when Liliana arrived.

"I'm glad you're here, because I'm already a little late for a meeting, so I must leave right away," Pablo said with a hint of relief as he embraced his sister briefly and warmly. "Please take good care of my patient."

The Family

Liliana took Lucien's hand. "Lucien, has my brother been taking good care of you?"

"He has shown me more kindness than I could have expected. Before you came, he was telling me about his work, and it certainly sounds interesting."

Lucien and Liliana were sitting in Pablo's vast living room. The pair had spent a morning chatting, getting to know one another.

"He will likely share his work more with you than he does with me," Liliana affirmed. "He would probably enjoy working with you, because he loves his work, and you two seem very compatible. He is very dedicated and is constantly trying to recruit people, so at some time, he will probably try to recruit you if he thinks you can be of help. But Lucien, I am anxious to know how I can communicate with my sister."

"There is a business card in my wallet for 'Adivinaciones' that has her address on it."

Liliana glowed. "Tell me again, does she look healthy and happy?"

"Very much so. She is almost as beautiful as you."

"Be careful what you say, Lucien, or you may make me jealous and I might slap you again, even in your helpless condition! You know that I'm only joking, and I can never again be mean to the man that brought my sister back and made a dream of mine come true!"

"How long has it been since you last saw her?"

She paused before answering. "It's hard to believe that so much time has passed so quickly. It has been about twenty years, but our separation is as fresh in my mind as if it had happened yesterday."

"Please tell me about it. I want to know everything about you, so I hope you're willing to share with me."

Liliana had made them tostada con tomate—Spanish tomato bread consisting of juicy tomatoes and extra virgin olive oil on toast—which served as a light, easy brunch. On the ornate coffee table in front of them sat two cups that displayed an artful design of a "vieira" or scallop shell. Lucien knew that icon to be a symbol of the Camino de Santiago, a sign that was once typically attached to pilgrims' cloaks or hats on their journey to Santiago.

She poured a hot tea to soothe Lucien. "I want you to know me as a person, not only as a performer," she confirmed. "And Lucien, you don't feel that you need to tell me about your own life, because what you have done in the past doesn't matter much to me, since I try to live in the present as much as I can. So, you may share what you wish and withhold what you wish."

"Liliana, you can ask me anything about my life. I have nothing to hide from you."

"I feel the same way. You can ask me about anything you wish."

"Please tell me about the pendant. Why did your sister, Mariana, have one half and you the other half? How were you separated? Why did you not know where she lived? Please don't feel that you have to answer me if they are too personal, because I don't want to be overly inquisitive."

"Those are very personal questions, but they are an important part of my life that I want to tell you about, so I will not hold back anything." She sat back. "I remember our parting very clearly, even though I was only about five years old. As I became older, I learned more from other people. What I am going to tell you is also painful, so I ask you not to interrupt me, and don't stop me if I start to cry, because crying is good for me."

Lucien agreed.

"…I will start when I received the pendant from my mother, and tell you that she gave it to me at the time she was sending us all away. That included me, my sister Mariana, and my brother Pablo. She was sending us away, not willingly, not of her own accord. She was sending us away because she was forced by the circumstances that took place in the aftermath of the Spanish Civil War. Do you know anything about that war, Lucien?"

"Nothing really. I only know what I have read in a novel, so you had better tell me what I need to know."

"I won't bore you with details, so I will tell you only the bare essentials. The war was fought between the years 1936 and 1939. Most people think that the war was only between two major combatants, the Nationalists under Franco, and the Republicans, which refers to the Republic of Spain. But it was actually more complicated than that, because there were many smaller factions in the major groups. The Nationalists began as a military coup under Franco, and were given a lot of military help from Hitler and Mussolini. The Nationalists were a more coherent group than the Republicans, who were made up of international volunteers that included Americans, anarchists, Spanish patriots and communists, so they received military help from Russia. The Republicans were not as tightly organized as the Nationalists, and sometimes fought with each other at the same time they were fighting the Nationalists, because each faction had a different objective. My father fought on the Republican side, the losing side.

"After the Nationalist victory in 1939, Franco remained an

absolute dictator until 1975, and Spain remained in turmoil a long time after the active fighting had ended. His government passed a law with the purpose of taking revenge on political forces that remained in Republican areas. Under this law, a minimum of thirty-five thousand official executions took place, and if unofficial executions are included, the total number probably reached fifty thousand or more. My father's death was one of the 'unofficial' deaths.

"…Many deaths occurred after Franco died. They took place when old grudges that had been festering for years, with roots in active fighting, were settled unofficially. I do not know who killed my father, or why. I have tried to find answers, but without success.

"Before I go on, Lucien, I want to be sure that you won't be offended if I discuss atrocities caused by war."

"Don't hold back on my account. I know they happen, although I have not experienced them directly."

"Then you know that during a war, many women are raped, and children are killed. My mother was a wise woman and aware that if her husband had been killed, someone must have had sufficient reason to kill him, and that revenge or retribution extended to the family of the offender. She expected her own death to come at any moment. My mother was very attractive, so she knew that before being killed, she would be used and her children would be used as hostages to ensure cooperation. After that, they would all 'disappear' without a trace.

"Mother prepared quickly and carefully. She sold her jewelry and small things of value in a way that would not attract notice. Then she gave the money to a cousin whom she thought was trustworthy, who was to deliver all three of us to a maternal aunt already living in France.

"We were in sight of the Pyrenees mountains, already close to the French border, when Mother's supposedly trustworthy cousin sold me and my sister, but not Pablo. Pablo was six years older, and managed to escape and arrive safely in France. The woman who sold us kept the money that my mother had given her, and the money that she received for selling us. Mariana was sold to a family fleeing to Mexico, and I was sold to a Gypsy caravan. The Gypsies later said that they had bought me because they had seen me walking, and I seemed to dance as I walked.

"While with my Gypsy family, I learned their music and dancing and their way of life, all of which I use in my work. I stayed with them until I was old enough to run away, and then I returned to Seville. A few years later, my brother found me dancing in the flamenco bars, and by then he had become a doctor, and returned from France to practice in Spain. He has been taking care of me ever since, much like a good brother or a good father."

Lucien nodded lovingly, trying to keep his rising emotions at bay with a stern face.

"As for Mariana, we had no idea what had happened to her after we were separated, and did not know whether she was alive or dead. We have always been close, and have never forgotten her. I assumed she was dead, and didn't expect to see her again. And then *you* came into my life!"

Lucien found that there were hot tears flowing down his cheeks. He could no longer control the emotions that were flooding him. "But are you completely certain that the woman in Mexico City is your sister?" he asked.

"I had forgotten to tell you about that. As my mother was saying goodbye for the last time, she was crying. She took a pendant she had and broke it into two. She placed one half of the pendant on a string around my neck, and the other half around my sister's neck, and asked us to wear them under our clothing. You saw for yourself that the pendants match perfectly, so the other half must have come from my sister. Then after you told me that we looked similar, I was certain."

"True, you do look alike in many ways. But how would Mariana have known that I would ever meet you? When she gave me the pendant,

I had no idea of ever coming to Seville."

"I don't know why she gave you the amulet, but she must have had a good reason. She must have seen that you are a good person, and it was important that you should have it. Because I know that the pendant was as important to her as mine is to me, she would not have given it to you without a compelling reason. God works in strange ways, and I think Gypsies may be more attuned to God's ways than most people. My sister and I are both very much like our mother. She could trace her ancestry to a Gypsy soothsayer who was an advisor to the Moorish court in fifteenth century Spain. At the time that Boabdil, the last Moorish Emperor of Spain was born, half of his advisors interpreted the omens of his birth as favorable; the other half interpreted them as bad, and predicted that with Boabdil as emperor, all of Moorish Spain would be lost to the Christians. The two factions could not come to an agreement, and my mother's ancestor was made responsible for breaking the tie. Our ancestor made the decision that the omens were bad, and because that was not pleasing to the other half and they had enough power, they put him to death. History, however, has proven my ancestor's decision correct, and the Moors were driven from Spain in 1492 during Boabdil's reign as the last Moorish emperor.

"Perhaps my ancestors may have helped my sister to see something important enough to make her part with her pendant. I have no other explanation."

Lucien put down his cup accidentally with force, an inspirational energy coursing through him. "Before you finish, Liliana, please tell me what happened to your mother, if that is not too painful."

Liliana nodded with tears in her eyes. "She died a few days after we left, without anyone having seen her leave her house. She was seen on the plaza of the Seville Cathedral, dressed in her best clothes, as if on her way to a wedding, or a funeral. After that, she was found dead on the pavement directly below the cathedral bell tower. Whether she had jumped of her own volition or had been pushed, we will never know."

Liliana was overcome with emotion, and tears streamed down her face. Lucien held her tightly to console her. She kept sobbing until they fell asleep in each other's arms. When Dr. Penafiel came home, he saw them and went quietly to his room without disturbing them.

EDICES

T he following day, Pablo embraced Liliana, kissing her on both cheeks. "I am sorry that I need to leave again so soon," he reassured them, "but you two should have no problems. Lucien was a good patient and was somewhat weak earlier, but he is better now. I won't be long. There are plenty of healthful snacks in the kitchen if you get hungry. Liliana, please take care of my patient!"

As Pablo left for work, the pair assumed their seats back on the couch. Liliana sat next to Lucien and snuggled familiarly against him. She held both of his hands in her own, her eyes still having that loving look. Lucien's face showed complete happiness, with only a touch of disbelief that what was happening was real. Infrequently, Lucien moved both hands away and placed them on the sides of his bandaged head.

One of those moves prompted Liliana to say, "Let me fix you something substantial to eat. I will see what else is in the kitchen." Liliana now knew that since Lucien lived in France for part of his life, he had very good taste. "I am learning about what your preferences are, but if anyone asked me about you at this point, I would have to say that you subsist on manzanilla! But Spain has many good things waiting for you."

In the kitchen, she went immediately to the cabinets on the right-hand side of the stove, withdrawing a long, thin, flexible knife from the top drawer—cutlery designed for slicing meats. She uncovered a whole leg of Serrano ham, a Spanish delicacy much like Italian prosciutto ham. She cut a stack of paper-thin slices onto an oval platter. Then she sliced some bread from a loaf much like a baguette, only larger. She went on to cutting portions of Manchego sheep's milk cheese. Finally, she dashed extra virgin olive oil onto the bread before stacking the ingredients into delicious tapas. She found a serving tray, and with the tapas and a bowl of large green olives, presented it to Lucien.

Then she headed back into the kitchen to a dual-zone, counter-high wine cabinet, pulling out a bottle of Spanish red wine—a Rioja—and another bottle of Spanish white—an Albariño—from the cooler, lower zone. "Try one of these with your tapas," she called to Lucien, "and you can have some manzanilla sherry afterwards if you'd like!"

"Thank you for being so kind, Liliana! I will have the red, I think it would better suit me."

Liliana then went to the crystal cabinet and brought out two long-stemmed wine glasses that she filled with Rioja wine. She returned to sit next to Lucien on the couch, clinked her glass with his, saying, "Welcome, Lucien! I drink to your quick recovery. After our snack, you can tell me how to communicate with my sister."

When Pablo returned that evening, he sat down with Lucien to have a more in-depth conversation with him. "Lucien, before you went into the hospital, were you staying in a hotel?"

"No, I rented a pension in the Arenales District," Lucien answered.

Assuming a tone of professionalism, Pablo said, "Speaking as your doctor, I think you still need someone to keep a watch on you for the next several days. I am not comfortable leaving you alone at this time. The simplest way to take care of the matter would be for you to stay in my apartment for a few more days, where Liliana and I could watch over you. Perhaps we could bring over some of your personal belongings so that you can be more comfortable here?"

Lucien agreed. Sometime later, a driver returned to Lucien's pension for his personal items. It was during the afternoon that Dr. Penafiel noticed the book of Hebrew grammar that Lucien had left on a table in the living room alongside René Descartes' *Meditations*.

"Lucien, I see by your books that you are a serious reader," Dr. Penafiel noted. "Are you learning the Hebrew language?"

"No. That book was given to me by a priest back in Arizona, and it is one of the reasons for me being here in Seville." Lucien pointed out the paper where the priest had written the biblical passages on it, where he had crossed out the letters in "servilleta," that had left only the word, "Seville."

The doctor looked puzzled and thoughtful for a moment. "What was the priest trying to tell you? What did he mean by, 'Open the door, enter and close it'?"

"I am only guessing, and I don't want you to think I'm crazy, but I think that he was asking me to continue his work that he had been unable to finish before he died," answered Lucien sadly.

"Do you know what he was working on?"

Lucien gave the question some thought. "He said that he wanted to prove in a scientific way that Jesus of Nazareth was real."

"What makes you think that I would consider that to be a crazy notion?"

Lucien paused before he answered the question, because he felt a little ashamed, but he made an effort to be honest and truthful as he made his reply. "Because I think the old priest was really a ghost, and I have been foolish enough to travel halfway across the world to Seville simply because a ghost crossed out three letters in 'servilleta' and meant to tell me to come to Seville!"

"Seriously, is that why you came here?"

"Pablo, I'm ashamed to say that the truthful answer is 'Yes.' But I also think that he was asking me to help him do something that he considered to be very important."

In the soft light of the evening, the two had to remember to hush their tones, as Liliana was exhausted from the recent events and had retired to her quarters to rest.

"Lucien, I have changed my way of thinking dramatically since I have started working on this case that I am currently working on, so I don't think you're crazy at all. I think that you may have been directed to Seville for a specific purpose. And I certainly do not think that trying to scientifically prove the reality of Jesus of Nazareth is a crazy notion. You may be surprised when I tell you that I am employed by an organization with a purpose—although in a very indirect way—of proving exactly the same thing that the ghost—the priest—was trying to prove! I work for an organization that is also trying to prove that Jesus of Nazareth was real, and they are trying to prove that by scientific means!"

Lucien was so startled by Pablo's words, and reacted very emotionally. He could only say, "Pablo, I hope you aren't trying to make fun of me."

Pablo responded to Lucien's emotion and said very gently, "Not at all. I am being absolutely truthful. I have already told you that I am not a practicing physician. My work is forensic medicine; I work for EDICES, and have been working for over ten years on the same case. I have told you a little about EDICES earlier."

"Pablo, my mind is trying to absorb what you said…that you have the same objective as the old priest: to prove scientifically that Jesus of Nazareth was real!"

"No, Lucien, I would not be joking about something as serious as that."

"This is too much for me. I want to know more about EDICES, the organization you work for, but I need more to give my mind a rest. Would you mind if I took a short bath?"

"Not at all. I will amuse myself with your book on Hebrew grammar."

Lucien headed into the bathroom and filled the old-fashioned clawfoot bathtub half full of water that bordered on being too hot, but just right for making his skin tingle and his mind relax. He wanted to think more about what Pablo had said, but the warm water quickly lulled him into a sense of reverie and slowed his mind almost into a dreamlike mood. He thought that he was hearing, through the open window that fronted onto the Guadalquivir River, the voices of men that through the ages had struggled upriver on this waterway that connected Seville to the greater waterway of the ocean.

At first he heard voices in the guttural sounds of the Goths and Visigoths, then more moderate sounds of the Arabs from Phoenicia. Next came the gentler Roman sounds that sounded closer to Spanish, then Moorish that had brought music, poetry and romance to Spain.

He awoke from his reverie when he realized that his body was slipping into the warm water that had reached his throat, and remembered that he must keep his bandages dry. He dressed himself and returned, wide awake and refreshed, to continue his talk with Pablo, who was absorbed in the grammar book.

"Pablo, may I interrupt you enough to tell me more about EDICES? I am still stunned by what you said, but now I want to know about your work even more."

"I am quite glad to do that. EDICES is an acronym for 'Spanish Team of Scientific Investigation of Sindonology.' It began as an organization that first started studying the Shroud of Turin, until an Italian cleric named Guilio Ricci saw the connection between the Shroud and the Sudarium of Oviedo. The Sudarium is located in Spain, so for that reason we concentrate on the study of the Sudarium and its relation to the Shroud. The Sudarium is my specialty, because of my training in forensic medicine."

"I have heard of the Shroud of Turin, but I have never heard of the Sudarium, as you call it."

"You need not worry, Lucien, you are not the only one. In my opinion, however, it is one of the most important objects in the world today, yet very few people know of it. The Sudarium is every bit as important as the Shroud of Turin, because the Sudarium is also one of the cloths that was found in the tomb of Jesus of Nazareth."

Lucien again reacted very strongly. "Forgive me, Pablo, but I find that hard to believe. Surely, you don't expect me to believe that the Sudarium is the same cloth that is referred to as a 'napkin' in the Gospel of John."

Pablo straightened himself which made him look taller, and then with a firm stare, he looked directly into Lucien's eyes, saying in a direct, reverent tone, "Yes Lucien, I mean exactly that."

Lucien's eyes grew wider in surprise and disbelief. "Pablo, I find that so hard to believe. I must sit down!" He half-collapsed into a larger leather chair, and sat quietly composing himself, unable to speak. After a moment, he mustered, "Are you telling me that you study an object that had actually been in the tomb with Jesus? How can you be so certain? How is it that I, and the rest of the world have never heard of it? How can you keep such an important secret all to yourself?"

"Lucien, I can sympathize with your reactions, because you are replicating my own feelings when I first learned of the Sudarium. You have been unexpectedly confronted with something that seems impossible to believe; too good to be true! I know that can be frightening, and it is only natural that a million questions will arise in your mind. I will not try to answer them now, because that would take a lot of time, and I don't think this is the right time. Instead, I will only give you an answer that you will probably not understand: The reason that I am so certain that the Sudarium is the same cloth that was in the tomb of Jesus is because of the scientific data that we have learned on the Shroud of Turin, as well as the Sudarium. The Sudarium and the Shroud tell matching stories. These matching stories are so remarkable because they match exactly with each other and correspond exactly with the Gospel of John!"

"Pablo, now you are asking me to take an even greater leap of faith. I don't feel able to take that leap right now."

Pablo nodded. "Lucien, I can see your agitation, and I understand it completely. But if you are really interested in knowing more about the Sudarium, I think I can convince you that what I have said is true." Pablo had made his statement in a very calm, confident tone.

"Pablo, you know me well enough already to know that if you can convince me of what you said, you would be doing me a favor beyond belief! But at this stage of my disbelief, may I ask you still another question?"

"Sure, go ahead; but I hope that your question will not require too long of an answer, else we will not get anything of your unpacking done!"

"What makes you so certain that the cloth you study is the same cloth that is referred to in the Gospel, Pablo?"

With only a slight hint of frustration in his voice, Pablo responded calmly. "Your question cannot be answered in a short way, but I will try to give you an answer before Liliana wakes, one that will rid me of a pet peeve. I want to say that many of the things we believe, we first learned in childhood, and we believed them based on faith without ever having given them a mature examination. But how should we believe things as adults? What standard should we apply in testing those beliefs?"

"Logic and reason, of course!"

"You are right, but how much logic and reason do we need to

apply? How much logic and reason should apply before we can accept something as true? What standard should we use? Preponderance of the evidence? Beyond a reasonable doubt? Overwhelming evidence? What would you, Lucien, need to convince yourself of the truth of the statements I have made?"

"I don't know, but I suppose that I would want overwhelming evidence before I could believe certain things that you say, which are based on faith alone. I think that is what the old priest would want me to do. Can you give me an example, just to make sure I understand?"

"Why don't I use the question that you asked earlier: How can I be certain that the Sudarium was the same as the cloth in the tomb of Jesus? In trying to answer that, the problem becomes part of a more general problem: How can we be certain of anything? Do you realize, Lucien, that if I had Jesus Christ himself hold the Sudarium in his hands, and say to you, 'This is the napkin that covered my face when I was taken down from the Cross and laid in the tomb,' you might believe it then, but there would still be many 'doubting Thomases' that would doubt the truth of Jesus's words. They would ask, 'How can we be sure you are Jesus? If you are Jesus, how would you know that you are holding the correct napkin, since you were dead at the time?' There would be many questions after questions, all expressing doubt after doubt."

"I have never given much thought to the problem. What standard do scientists use?"

"The standard way to prove something scientifically is to use the demonstration method."

"I don't know what that is."

"Let me give you an example. Say that your hypothesis is that one particular thing is the cause of a certain effect. First, you run a procedure without that particular thing that you want to test, and you do not get the particular effect that you want. Next, you run the same procedure, but this time you include the particular test ingredient that you want to prove as causing the particular desired effect. If this time, the desired particular test is achieved, you have proven that the particular ingredient is the cause of the effect. I know that I used too many generalities, but, did you understand what I was trying to say?"

"I'm sorry, Pablo, I couldn't follow you because it is too abstract. Would you be able to use that technique to show me that Jesus of Nazareth was real?"

"I suppose that I could, if it could be possible for me to set up the initial conditions of the experiment. But do you know how difficult that would be? I would have to start with a human being, subject him to the same tortures to which Jesus was subjected, meaning he would be hung on a cross until he was dead, then placed in a tomb and left alone for three days. If he completed all those tasks, that would be a demonstration that the man was either Jesus, or someone else with the capabilities ascribed to Jesus of Nazareth. But obviously, a demonstration such as that would be an impossibility."

"The difficulty of such a demonstration leaves me completely discouraged, Pablo. It makes me realize that what the old priest wanted me to do is completely impossible. If I had not met Liliana, I would be thinking about going back home, and try to forget all this. But how can you continue to study what seems to be an impossible task?"

"I don't agree with you that the task is impossible. There is one remaining method that may still continue to provide useful information. I am proud of what I and other scientists at EDICES may still accomplish, and that is a worthwhile task."

"There is another method? What would that be?"

"Look, Lucien, why don't you get your unpacking done before we talk any further?"

"Thank you for reminding me, Pablo. I am so interested in what you were saying, that I had completely forgotten! How long will I be staying at your place?"

"I would say three or four days."

Grateful for the quiet break, Lucien retrieved the smallest of his suitcases and set it open upon his bed, alongside one of the dresser drawers that contained a few articles of clothing. First he transferred the socks that were rolled together at one side of the suitcase and tucked them towards the edge of the drawer, keeping them in their tight arrangement. Then, not wanting to take up too much space, he placed his underclothing in the middle, under the folded short-sleeved shirts. Lastly, he positioned the long-sleeved shirts and pants neatly in the bottom drawer, and they were held in place by two wide belts.

When he was finished, he closed the case and returned to Pablo, situating himself next to him. "Okay, I am ready. If we have time tonight, will you tell me about this other method?"

"This is a method that I call 'overwhelming evidence.' It is something that I have developed on my own that I find useful. I can best explain it to you by using this example: If, as I did earlier, tell you that the Sudarium and the Shroud match each other and the Gospel of John, without giving you more information, you could accept or reject that as truth, but you would be making that judgment based on faith only. But if I back up that statement with two decades of credible scientific research by scores of expert scientists, that would add overwhelming evidence."

"Have not some scientists already concluded that the Shroud is a medieval fake?"

"Thank you for mentioning that 1988 carbon-14 test, Lucien. You are correct that that test concluded that the Shroud was a medieval fake. But let me use that as another example of overwhelming evidence. Based on my personal work and training in forensic medicine, coupled with about forty specialized experts in the scientific fields such as radiation physics, optics, ancient textiles, entomology, photographic and computer images, ancient history, ancient customs, and biblical and historic scholars who have been studying the Shroud all that time since 1988, we have unanimously concluded that both the Shroud and the Sudarium pre-date 1988, and neither is a fake. With this mountain of evidence on one side, and the carbon-14 test being the only test to conclude differently, I consider that to be overwhelming evidence that the Shroud is not a medieval fake."

"Pablo, I have learned what you mean by overwhelming evidence."

"Let me hear you."

"Your sister, merely by looking at her, gives overwhelming evidence that she is an extraordinarily beautiful woman! Seriously, I have no basis to contradict what you have said, and you have driven any thought of leaving completely from my mind. You have made me want to learn everything I can about your work, the Shroud, the Sudarium, and EDICES."

"That is fine, but don't expect me to go on all night tonight; we can talk more on that later. If you are unpacked, we should get some rest, too."

There was a knock at the door. The two men exchanged looks of confusion, and soon afterward started moving towards it. Pablo reached the door first.

The woman standing at the entrance was Peg Ledbetter from UNITA. She looked surprised when she saw Dr. Penafiel, but quickly recovered when she saw Lucien behind him, and said, "Oh, there you are, Mr. Christopher. Were you hurt badly? I learned that you were hurt in some way, and I am glad to see that you are all right, and that there is someone to take care of you."

Dr. Penafiel invited her in, but she declined. "That won't be necessary; I won't be long. I only want to assure myself that Mr. Christopher was not seriously injured." Cocking her head in Lucien's direction, she continued, "Lucien, please call me when you are more recovered, please. You are required to meet with me regularly so that

I can keep Mr. Mason informed. He has asked me whether you have chosen a research subject yet. There is no rush, but Mr. Mason is interested in knowing."

"Please tell him that I have not chosen a subject yet, because I am constantly finding new things of interest," Lucien replied shakily, still recovering from the initial shock of seeing Ms. Ledbetter at the door. "I will let you know when I have narrowed things down a bit. Thank you for checking on me."

In parting, she added, "Don't forget that you have to communicate with me regularly." Swiftly and curtly, she exited.

After he closed the door, Pablo asked in a friendly tone, "Lucien, I don't want to be nosy, but is she a romantic interest?"

"Not at all. She is only my contact person with the organization that gave me my grant. Sometimes she gives me the impression that she would like a more friendly relationship, but our relationship is strictly business as far as I am concerned. I did not invite her here, I had not told her where I lived, and I don't know how she learned that I was injured. Somehow, she is well informed of my actions."

Pablo's expression became more serious and asked, "You are not interested in her? She is an attractive woman."

"Pablo, I am interested in Liliana and nobody else. I am glad that she was not in the room when that woman arrived, because I would not want to upset Liliana. I am serious about her."

"Well, I'm glad to hear you say that, because I am very protective of Liliana, and I don't want her to be hurt. You must be aware of that."

"Don't worry. I understand that and we have no problems understanding each other, Pablo."

The Feria at Sanlúcar

"I need to be in a conference with scientists from Turin," Pablo explained, "and I'm not comfortable leaving Lucien alone. He should have someone with him in case of an emergency, such as if he starts to have severe headaches, becomes incoherent or loses consciousness. Hopefully nothing like that will happen, but I am not comfortable taking a chance. A trained nurse will not be necessary; we only need someone to act more like a companion to him. Do you know anyone, Liliana? We could pay them, of course."

Liliana, having just come downstairs after her nap, pondered for a bit and then answered, "Tell me what you think of this idea, Pablo. The feria of Sanlúcar de Barrameda starts tomorrow, and as you know I had made plans to attend again this year, as always. But now Lucien has turned our lives upside down. But what if I went to Sanlúcar and took Lucien with me? He would enjoy seeing a small-town music festival and hearing all the flamenco music and dancing that goes on. That would keep him awake with no problem. What do you think of that idea?"

Pablo's face lit up. "A wonderful solution! If you're going to be in the company of a man all that time, you may need to disguise yourself, don't you think? You don't want to upset all your admirers!"

Liliana stared directly at Lucien with a look on her face that said,

"Please come with me!" She asked aloud, "Would you like to go with me to Sanlúcar, a small town on the coast near Cádiz? It hosts a flamenco festival every year, when the local people have a great time singing and dancing flamenco all day. It's a great festival. Would you go with me?"

"That sounds exciting! You already know that I would enjoy being anywhere with you, even without music and dancing!"

"That settles it. We will start at nine o'clock tomorrow morning. We will have a great time!"

Pablo suggested that they have a light dinner, and have Lucien retire early so that he would be well-rested for the following day. They enjoyed a simple meal of olives, bread and olive oil, and a fish soup, washed down with a white wine.

After supper Liliana wished them all a good night as she ascended the stairs. "Until tomorrow!"

Lucien slept peacefully, knowing that Liliana was safe and close by.

The next morning came too quickly. Lucien, feeling much more awake and stronger, heard a gentle knock at the door. A nurse in a starched white cap and gown stood next to a wheelchair and whispered cheekily, "Good morning, sir. Did you call for a nurse?"

Lucien responded, "No, I didn't…" but then recognized the voice. "Liliana! You fooled me by hiding all your hair in a cap, and the dark glasses you're wearing. You would have fooled me even without the wheelchair!"

"Then the disguise will work fine. Are you ready to go?"

Lucien walked to the car, where Liliana was already folding the wheelchair into the trunk. They left Seville on the road that followed the Guadalquivir River as it flowed toward the ocean, before it filled with salt in the 1680s so that ocean-going ships could no longer sail upriver to Seville. As they neared Sanlúcar, Lucien could smell the salt air from the Atlantic Ocean while Liliana was talking.

"You are going to enjoy yourself, Lucien. Sanlúcar is a very historic town, from where Magellan and Columbus left from Spain on their voyages of discovery. Sanlúcar is much like Seville, with an early history of flamenco, but hosts a much smaller festival. I like that better because I can get closer to the people. It is an informal festival; people of all ages participate, and you can see young children and old people dancing and singing in a very natural way, with a lot of heart. That makes this festival more fun than Seville's. In Sanlúcar, nearly everyone is an amateur, except for an occasional professional."

They arrived, and Liliana gave Lucien a tour of the town. She drove through the old port section, with houses that faced the ocean, and parked near the center of town, at a small restaurant that had an outdoor eating area. It had enough space for Lucien to sit in his wheelchair alongside the table where Liliana had seated herself. From there, they could hear ocean waves breaking, as well as music coming from all directions. The streets were nearly empty of automobiles, but there were many people dancing on the roads and sidewalks. Men who were older and young boys played guitars as extensions of their bodies. They played alone or in groups that constantly formed and dissolved frequently. There were all types of dancers, but the majority were women wearing colorful skirts and solid-colored short-sleeved blouses. All were singing and clapping their hands and dancing with tapping heels.

They both listened to the music, sitting in brilliant sunshine after the morning clouds dissipated by the cool breeze bringing a briny scent to their senses. After listening for a while, Lucien complained that he could not understand the words of many of the songs.

Liliana consoled him. "Don't worry, Lucien. They are singing partially in an Andalusian dialect, and some of the words are different from the normal Spanish. Occasionally, they drop the final consonant and add a vowel, something done sometimes in flamenco music. I can understand them, and I listen carefully to the details in their lyrics. They are singing about their dreams, failures, frustrations, their loves and their joys."

During one instance, when there was a lull in the music and ongoing festivities, Lucien looked around and saw a sign on a building across the street that had a picture of "La Gitana" on it—the same woman shown on the labels of the manzanilla sherry bottles he had shared earlier in Seville with Liliana.

"Is that your business across the street, Liliana?" Lucien inquired.

"No, I wish it was. The owner, however, is a good friend of mine. Would you like to have a drink with him?"

Lucien agreed gratefully, honored that he could meet the person who created such an amazing drink that he had enjoyed throughout his visit so far.

The couple reached the building with the manzanilla label, where the proprietor stopped them at the door. "I apologize, madam, but I'm afraid our premises are not suitable for wheelchairs."

"Don't you recognize me, Mr. Hidalgo?"

The gentleman took a closer look, and after he recognized Liliana, he kissed her on both cheeks and apologized, stumbling over his words. "Forgive me for not recognizing you sooner! Because I didn't know that nursing was another of your many talents. I hope that I did not offend you by my failure to recognize the best promoter of my sherry! You know that you are always welcome here; please come in, both you and your patient."

Lucien was strong enough to be able to stand for periods of time, so arose from his wheelchair, folded it, and carried it inside the business, whereupon Liliana made introductions. "Mr. Hidalgo, this is Lucien Christopher, someone I met recently who has become a dear friend. I brought him with me to enjoy the feria, but he is only partially a patient. He is also a part of my disguise!"

"I understand! But if he should tire of being attended by the most beautiful woman in Spain, I will be glad to take his place!" He shook hands with Lucien. "Please, call me Hidalgo, at your service. A friend of Liliana's is a friend of mine." Turning back to Liliana, he asked, "How long can you stay this time? Is there anything I can do for you?"

"Would you be kind enough to share some of your sherry with us?"

"I would be most honored! Please come sit down in our waiting room. It might seem dark, having come in from the sun, but your eyes will quickly get used to it. I have some aged Manzanilla Pasada that I save for guests like you. Your friend might recognize it as Fino Amontillado. It is from my oldest solera, and I would like to join you, with your permission. Mr. Christopher, would you like to know a little bit about our sherry?"

"Thank you, Mr. Hidalgo, I would like that, since I know very little about sherry. But first I would like to ask you a question… Is the woman on your sign one of Liliana's relatives?"

"To be honest, I think so, yes. It is probably one of her maternal ancestors, one of the long lines of beauties that she comes from. One of my own ancestors very likely was in love with the woman on the label, as I am now with Liliana! But I am afraid that I do not know the name of the woman on the label, because my family has been making sherry a long time."

"The fine taste of your sherry is proof that you have been making it long enough to perfect your process. About how long would that be, Mr. Hidalgo?"

"My family, in this business and in this place, goes back more than *five* generations. But the business of growing the Palomino grapes for this sherry goes back much farther than that. The first grapes were planted in this area by the Phoenicians in 1100 B.C., and after that came the Carthaginians, the Romans, the Moors, and Christopher Columbus."

"I didn't know Columbus made wine here."

"He didn't *make* wine, but he *took* sherry from here on his third voyage, in 1492, so it is almost certain that our sherry was the first wine to reach North America. I don't want to bore you with history. So, tell me, how you like my sherry, now that you have had a chance to taste it?"

"Obviously you have had a lot of time to learn your business! But I notice that this particular sherry has a salty taste. What gives it that taste that other sherries do not have?"

"You have a fine sense of taste, Mr. Christopher, so I consider your observation a compliment! The salty taste is achieved naturally by fermenting Palomino grapes in an open container that is exposed to winds that blow constantly from the Atlantic." He raised a toast to their friendship.

After more wine and pleasantries, Lucien and Liliana wandered and eventually returned to their table nearer to the sea, in a more relaxed and intimate mood.

Feeling happy from the music, sunshine, and sea breeze, with their ever-increasing contentment, Liliana moved closer to Lucien. "Lucien, maybe I feel that I want to talk more, but I don't want you to think that it is only the sherry that is talking. I want you to know more of me, to know me better, so I am going to tell you one of my important secrets."

Lucien took his attention away from the activity and gave her his full attention.

"Don't you think it odd that I come here to see more flamenco even on my days off, even though I dance flamenco all the time?"

"Yes, I confess that came to mind, but I attributed it to your great devotion to your art!"

"You are partially correct. I do come here for my enjoyment, certainly, but I also come here with another, more serious purpose, and that is to listen very closely to what the people are singing. I want to learn what they are feeling, to learn what is important for them to sing about. Then I try to incorporate into my own performances what I have learned from them. That is how I keep myself current and relevant to my audience. In my performances, I try to convey their own emotions back to my audience as artistically as I can. I want them to be able to hear, without them knowing it, emotions that are really their own played back to them! If I am able to please them, that gives me a sense of satisfaction that pleases me, as well."

After a breath, Liliana continued. "Lucien, I would not have said any of this if you had not made me feel comfortable enough to talk about myself that way. I also want you to know that I grew up just like that little girl on the corner over there… That one who looks like she is dancing her first dance, and that when I grow old, I will look just like those older ladies farther down the street who are trying to recapture the grace and fluidity of their youth. These small-town fairs capture the heart and soul of Spain. That is why I come to this festival. Whatever success I may have, I owe to this method. I can feel the emotions of my audience, sometimes before they are aware of them. I love what I do, and I will keep doing it as long as I can. Flamenco is such an important part of me. I cannot change that, even if I wanted to."

Lucien reached out his hand. "Liliana, the more time that I spend with you, the more I learn about you, the more my love for you keeps growing. I have come to realize that I love you exactly as you are. Please don't change in any way!"

After he had said the magic words, "I love you," Lucien realized that they had come naturally—not from his conscious self, but his inner self. He retracted. In silence, he reflected on his thoughts, his past, and his future.

He had no problem accepting that Liliana was from Spain, totally committed as an artist, and completely a "woman" to him in every sense of the word. He knew that Liliana would be unable to flourish anywhere else but here, where she could be unequivocally herself, and that if he committed himself to her, he would also be committing entirely to her way of life. He contemplated about his own life prior to meeting Liliana, and it seemed to only be a succession of events without a lot of passion or heart, lacking many things that made life worth living. He concentrated again on the little girl who was still dancing her first steps and putting all of herself—her concentration, her emotion, and her passion—into every movement. He carved that little girl into his memory and decided to live the rest of his life that same way. At that moment, his future became his present, and he confirmed to himself that living close to Liliana—that having her as a reminder and as a model—was his best way to assure himself of the future he wanted.

Enough time had passed while Lucien had been absorbed in his thoughts that Liliana became concerned and interrupted him. "Lucien, are you all right? This is your nurse speaking!"

Lucien raised himself from the wheelchair and stood tall. He turned and faced Liliana directly. Then he said with conviction, "Liliana, will you marry me?"

Without showing any concern for nearby people, she placed her arms around his neck and kissed him full on the lips. "What took you so long to ask me? When we first met on the bridge, if you had asked me to marry you then, I would have said 'Yes!' I knew that you were the man that I had been waiting for all my life!"

"Liliana, I'll confess that I, too, when I first met you on the bridge, wanted to ask you to marry me, but I did not want you to think that I was a foolish and impulsive person who would make such an important decision without giving it some serious thought. But now I am finished thinking it over, so I am begging you to be my wife. Without any reservation. I give you my total commitment, forever."

Liliana's tears flowed freely. "Lucien, I gladly accept your proposal! Don't ever let me go."

"I already love you more than my life. I knew that when we first met on the bridge, when I felt your soul speaking to me."

Love, finding no obstacles, entered their world and transformed it into loveliness.

The Sudarium

Their world had changed; they were seeing everything through new eyes. Their priorities had shifted abruptly. Now it was important to return to Seville, to inform Pablo of their circumstances.

It was now nearing the end of the day, so they expected to find Pablo at his apartment.

"You are both glowing and flushed!" Pablo exclaimed when Lucien and Liliana were invited in. "Have you found the fountain of youth, or the secret of eternal life?"

Liliana overwhelmed him with excitement. "Pablo, we are going to be married! Lucien proposed to me in Sanlúcar, and we had to leave immediately to share the good news with you!"

"I should have been able to guess that," Pablo laughed, and put his arms around both of them. He separated himself from the embrace and stood back, facing his soon-to-be brother-in-law. "Let me be the first to congratulate *you*, Lucien. You must be very special, because I have long thought that she was perhaps overly particular, judging by the number of good men that she had rejected. But I fully expected that some time she would make a choice, and I could never picture her as an old maid! Lucien, I would be honored if you would let me be your best man."

Lucien beamed. "Pablo, you immediately came into my mind, but I was afraid to be too presumptuous. Thank you for your offer. No one could be more appropriate. The honor is all mine."

After they shook hands and embraced, Pablo asked Liliana, "How soon will the wedding take place?"

Liliana did not hesitate to answer. "I would not want anyone else except for my long-lost sister to be there for sure, so the date will depend on how soon I can inform her, and how quickly she would be able to take the trip. I would like our engagement to be a short one; I don't need time for more consideration."

Pablo opened a bottle of Pinot noir, filled three glasses, and they settled down. Lucien and Liliana sat in the living room holding hands with each other, facing Pablo, who asked them about the rest of their time at the Sanlúcar fair.

"Dear brother," Liliana said, "if I had not received Lucien's proposal, I would have probably been quite disappointed, because no one recognized me—not even Mr. Hidalgo. Nobody asked me to sing or dance this time, so maybe my disguise worked too well, or nobody cares about me anymore!"

Pablo consoled her. "My guess is that the two of you were so wrapped up in each other that nobody wanted to disturb you!" Pablo changed tunes and asked a few general questions about the feria before saying to Lucien, "Well, brother, it looks like you will become a permanent member of our family. That pleases me, and that will give me time to get to know you better…although I think highly of you, already. I know the two of you will be very happy. I congratulate you."

"Thank you, Pablo. That is very nice of you; thank you for welcoming me into your family. That makes me feel especially good. Before I proposed to Liliana, I thought a lot about my feelings for her, as well as my feelings for you, your way of life, and for Spain in general.

That even made me wonder whether Spain could possibly be in my genes, because I feel so comfortable being here. I, too, would like to know you better, and learn more about your way of life here."

"That should be no problem. But Lucien, what did you say about Spain in your genes?"

"…This is something that I have never shared before with anyone. But I feel very comfortable telling you and Liliana about my past. I learned a few years ago that I had been adopted as an infant, and I have never learned about my identity of my birth parents. But I have had such a strong affinity for Spain that when I landed in Seville, my first time in Spain, I had the feeling I was home! That is not a good reason for me to feel Spain in my genes, I know, but I can say that I felt especially grateful when I heard you welcome me into your family. I do want to know you better personally, as well as learning more about your work and the Sudarium."

"I already know of your interest in the Sudarium, so I will make an effort to share my work with you," Pablo replied. "Maybe when I return from a trip that I must make to Asturias, to meet with some associates that work on the Sudarium, we can sit down together and I will tell you more about it."

"Pablo, if you could plan to drive, could Lucien and I go with you, at least part of the way?" Liliana inquired with exhilaration. "You could tell us both about the Sudarium on the way there, and you know that I want you to share more about your work with me. I could also play tour guide for Lucien and point out interesting things, so that he can learn something about Spain at the same time. Could we go with you, please?"

Pablo nodded. "Yes, I think that is a good idea. Listen, are you feeling strong enough to make the trip to Asturias in the car? The Sudarium is in Asturias, in a monastery near the town of Oviedo. That is the reason why the Sudarium is known as the 'Sudarium of Oviedo.'

Asturias is the northernmost province in Spain, but you should have no problem if you have recovered your strength. Of course, I must check your injury under those bandages. May I do that now?"

Pablo carefully unwrapped the bandages. He went into his bedroom, returned with his first-aid kit, and did a little probing before saying that everything was healing quite well. Lucien said he felt fine, so Pablo cleared him to shower and wash his hair. "Everything looks ready to go. We can all leave for Asturias in the morning."

"I have realized that I cannot go all the way to Asturias with you," Liliana interrupted, with much disappointment, "but I can go as far as Madrid, because I need to return to Seville for a show. I can take the train back that will return me to Seville on time, and will still have a little time to look at current wedding fashions in Madrid. I hope that will not be a problem for the two of you."

It was agreed that Liliana would make only part of the trip.

The next morning was quiet and peaceful. Liliana brought hot chocolate and churros down to the men from her upstairs apartment. Everyone looked bright-eyed and happy. Each of them carried a small bag that they packed into the trunk of Pablo's new, small 1995 Fiat. Liliana insisted on driving so that Pablo could sit in the back seat and be able to tell them about the Sudarium without being distracted by having to drive. Liliana headed out of Seville on the highway to Córdoba and Madrid.

Once they had left Seville, the vista broadened out into vast rolling plains, where Liliana started to speak, pointing to the north, primarily directing herself to Lucien. "This part of Spain is called 'The Fireplace of Spain' because it is always so hot in the summertime. After only about eight miles on this next side road, there is an unrestored but partially excavated Roman ruin with a stadium large enough to seat forty thousand people. Maybe we can visit it together sometime. Also, that is the setting of Cervantes' *Don Quixote* of La Mancha. The 'La Mancha' in his title refers to the province of La Mancha, immediately north of Seville. Have you ever read the book, Lucien? It is one of my all-time favorites! Do you have any favorite books about Spain, Lucien?"

"Yes, I love *For Whom the Bell Tolls* by Ernest Hemingway. How about you, Pablo?"

"My favorite book…" he began, "is not about Spain, and not even by a Spanish author. The title of it is, *A Doctor at Calvary* written by Pierre Barbet, a French doctor."

Surprised by Pablo's answer, Lucien interjected, "I have never heard of it! Can you tell me more about it?"

"Yes, I will do that, but not now—although I will say that had I never become interested in the Shroud of Turin, the organization that I work for would not exist, and perhaps I would not have become a specialist in forensic medicine. Dr. Barbet has been very important in my life." Pablo appeared to be contemplative for a moment before deciding to speak again. "Right now I need to concentrate on the purpose of this trip—to share my information with you and Liliana, first about the Sudarium, and then about the Shroud. And since the president of EDICES is going to be in Oviedo, I would like to use this opportunity to introduce you to him. And if things go right, perhaps I can even ask permission for you to work with me. …I know that this is entirely of my own doing, but I have taken it upon myself to test whether you have been serious about wanting to learn more about the Sudarium and the Shroud, and also wanting to work with me. By the end of this trip you should know a lot more about both objects, and also whether you would like to spend part of your grant time helping me with my work. In order to make this happen, I need my president's permission, and this trip might be a good time to ask for it. May I continue to try to make that happen?"

Lucien was humbled and grateful. "Do you really mean what you have said, Pablo?"

"Yes, of course!"

"…Well, Pablo, you have been very sensitive in correctly gauging my feelings. I am honored that you have such a high opinion of me. I hope that you have not overestimated me, and that I do not disappoint you!"

"I know that you will not disappoint me, brother. Pay attention to what I say, because the president may ask some questions of you. With your permission, I will proceed, and on the assumption that you know very little—or nothing—about the Sudarium."

When the couple agreed to take everything in, Pablo switched gears as they drove through the changing landscape. "The first historical mention of the Sudarium is in the Bible, in the Gospel of John, where he says that he and Peter entered the tomb of Jesus and found it empty, but saw 'the linen cloths lying, and the napkin that had been about his head, not lying with the linen cloths, but apart, wrapped in one place.' And please take note, Lucien, that when I explain this, the word 'napkin' that is used by John refers to the 'Sudarium.'"

Lucien swiveled around in the front seat to face the doctor. "Pablo…I am not trying to be difficult, but how can you possibly be so certain that the Sudarium is the napkin mentioned in the Bible? The time of Jesus was more than two thousand years ago!"

Pablo smiled. "I knew that what I said would get your attention! I fully expect you to be doubtful to begin with. And I also believe that when we are finished, you will be able to accept that everything that I have said to you will be proven to your satisfaction. …And I do ask you to minimize your questions for now, but make note of each one, and after we are done, we can deal with each doubt, case by case. But if I am to continue, we should start by agreeing on some 'ground rules' as to how we should proceed—in order that we can accomplish as much as we can on this trip. And in the end, we can test whether our 'ground rules' were valid. Specifically, I mean that we should agree to accept John's statement about the empty tomb and the napkin to be true, so that we can draw reasonable inferences from them."

Lucien agreed.

"…The disciple entered and 'the linen cloths lying and the napkin that had been about his head, not lying with the linen cloths, but apart…' John saw them 'and believed.' But what did he believe? John doesn't say what he believed, but he did not mention that for good reasons—one being that they were afraid of the Jews, and another because there had been no body in the tomb. Because there was no body, the Apostles would have been accused of taking the body themselves and hiding it. If they had taken the position that Jesus had resurrected, they would have also been crucified for blasphemy.

"Can you imagine what would have happened if the Apostles had run through the streets of Jerusalem, shouting, 'You made a huge mistake! You crucified someone who was truly the Son of God! He has resurrected as He said He would, on the third day! Here is the proof that He left behind, but He did not leave His body!'"

Both Lucien and Liliana shouted simultaneously in their own ways, "We would have no Gospels! We would have no Sudarium! We would have no Shroud! We would have no Christianity!"

Pablo stopped the tumult when he said over their voices, "You are both right, of course! Let us thank God and be grateful that the Apostles considered the Sudarium and the Shroud to be holy objects that needed to be preserved. And they also knew that as long as both objects existed, that their own lives were on the line, if they were discovered. Nevertheless, they agreed to preserve the evidence. We know the Sudarium and the Shroud have not been destroyed, because they exist today."

Lucien could not hold back another interruption. "But Pablo, doesn't what you finished saying depend upon the objects in the Bible and today's objects, the Sudarium and the Shroud, being one and the same?"

"Good observation, Lucien. Yes, it does, but please reserve your judgment on whether the two are the same until I give you all the information. That they are the same may be hard to believe at the moment, but I assure you that later you will be convinced. May I go on?"

"Yes, of course. I'm sorry that I interrupted you again."

"Thank you. The Apostles' efforts at secrecy succeeded, because the first historical reference mentioning the Sudarium is by Santo Nino of Georgia, who died in 335 A.D.! Santo Nino said that the Apostle Peter had hid the Sudarium 'in one of the city gates of Jerusalem.' It took two hundred years more before the next reference appeared in 570 A.D., that said, 'seven nuns in seven cells looked after the Sudarium of Christ.' After that, the whereabouts of the Sudarium becomes more firmly established when it reached Seville in 616 A.D. and was left in the custody of Bishop Isidore of Seville. The chest containing the Sudarium finally reached Oviedo in 761 A.D. That is our destination right now."

Lucien's heart began to race. "Pablo, have you ever seen the Sudarium yourself?"

"Yes, I have. I have also personally done some testing on it."

Lucien was stunned. "If I get to see it, what will I see?"

"You will not see it on this trip, and may not ever see it, but if you do, you might see one of two things: You will either see a bloody linen rag, somewhat dirty, with dimensions of twenty-one by thirty-four inches. Or you might see something else in the same object—a sacred cloth that is somewhat dirty because it has been hidden in out-of-the-way places for over two thousand years; you will see that it is stained with blood that has a definite pattern, and note that in the blood stains are imprints of human fingers, that the blood stain pattern corresponds exactly with the injuries shown on the head and face of the man shown on the Shroud of Turin, and ultimately you may conclude that this dirty cloth was wrapped around the head of Jesus of Nazareth when He was on the Cross!"

"What! You can't be serious, Pablo! If you are correct, that would make the Sudarium one of the most treasured and venerated objects in the world! If what you say is true, where are the crowds?"

"Lucien…I may not be the best person to answer your question," Pablo replied sadly, "because knowing what I know, I clearly see the second option, and I am very biased. Don't forget that the Sudarium belongs to the Church. Perhaps at this time they do not want to deal with the problems involved with handling huge crowds. Another consideration is the involvement of EDICES that could want to continue further testing on the Shroud before making any public announcements. Knowing what I know, however, there is not the slightest doubt in my mind that I believe the Sudarium to have been on the head of Jesus of Nazareth at His Crucifixion."

"I cannot dispute what you have said, Pablo, but I regret to tell you that I am one of those people who would see the Sudarium as a rag. I hope this will not upset our relationship!"

"Don't worry; what you say does not bother me—because I fully expect you to change your mind as you learn more about the Sudarium and its relationship to the Shroud. I am saying this not only for your benefit, but also for Liliana's sake, in case that she was upset by your words."

"Pablo, that is very kind of you to consider me," Liliana cut in. "I trust you completely, and I know that everything you say always comes from a well-considered basis, so I fully expect that Lucien will come around to your point of view before long. In the meantime, that does not change my feelings for you, Lucien."

"Thank you, Liliana. I know that I must have hurt you, but I want to be honest with such important matters. I will make a good effort to listen to what Pablo has to say, and I hope that he can change my mind."

Pablo gave a sigh of relief before suggesting, "I think we all need a rest stop. Liliana, why don't we stop in Córdoba for refreshments?"

"We are already past Córdoba, Pablo."

"Really? Have we already passed the Roman bridge before Córdoba? Why didn't I hear you saying anything to Lucien about it?"

"I must have been listening to you and did not notice it myself! Linares is not far off; I will stop there."

Liliana took the Linares turnoff and parked at the first bar they saw—a pub like any other in Spain. This one, like many others, immediately gave the impression that it was not new or temporary. It had a low, varnished wooden bar running along the length of the left side of the room, opposite the round, solid wooden table where they were seated. A substantial stock of all varieties of Spanish red wine were stored in open-faced shelves hanging elaborately with carved wooden fronts, the shelves reaching all the way to the ceiling. A dozen whole, aged hams hung high at the back end of the bar. They were served two dishes of large green olives, a platter of freshly sliced bread, two modest dishes of olive oil, and a bottle of La Gitana sherry manzanilla.

As they sipped their drinks Lucien mentioned to Pablo, "Your discourse before we got here had some information that was shocking to me. It certainly got my attention!

"Just wait… There is a lot more coming!" Pablo laughed heartily.

Liliana changed the course of their conversation when she told them that Linares was the last bullfight of Manolete, and that he had died in Linares. Then Pablo and Liliana talked briefly about a prior trip they had made to Linares, and after they had finished their sherry, they were back on the road.

The Shroud of Turin

After they had driven out of Linares, Liliana, who was still driving, asked Pablo, "Are you tired of sitting in the back seat, Pablo? It seems a little crowded for you."

"Thank you, Liliana, but I'm doing fine. And enjoying telling you about my work. So now... I will start with the Shroud of Turin. Lucien, I will warn you that the travels and whereabouts of the Shroud are even murkier than the Sudarium—so I expect that you will doubt even more whether today's Shroud and Sudarium are the same objects mentioned in the Gospels. But don't worry; the more you learn, the more your doubts will start to disappear. With that said, I concede that your doubts are quite understandable."

The trio continued on their way.

"The reason I accept your doubts is that for more than one thousand years, the whereabouts of the Shroud could not be determined with any reliable accuracy. One source states that Thaddeus Addai, one of the first seventy disciples, took the Shroud at about the time of the Crucifixion to Edessa, formerly known as Urfa, in what is now Turkey. After that, the next known date is 525 A.D., when a cloth with an image of Christ was discovered in a niche above the west gate of Edessa, and thereafter stored in the same city in the Cathedral of Hagia Sophia. The

Shroud, which then or sometimes was known as the 'Mandylion,' was moved to Constantinople in 944 A.D., and was housed in the Church of St. Mary of Blachernae."

Lucien could not help but interrupt again. "Pablo, do you know for certain that the Image of Edessa and the Mandylion in Constantinople are one and the same as the Shroud that we have today?"

"No, I don't know for certain. My only basis for saying that they are the same is because of all the scientific tests that I am familiar with—which have since been conducted on the Shroud by my respected colleagues—that have not been able to prove that the Shroud is inauthentic. I know that the tests are valid; that the Shroud is not a fake. If you ever see the tests yourself, and test their methods and conclusions, you will also agree that today's Shroud and the cloth originating in the Bible are one and the same. And by the way, you will also learn that the 1988 carbon-14 test conclusion about the Shroud being a 'medieval forgery made between 1260 and 1390,' as reported by *The New York Times*, is incorrect."

Lucien stated that he did not know about some of the details that Pablo was talking about, so urged him to continue.

"From that point on, the trail of the Shroud becomes a little clearer, with the next historical mention of the Shroud in Constantinople in 1203 A.D. At that time, a Christian Crusader from France named Robert de Clari reported that he saw, in the Church of St. Mary of Blachernae in Constantinople, a 'shroud,' or 'sindone,' in which the body of our Lord was wrapped. Shortly after this event, Constantinople was sacked by the Crusaders, and the Shroud disappeared again, but only for a short time. It is not known how the Shroud reached France, but one theory is that it was brought from Constantinople to France by the Knights Templar, and into the hands of one Geoffroi I de Charney, master of the Templars in Normandy, France. This Geoffroi de Charney was burned at the stake in 1314, and then another man, also named Geoffroi de Charny and possibly a son of the first Geoffroi, but whose relation is unknown, came into possession of the Shroud, possibly as a gift from King Philip VI. I personally favor Dr. Barbet's theory, because both de Charneys (or de Charnys) were known to be acclaimed soldiers; the younger Geoffroi de Charny was killed in battle in 1356 while defending his king. In 1353, before his death, Geoffroi de Charny had received funds to build a church in Lirey, France. After her husband's death, his widow, finding herself in financial need, organized a fundraiser in the Lirey church in 1357, with the burial shroud of Jesus as the main attraction. Pendants and amulets were sold that showed the coat of arms of de Charny, his wife, and the front and back of a figure of a reclining man. These amulets are the first known representations of the full-length figures on the Shroud. One of these amulets was found in the eighteenth century in the Seine River upstream from Paris, and is now in the Musée de Cluny in Paris."

Pablo broke off from his explanation to address the couple directly. "Lucien and Liliana, now you know the historical significance of the amulets you both wear! It is important because it helps establish that the Shroud was in France in 1357."

Lucien fingered the design on his necklace, still allowing himself to be open to the information. "Thank you, Pablo. With that, and the information about the importance to your family, knowing that I would never have met you or Liliana if Mariana had not given it to me… Now I treasure this amulet even more."

"The planned 1357 exhibition never took place because it was stopped by the local bishop, who did not believe that the genuine Shroud of Jesus could possibly be in the possession of such a humble family as the de Charnys. But that was not the end of the family's efforts. Again, in 1389, they tried to stage another exposition of the Shroud, but again were stopped by the local bishop, who wrote a letter of protest to the Pope. The bishop protested that the Shroud had been 'cunningly painted with…a clever sleight of hand, and could not possibly be authentic' because it had not been mentioned in the Gospels."

At this time, Pablo's face broke out into a big smile, and in a voice that betrayed his amusement, he said, "I always enjoy this part of the Shroud's history, because the words that the bishop used to dismiss the Shroud, 'cunningly painted…with a clever sleight of hand' are in retrospect so simplistic that today they seem almost comical! Of course, the bishop could not have known that even six hundred years later, with all the tests that we have run using space age technology, we still have not even been able to determine how the Image was formed on the Shroud! Nevertheless, although we have enough evidence to learn that the Shroud is not a forgery, we have also learned that the Shroud was not 'cunningly' or 'cleverly painted' because there are no paints, dyes or chemicals on the Shroud. Even so, we still have much to learn about the Shroud."

Lucien turned from his place in the front seat and spoke. "Please, Pablo, if you want to keep my attention, could you please give me something to help me believe that the bishop at the time of Lirey was wrong? Or please tell me something about one of your current tests?"

"I understand how you feel, Lucien, so I will turn to the scientific focus on the Shroud."

Before Pablo could speak, Liliana had something to say once more. "Pablo, I purposely did not interrupt you while we were climbing the Sierra Morena, but now we are crossing over into La Mancha, and I want Lucien to know about the windmills that still exist here, mostly to give more reality to Don Quixote."

Pablo, very considerately, told her to go ahead.

She glanced slightly at Lucien. "You can see how enthusiastic I am about my country! There are many more reminders around here of Don Quixote other than windmills. In Puerto Lápice, not far off the road, there exists an inn called the Don Quixote Inn that the villagers claim is the actual inn that Cervantes used as a model in his famous novel. We are also approaching Valdepeñas, part of our wine-growing areas, where their wine storage vaults are so large that they are called 'cathedrals'! Spain grows more wine than either France or Italy!" Then she told Pablo, "Thank you, brother. That is all I want to say. For now."

Pablo thanked her. "And you, Lucien, I can see that it will be more difficult for me to convince you quickly about the authenticity of the Shroud, so I should start to tell you about the scientific studies. Perhaps that will help you to understand why I am so convinced that the Shroud and the Sudarium are not forgeries or fakes."

He carried on. "The first 'scientist' that contributed much to the serious study of the Shroud was a photographer named Secondo Pia. In 1898, he took the first photograph of the Shroud of Turin, and the results were both shocking and groundbreaking. You should know that the image on the Shroud, when seen with the naked eye, is vague and indeterminate, and makes it very difficult to establish where the Image begins and where it ends, because the Image seems to disappear into the cloth. But when Pia developed his photograph, the figure of the man was presented sharply and clearly, with lifelike highlights and shadows. Pia recognized that the image was a photographic negative that reversed the lights and darks, so that apparent blood stains showed up white! That meant that if the Shroud was painted by someone, the artist would have needed to paint in reverse, with dark portions needing to be portrayed as white portions!

"…The injuries to the man represented in the cloth were easily discernible; injuries to the head, face, crown, feet, and chest showed plainly; the blood flow could be easily traced as white lines and marks. Such details, like the flow of blood from a crown of thorns wrapped tightly about the head of the man, the mark of nails on the wrists and feet, showed plainly."

Lucien could not contain himself. He exclaimed excitedly,

"Pablo, you are describing the Gospel accounts of the injuries suffered by Jesus of Nazareth at the time of his Crucifixion!"

Pablo nodded. "Lucien, you are exactly right. The correspondence is so exact that it causes you to think that the Gospel accounts were written by eyewitnesses having the body of Jesus laid before them on an autopsy table! Of course, the relation between the Image and the Gospels is what prompted the scientific effort to determine the authenticity of the Shroud.

"Because of their clarity, the Pia photographs also attracted the attention of people with medical training who wanted to determine if the injuries were medically accurate. One such doctor was the chief surgeon at St. Joseph's Hospital in Paris, one of the largest teaching hospitals in the city. In that capacity, he had much access to corpses and freshly amputated limbs upon which to conduct his experiments. Dr. Barbet worked initially from photographs, but he describes, in his own publication, his own emotional reaction when he first saw the Shroud directly. His first exposure took place on the last day of an exposition of the Shroud in the Cathedral of Turin, in 1933. In front of twenty-five Church prelates, soldiers and a vast crowd that filled the square in front of the cathedral, Dr. Barbet, standing at the front of the crowd, was able to see the Shroud in direct sunlight. I am now quoting from memory, as best as I can, Dr. Barbet's own words that describe his emotional reaction to what he had seen:

> "'I have thus seen the Shroud by the light of day, without any glass screening it, from a distance of less than a yard, and I suddenly experienced one of the most powerful emotions of my life. For, without expecting it, I saw that all the images of the wounds were of a color quite different from that of the rest of the body; and this color was that of dried blood which had sunk into the stuff. There was

thus more than the brown stuff reproducing the outline of a corpse. The blood itself had colored the stuff by direct contact...but a surgeon could understand, with no possibility of doubt, that it was blood which had sunk into the linen, and this blood was the blood of Christ! As for me, my soul, both as a Catholic and a surgeon, was overcome by this sudden revelation. I was quelled by the Real Presence, the evidence for which was so impressive, I went down on my knees and I adored in silence.'"

When Pablo finished reciting the words of Dr. Barbet, everyone in the car hushed in silence for at least the next twenty miles.

When their moment of reflection and contemplation had ceased, Pablo felt that he could keep speaking. "Dr. Barbet continued to study the Shroud, using his knowledge as a trained surgeon. From the photographic evidence, he confirmed that the medical cause of death of the man in the image was death by asphyxiation as a result of crucifixion. Dr. Barbet noted details on the body that corroborated the torture of Jesus described in the Gospels, such as the scourging, the Crown of Thorns, and the bruises on the right shoulder such as would be caused by the carrying of a heavy cross. He also explained things that no one—not even a trained doctor—would have been able to explain before the study of human anatomy began in the sixteenth century: Dr. Barbet pointed out things on the Shroud that can only be explained medically, such as why Jesus was, in fact, nailed to the Cross with nails though the wrists, and why no thumbs are shown on the hands in the Image. He determined that Jesus had been nailed to the Cross through the space of Destot near the wrist, the only space that is capable of supporting a crucified man's weight."

"What does 'the space of Destot' mean?" asked Lucien.

"Étienne Destot was an anatomist born in France in 1864, and the Destot space is a place on the wrist, bound by the hamate, capitate, triquetrum and lunate bones."

"Pablo, that doesn't mean anything to me besides that Destot's space is on the wrist. Why is that so important?"

Pablo replied, "Had the nails actually been driven through the palms, as is usually artistically depicted, a man's weight would have pulled the nails through the space between the fingers. Could a forger in medieval times or earlier have known this? Dr. Barbet further explained that nails driven through Destot's space would have impacted the median nerve of the body, that would have caused the thumb flexor muscle of the thumb to drive the thumbs into the palms of the hands, where they would not be visible. Could a forger have known this? Also, Dr. Barbet said that such nails would have damaged the median nerve, and thereafter would have been sending unbelievable messages of pain to the brain, causing the worst torture imaginable! Jesus endured this torture for three hours!"

At this time, Lucien treaded lightly, but retorted. "Thank you Pablo for the anatomy lesson, but since I have no medical training, more medical details would be wasting your time. Can you tell me of more recent tests that have been done?"

"You are right, Lucien; perhaps I have already given you too much medical information—but I do want to say that you made me think a lot about Dr. Barbet. He is someone that I respect and admire very much. In fact, the book is the reason that I specifically chose the work I do for EDICES, because of a question that Dr. Barbet raised in his book. Would you like to know what that question was?"

"Of course!"

Liliana included, "Pablo, you have never told me about this before! Please, I want to know."

"I will be glad to oblige. I have already told you about the scourging and the Crown of Thorns and the beatings that had left Jesus in a state of exhaustion near death and covered with blood. Part of this blood was live blood that came into direct contact with both the Shroud and the Sudarium, and left the marks of congealed blood. That raised a question in the mind of Dr. Barbet. Now, Liliana and Lucien, I am certain that you both have had at least some experience in removing bandages from injuries with congealed blood—just like we had to go through with you, Lucien, from your most recent injury! And you don't need medical training to know that you can't lift off the bandage without disturbing the congealed blood on the wound. So, Dr. Barbet asked himself, 'How could a corpse covered with wounds have left the Shroud while leaving behind a fine and unblemished impression of the body and the marks of its bleeding?' He said that 'humanly speaking, that would be a physical impossibility.' I have to admit that I have taken that upon myself, either through recklessness or ignorance, to try to achieve something that Dr. Barbet thought inhumanly possible."

"Pablo…I am impressed that you accepted the challenge. Have you had any success?"

The doctor's response came in a single word, "No," but after a pause, he went on to add, "I am beginning to think that Dr. Barbet was right—that it is not humanly possible," emphasizing the words "humanly possible." "But I have not given up yet, and I am planning other tests."

A brief silence ensued until Pablo finished his explanation. "Lucien, in response to your earlier request for information on later tests that have been run, I will only be able to summarize two of them briefly. The blood group on both the Shroud and the Sudarium is human blood, type AB. One of the latest tests was able to produce a three-dimensional figure of the Image on the Shroud. When this three-dimensional figure was overlaid with the two-dimensional Sudarium, they were coincident in seventy locations! And furthermore, this latest test also showed that the Image on the Shroud was not made by direct contact, but that the intensity of the Image corresponded to its distance from the body. In other words, the intensity of the Image corresponded to the distance between the cloth and the body! For me, this implies that the Image was formed by some form of radiation from the Body of Christ, which would explain how the Sudarium could have been removed, while leaving only a 'fine and unblemished' outline of a body. As I said earlier, I still have work to do."

After all these words, all three people were lost in their thoughts. They rode into Madrid, and the city's principal train station, in silence. Once there, both men escorted Liliana to the train car, where she left them each with an embrace and, "I will see you tomorrow night! Come see me after I have finished my show!"

Segovia

After leaving Liliana at the train station, Pablo continued to drive through Madrid, westward along the highway toward León and Oviedo. When they reached the area of the university, Pablo spoke about the heavy fighting that had taken place there during the Spanish Civil War.

"My father was wounded badly in this battle to defend Madrid," he shared with Lucien. "He was lucky to have been shot while he was in an area where there was access to a surgery center, otherwise he might not have survived. Of course…he did end up being executed. I am sure Liliana told you more details about our family history. Do you know anything about the Spanish Civil War?"

"Yes, Liliana told me about your family. Other than that, I only know what I have read from *For Whom the Bell Tolls*, and that is a favorite book of mine. I even memorized the words from which Hemingway used for the title: 'No man is an island, entire of itself; every man is a piece of the continent, a part of the main; if a clod be washed away by the sea, Europe is the less, as well as if a promontory were, as well as if a manor of thy friend's or of thine own were; any man's death diminishes me, because I am involved in mankind, and therefore never send to know for whom the bell tolls; it tolls for thee.'"

"Well done, Lucien! I, too, like to study the Spanish Civil War, but for different reasons. I have told you already that my father was killed because of some incident that happened during the war. I'm glad to know that you liked Hemingway's novel. We have made more progress than I expected, so we can take time for a detour through the Sierra de Guadarrama, instead of driving directly through it."

Past Madrid, Pablo turned off the highway onto a smaller road heading in a northeasterly direction. They passed a small town named El Escorial, where the road started climbing higher into the mountains. Soon they reached a narrow gorge.

"Do you know where you are?" Pablo asked.

"No, I have no idea. I have never been here before."

"Maybe you *have* been here before, but only in your imagination. You are crossing the Sierra de Guadarrama, the likely setting of *For Whom the Bell Tolls*."

Lucien recalled that when he first read the book, it had taken place in some faraway land he never expected to see. But here he was now, in the actual place! He imagined himself being in the real spot where the hero had first observed the bridge that he had been ordered to demolish, and a little later, at the wide area in the canyon where the hero was killed.

Pablo must have noticed Lucien's emotion. "I thought that you would appreciate this detour."

"Thank you, Pablo. I am very grateful. Even though I know that the work is fiction, I felt the same emotions as when I first read the book!"

"That is a measure of Hemingway's skill, to be able to make you feel that emotion. Your own sensitivity could make you a good writer, too. EDICES could use a good writer. Would you be willing to work as a writer if I can get approval to hire you?"

"I sure would, if you think that I could contribute in some way!"

Pablo gave a sigh of relief. "I'm glad to hear you say that, because I have already spoken to the president of EDICES. …It is one of the main reasons I wanted to bring you on this trip. That, and being able to inform you about the Shroud and the Sudarium." Pablo continued driving through the mountains until they reached Segovia.

Lucien was immediately impressed with the historical city of Segovia, particularly with the great Roman aqueduct, cobblestone streets and Gothic cathedral. Lucien practically begged Pablo to stay overnight so he could fully explore the charming city. Pablo agreed to stay as long as they departed Segovia early enough to reach their destination by mid-morning the following day. First, they secured a small hotel for the night and spent the rest of the day exploring Segovia.

Lucien was missing Liliana terribly. After a good night's sleep and enjoying a hot chocolate with churros for breakfast, he strolled to the front lobby to check out, all the while having thoughts of her on his mind. Pablo was already sitting in one of the comfortable leather chairs near the entrance.

"Sir, a lady left this for you last night," the clerk called out, handing Lucien an envelope before they could leave. "She told me that it was very important, that I was to personally hand it to you before you left."

Lucien checked the handwritten note.

Lucien, this is an urgent warning! Please take this message very seriously. You should not tell UNITA that I have given you this explicit warning. If you did, that would put me in serious trouble. You have made things very difficult for me by not reporting to me as you are required to do.

This may be my last chance to help you avoid trouble, so take my warning: DO NOT GO TO OVIEDO! If you persist in going, there may be serious consequences that I will be unable to prevent. If you won't do this for yourself, please do it for me.

Affectionately,
Peg Ledbetter

Once in the car, Lucien asked, "Are we going to Oviedo?"

"Yes, that's our next destination. I thought you knew."

"I thought we were going to Asturias," Lucien pondered, his thoughts wandering to Liliana. "I must not have realized that we were going to Oviedo."

"Asturias is the province in which Oviedo is located. I may not have been very clear, especially with all the information I have been telling you. Is that causing a problem for you?"

Lucien clenched his fist around the envelope. "The clerk gave me a letter that was left for me by that lady you met, my contact person. She warned me not to go to Oviedo, but she did not say why I shouldn't go there."

Pablo was silent for a few moments. "I saw the clerk hand you something, and you got a worried look on your face. Lucien, if you don't want to go to Oviedo, you can wait for me here and I will go on alone. I don't want to cause you any problems."

"I want to work with you and eventually see the Sudarium that covered the face of Jesus of Nazareth, if that ever becomes possible. You can't keep me away."

The doctor nodded. "I'm glad that you feel that way. When we meet the president, I will ask for his approval to have you work with me. And I expect to get that, but you very likely won't have permission to see the Sudarium. Don't feel bad, because even the King of Spain was once denied permission to see it, even when kings were all-powerful!"

"What you have already told me about the Sudarium makes me wonder why Oviedo is not recognized as a holy place. It should be one of the most visited shrines in the world!"

"Perhaps it should be. But we are not ready yet," Pablo looked at Lucien with a knowing smile, and Lucien could see that he was excited like a child through the beam of his dark eyes. "Perhaps one holy place is all we need. And there is already the pilgrimage to Santiago de Compostela! Thousands of pilgrims walk all the way from Chartres, France, but even they pass Oviedo without realizing that one of the most precious relics in existence is there. In Spain there is a saying, 'A pilgrim who goes to Compostela and bypasses Oviedo has gone to see the servant and not the Master!'"

Monsacro: Sacred Mountain

They drove out of Segovia in silence through the plateau of northern Spain, through Valladolid and León. Lucien remained in deep thought about Liliana, wondering what she was doing, what she would be having for breakfast, and if she was dressed today like she was when he first met her on the bridge. That memory remained fresh in his mind and he was enjoying its recall.

After some time, Pablo interrupted the quietness when he observed mountains in the distance. "We're close to Oviedo. But first we must cross another mountain range called the Cordillera Cantábrica."

As they entered the Cantabrian Range, they began to descend, the temperature dropped ten degrees, and the air became cooler, more humid and smelled of salt water. A few miles before they reached their destination, Pablo left the main road and drove onto an unmarked dirt road that wound around low hills, until they reached a stone building that blended so well into the terrain that it could be easily missed. Before they could get out of the car, a man in shepherd's clothing that was holding a rifle held across his chest appeared in the roadway.

Pablo recognized the man, lowered the car window and asked him, "Juan, what is going on here?"

The man lowered his weapon and scrutinized them from afar.

"Oh, it is you, Doctor. I don't know what exactly is going on, but I was told to be alert. Apparently there was some suspicious activity around here yesterday. Other than that, I know nothing. Who is with you?"

"A colleague of mine from Seville. I will vouch for him. Is the president already meeting with the other group?"

"Yes, he should be finished by now. You are scheduled at eleven thirty-two, and you're right on time, so you may go right in."

They soon entered an austere anteroom, windowless, dimly lit, with earthen-colored walls and a dark floor. Six well-dressed men, two of whom were dressed more casually—each carrying a briefcase—came out of an adjoining room. They were chatting among themselves, but when they recognized Pablo, everyone stopped to greet him.

Pablo met each of them by their names and titles. "Good morning, Dr. Enrique; good morning, Dr. Romano; good morning, Dr. Heinrich; good morning, Dr. Anderson." Even the two more casually dressed men were also addressed as doctors. Lucien thought at first that this was a medical convention, until he realized they were doctors in many scientific fields. Then Lucien followed his soon-to-be brother-in-law into the inner room.

The inner room had a long, rustic wooden table surrounded by straight-backed wooden chairs without cushions. There were more chairs along the wall. Only two other people were sitting at the table— one obviously a monk, the other looking like the president with his commanding presence. The monk was dressed in a brown cassock made of coarse material, with a hood over his head. Since the monk had said nothing when they had entered but only nodded, Lucien concluded that he was an observer with a vow of silence. The other man was dressed in a business suit, middle-aged, and wore glasses with a silver-gray frame that matched his hair color. The man's face expressed familiarity with Pablo, and pleasure at seeing him.

He shook hands and then embraced Pablo warmly. "I apologize

for the tight schedule this morning, Dr. Penafiel, and having to drive such a long way. I wish we had more time to spend."

"Please, you needn't worry about that," Pablo glowed. Then, turning to Lucien, Pablo introduced them. "Dr. President Molina, this is Lucien Christopher…"

The president warmly shook hands with Lucien. "We need not be so formal. You can call me Juan or Thomas. Pablo has spoken to me about you, and I am pleased to meet you."

President Molina took Lucien to the monk and introduced them. "Brother Francis, this is Lucien Christopher. Pablo would like to work with him."

Brother Francis, in the hooded robe, nodded with a hint of a smile on his face.

"Is this the man we spoke about?" the president asked Pablo.

"Yes," Pablo responded deferentially. "After spending some time with him, I'm convinced that he can be of help to us, so I would like your permission to have him work with me as an editor. I believe that he is a good man. My sister is of the same opinion, since they are planning to be married! She sends you her regards."

"Ah yes, your sister. Has she finally met a man she considers sufficiently worthy? He must be truly special. You know, Pablo, I often trust a woman's judgment more than I trust my own. But don't forget to tell your sister that she has broken my heart, and that I will still wait for her, although I can't wait too long, because I am not getting any younger!"

The president then looked intently at Lucien, giving him a silent examination. After a brief moment, he spoke in the calm, measured tones of a man accustomed to choosing his words carefully. "Young man, are you acquainted with the philosophy of subjectivism and its derivatives, naturalism and rationalism?"

"Yes sir, I am."

"Then you will save me a lot of time and explanation if I can get directly to the point I wish to make. For the last five hundred years, more or less, Europe and the entire Western World, beginning with Luther, have come to believe that reality consists of a subjective private judgment—that man's own will has replaced reason. Then Immanuel Kant came along and built upon that to say that man cannot know the truth of things; that the intellect is shut within itself without reference to the outside world, which leads to the conclusion that there is no external God. Kant was followed by Hegel, who said that God does not exist; that He is only becoming; that He is still in the making; that God does not preexist man. Consequently, we are to believe that reality consists of only what we perceive with our intellect, and beyond that, there is no reality. Do you agree with what I just said, young man?"

"Yes, sir, I am afraid that I must agree with you, but I do so reluctantly."

"I am glad you agree with me. Had you disagreed, I would have been more inclined to think that you would not be the right man for Pablo. You do agree that we perceive with our senses, do you not?"

"Not exactly, sir. I believe that we perceive with our senses, but without intellection."

"Wonderful! I stand corrected, young man. Let me ask you this: Do you believe that the intellect should conform to reality, or that reality should conform to what the intellect believes reality to be?"

"Let me answer you this way: I believe your question refers to liberalism. Liberalism as a philosophy, not political liberalism. One of the components of liberalism is subjectivism, and you are referring to subjectivism specifically, am I correct?"

"I am referring to precisely that. Please continue."

"What you are asking involves a difficult and controversial question. It is exactly the question that Pontius Pilate asked of Jesus of Nazareth, 'What is Truth?' That is really the same question as, 'What is reality?' The answer to that is given by philosophers after Descartes and Kant, who are known as modernists, who state that Truth is what the intellect believes it to be. I don't agree with those philosophers, but instead believe the teachings of Thomas Aquinas and Garrigou-Lagrange and Dominique Bourmaud and other philosophers who say that 'Truth is that which Is.' When Moses asked God what His name was, God answered, 'I AM WHO I AM, He Who Is.' Therefore, I believe that the intellect must conform to reality and not the other way around. In other words, there is a reality that is objective and exists in and of itself; reality does not depend on the subjective intellect for its existence."

"Young man, I have had this same discussion with others, and we have spent hours arguing without ever reaching the basic question. I can see that your mind cuts directly to fundamental issues, so I know that you will have no issues dealing with the challenges that Pablo first brought to my attention. I agree with him that we have a communication problem within our organization; that although scientists at EDICES and the Shroud of Turin Project publish many scientific papers, the general public continues to believe that the Shroud is a medieval forgery, and is not even aware that the Sudarium exists."

The president remained quiet for a minute before he said, "Pablo, I am glad to have this man work with you. It is important to inform the world of our work, and he could be of great help to you and EDICES. If we can do a better job of conveying our scientific findings to the world, we may be able to inject a measure of faith and morality into this cynical world. But I want you to be careful with him; I don't want his body to be fished out of the ocean, like that other man who worked with you two years ago." He turned to Lucien. "What is your name again, young man?"

"Lucien Christopher, sir."

"That name is a good omen," the president commented,

"because the root of 'Lucien' is 'light.' That was the given name of Seneca, one of Spain's most brilliant philosophers."

"Very respectfully, sir, I believe his given name was Lucius."

"Pablo, you have my full support, so you may share with Lucien any information that we have," and shook Lucien's hand with a welcoming smile. "Oh, and one more requirement before you can do that. He must first pass the Barbet test."

Pablo interjected. "Sir, I have a special request. May Lucien be permitted to see the silver chest where the Sudarium is kept? Of course, we do not ask permission to open the chest."

The president glanced at the monk, who assented only with a slight nod of his head. After that, Lucien was blindfolded and taken through a series of underground passages that changed directions several times and were partitioned by solid doors. They stopped, the blindfold cloth was removed, and Lucien stood facing a heavy wrought iron grate that barred access to a silver chest that was illuminated by a single spotlight. The lettering on the side of the chest said in Latin, "The Sepulcher of the Lord, and of His Sudarium, and of His Most Holy Blood."

Lucien felt paralyzed, as if he had lost his senses and strength. He felt that he was in the presence of something very spiritual and powerful, and could only fall to his knees.

Lucien remained kneeling and praying, with his eyes full of tears, and his soul full of gratitude, comfort and wonder.

Sometime later, he felt Pablo gently place a hand on his shoulder and heard him say, "Lucien, you have passed the Barbet test. We can leave now."

Lucien stood up, feeling emotionally exhausted and physically very weak. The last time he had felt this way was when Liliana had unexpectedly slapped him across the face, and his mind was in the same jumble of confused thoughts. He had difficulty remembering what he had read in the Bible: that there were events of long ago recounted in a book of ancient origins. Now, here before his face, one of those events had become something concrete—something true that spoke to him across the centuries. It made him wonder if he really believed the Bible. What chances would be required in his life if the past came into his present?

Both he and Pablo left the complex in deep silence, with Lucien still thoroughly confused.

Long after they left, while they were driving on the straight path back to Seville, Lucien was the first to break the silence. "Pablo, in my entire life, I have never been so moved, so shaken to the depths of my being. A different type of work has no meaning for me now. I want to become involved with you and your work in whatever way I can help. I was very impressed by your president, and I am glad that he gave you his permission."

"I think you impressed him, too."

"Thank you for that, Pablo. But I want to say that shortly before we left, he said something that bothered me…something he said about a man who had worked with you was fished out of the ocean. Is that anything that I have to worry about?"

"I hope not, because I don't want to go through something like that again, and even now it still bothers me to think about it or talk about it. But you deserve to know, so I must tell you about it." Pablo knew the route back to Seville by heart. To Lucien, it looked like he was retrieving a difficult and painful memory from the expression on his face. "He was from America, and worked with me for about six months, without pay and said he wanted to learn about my work. I think he was a journalist because he was always taking notes. Although he tried to be secretive, the questions he asked indicated that he wanted to know more about any correlation between the Shroud and the Sudarium. One day, he did not show up for work, and about a month later, I learned that his body had been washed up on the beach near Cádiz. There was an investigation that turned up no results. I don't know anything more."

"Did he ever tell you who he was working for?"

"I don't recall him telling me about that. As I said, he was always secretive. There was an investigation, but nothing ever came of it."

"I don't think that sounds like anything I need to worry about, and it would take a lot more than that to stop me from working with you," Lucien strongly affirmed.

After more silence, Pablo reopened the conversation. "Lucien, I know the emotional turmoil that you are going through, because I had the same reaction when I first saw the Sudarium, and what I told you about not being able to work for a week was true. That happens when you are in front of something that leaves you in total awe, that gives rise to a fear of the unknown, a fear of something powerful enough to change your world. You might be forced to believe that the biblical narrative regarding Jesus of Nazareth is true, even if, in the past, you may have thought of it as an interesting story, although one that you did not quite believe. But I know all that can change when something very real is before your eyes. I know what you are feeling, and your mind will need some time to recuperate. After that happens, I will give you copies of the scientific papers that EDICES has published, and then we will discuss how you can make a contribution to EDICES."

"Thank you for your offer of support and confidence, Pablo, but right now I don't feel that I am able to contribute anything," Lucien dismissed. As they drove, Lucien's thoughts slowly began to trickle more and more to Liliana. "I want to tell you, though, that I am surprised you felt the same as I did when you saw the Sudarium. I thought that doctors were trained to be completely unemotional!"

"You are partially correct, Lucien, because the control of our emotions is necessary in our work, and enables us to do the work that we do. But there is another aspect of that emotional control. Because of my training in anatomy, for example, I am much more aware than the average person about death by crucifixion, which is by far one of the most horrible ways to die. The person crucified dies of slow suffocation because the weight of their own suspended body prevents inspiration of the lungs, and the only way to breathe is to push against the pain in order to raise the body. Death ultimately comes by asphyxiation, after simulating drowning continuously in pain for three days. Jesus had nails driven through his feet and wrists in locations where the nails affected the central nerve trunk, causing more suffering than can be imagined. How long would any normal human be able to withstand that level of pain? The only doctor in the group of Apostles was Luke, the only Apostle to discern the pain and torture that Jesus was undergoing." Pablo kept speaking with a weary look in his eyes. "Luke tells that when Jesus was in the garden of Gethsemane, the sweat of Jesus 'became like blood.' Medically, this condition is known as hematohidrosis, which is when capillaries under the skin burst and allow blood to enter into the sweat glands. Hematohidrosis is rare, and only occurs as a result of severe trauma, injury, or great fear, often shortly before death. Jesus told of his own condition when he said, 'My soul is sorrowful unto death.' He could have well said, 'My soul and body are sorrowful unto death.' The pain, the torture, the exhaustion that Jesus was forced to endure was beyond the capability of any mortal man. He was not only a man, he was truly a superman."

After that conversation, they completed the trip mostly in silence, and arrived after Liliana had finished her last act. It was a long drive and by the time they settled down, it was nighttime, and both were exhausted. Pablo assumed his usual table near the stage, this time with Lucien accompanying him.

When Liliana finished her last act, she came to their table, greeting Pablo with her usual warmth, but she greeted Lucien in a colder manner. Her eyes looked cold, puzzled, and hurt.

Lucien immediately asked her, "What's wrong?"

"I am very worried!"

"You are not worried about marrying me, are you? You have not changed your mind, I hope! We are still getting married, aren't we?"

"That depends on what you may have done. Earlier this evening, a very elegant-looking woman, an American woman, came with two strong-looking men, and inquired about when you would be returning from Oviedo! I reasoned that if she knew you were in Oviedo, then the two of you must have been in communication with each other. That made me wonder about your relationship with her, and brought to my mind the differences between me and her, what she represents, and what I am. If you are still interested in a relationship with her, your marriage to me would be a major change in your life that makes me wonder if you have had enough time to carefully consider your decision to marry me. Of course I still want you as my husband, but I don't want you to marry me in haste and have regrets later. I want to be absolutely sure that nothing stands in the way of your commitment to me."

Lucien stood up respectfully to look at Liliana, so she could see the truth in his eyes. "Liliana, before you say anything else, I want you to know that there is nothing between me and that woman. She is only a go-between for me and the company that gave me my grant, and apart from that, I have no interest in her. If that causes you a problem, I will give up the grant so that I will never have to see her again. I have no romantic interest in her, and I did not see her on this trip; Pablo can confirm that."

Pablo nodded.

"The only communication we had is that she left a note for me at the hotel where we stayed in Segovia, but I did not even see her. Her note said that there could be 'serious consequences' if I went to Oviedo, but I ignored the note and went to Oviedo anyway."

"What did she mean by 'serious consequences'? The two

men with her looked quite strong. I hope they were not part of the consequences! I don't want you to be hurt in any way!"

"Do you mean that you love me and we are still to be married? Has your sister agreed to come?"

"Yes, I have managed to contact her using the information you gave me about 'Adivinaciones.' Although I do not want to spend time away from you again, the day apart allowed me to collect myself and speak with her after all this time. We had a long cry together, and she is as excited as I am! She said she could come in two weeks, but I told her to be here in a month. I would like you to take two weeks of that time to give some serious thought to our marriage, so that you can be absolutely certain that you want to marry me."

"I am certain at this moment, Liliana, so please continue to make the necessary arrangements. But I am willing to do anything to reassure you, even if it means a short postponement, but no more than two weeks."

"You are a darling, Lucien! But I want you to wait for two weeks, starting tonight, and I absolutely forbid you to have anything to do with that woman!"

"Liliana, because I love you, I accept your conditions, and I will ask Pablo to start me off with the work for EDICES, starting tomorrow."

She gave Pablo a kiss on both cheeks, and a warm hug and kiss for Lucien. "Goodbye for now, my love. When we marry, we will never be apart again. I hope that this does not keep you waiting too long, *mi amor*."

She left, Lucien turned to Pablo and said, "What a complete surprise! I was not expecting anything like that!"

Pablo could only say, "That is why we love women so much. You can't foresee what they will say or do next!"

The Stumbling Block

Lucien's imposition of two weeks of isolation meant that he could not stay in Pablo's apartment, so he reluctantly moved back into his own place—his modest pension in the Arenales District. However, it was not a pleasant experience. Everything in the space reminded him of his former life before meeting Liliana, and how much life had changed in a short time. He realized that before meeting her, he had been alone in the world, without direction or a future. But now, without becoming fully aware of when it had happened, he felt that he was part of a family with Liliana and Pablo, and strongly understood their importance in his life.

He also felt that he had a sense of direction in a line of work in which he could devote himself.

He wondered about whether he could tolerate being apart from Liliana for two weeks, without hearing her voice, without being able to plan their wedding together. He wondered what their new living arrangement would be, and what other numerous decisions would have to be made that would require her input.

To prevent himself from worrying about certain aspects of his situation, he planned to throw himself for the next two weeks into the work that Pablo gave him. His soon-to-be brother-in-law had given him

EDICES research papers to look over before his employment could be truly finalized.

The night before he left for his Arenales apartment, Lucien slept well and was ready for when Pablo came upstairs to greet him.

"Good morning, brother!" the doctor said. "I have gotten so used to you being in my life, that I am going to miss you!" He parted ways with Lucien after leaving him a box that contained a hefty load of research papers from EDICES.

"Pablo, since I am to have no contact with Liliana, as she has requested, I may not be seeing you, either. I will need to find somewhere else to hide for two weeks, hoping that will prevent my liaison from finding me. I will not contact you for any reason, except for an emergency or something extremely urgent. If you don't hear from me, assume that everything is fine, and don't worry."

"Good luck, Lucien."

Lucien could not stay at his apartment for too long. To assure himself that he would not be too distracted, he took just enough clothing and essential personal items, a book about Thomas Aquinas and his Bible. He left behind his UNITA telephone. He placed his belongings and the box of research papers into the trunk of his rental car and headed toward Sanlúcar de Barrameda, where he felt familiar—a place that had good memories for him.

Sanlúcar was much quieter this time than during his previous visit. He found the same sidewalk café near the bodega of Mr. Hidalgo, ordered some snacks, and prepared himself to examine the box of technical papers.

Inside, resting on top of the technical papers, was a handwritten note from Pablo:

I have arranged these papers in a way to make your study easier. The Shroud papers are separated from the Sudarium papers. Each section is in chronological order to make it easier to follow the development of research. Some labeled "STURP" are from the Shroud of Turin Research Project. The others have been generated by EDICES scientists.

On the subject of the Sudarium, I suggest you read the Shroud papers first, even if the Sudarium papers are of greater interest to you.

Good luck with your efforts. If you need anything, don't hesitate to come see me.

Pablo

Lucien made a decision to keep a separate journal of his own, so that he could make a record of the important information in each paper that would be helpful in later discussions with Pablo.

After he finished his cup of hot chocolate, he began to read the first slip of paper on the top of the pile, eager to learn what reading technical papers would be like.

Even with only a quick read of the first article, it was obvious that the writer was an expert in his field. He looked through the titles of the other papers and saw that they contained research in the fields of botany; palynology (which he had determined was the scientific study of spores and pollens); Greek and Roman history; chemistry; the mathematics of topography; types of fabrics and their dyeing and weaving practices; pharmaceuticals; entomology; and early histories of Spain, France, Palestine and Turkey.

There were also many biblical studies with references. The combined papers covered such a wide range of knowledge, that it made Lucien realize that even a cursory reading of the material could easily take longer than two weeks.

He was pleased to discover that the things Pablo had orally told him about the Shroud and the Sudarium were supported by the research contained in the papers, but he was disappointed to see that with his limited knowledge of science, he would not be able to contribute much. He read articles until past the lunch hour, then collected them back into the box and into the trunk of his car. Then he turned his attention to finding a place to stay for as long as he needed.

The room that Lucien rented in Cádiz was as comfortable as the bed that enabled him to get a good night's sleep. He awoke refreshed and eager. He returned to the café and ordered another hot chocolate, one of his favorite drinks. He began to lay out some papers on the tabletop, but it was not large enough to hold everything. A fresh, salty breeze from the ocean blew one of the articles to the floor. As Lucien bent over to pick it up, he heard someone ask in broken English, "Are you having a problem, Mr. Christopher?"

Lucien looked up and saw Mr. Hidalgo from his former visit. "Oh, it's you, Mr. Hidalgo! I was hoping that I would run into you!"

"Have you recovered from your injury? Where is Liliana?"

As he retrieved the article, Lucien responded, "Why don't you join me for a hot chocolate? I would be glad to talk after I organize these papers."

Mr. Hidalgo joined Lucien, and over hot chocolate, Lucien told him about his wedding plans with Liliana, the reasons for their two-week sabbatical, and the technical papers he had with him.

"I congratulate you on your marriage! You are a very fortunate man to have been chosen by Liliana. She is a wonderful woman, and I hope to see more of both of you in the future." Then, he frowned. "I understand that you enjoy the sea breeze, but instead of working out here in public, I invite you to work in a room where you could work undisturbed. It has a private entrance, so you will be able to work as early and as late as you wish. It is nice and quiet, and I think you will like it if you don't mind the aroma of sherry fermenting in open casks!"

Lucien nodded with a warm smile. "Mr. Hidalgo, I gladly accept. I love the aroma of sherry that energizes me!"

Lucien paid the tab on his personal card, and they walked together to what would be his new study. It was sparsely furnished with only a rectangular wooden table and four sturdy wooden chairs. The room had a one-foot gap between the walls and the ceiling to allow in sunlight and outside air from the ocean. Lucien could not have asked for a better workplace, and immediately thanked Mr. Hidalgo and spread out his papers. He made a note in his journal to inform Liliana of their friend's generosity.

Thankfully, Lucien's studies to become a professor rushed back to him. He took each paper out of the boxes and arranged them by title and subject matter. The topics covered not only the Sudarium and the Shroud, but a wide range of subjects he had seen earlier when he first skimmed through everything, including Jewish burial customs and biblical exegesis. He felt overwhelmed by the immense task of trying to understand everything before him—something that he saw to be impossible in the short time available to him—and saw the need to organize everything further by creating an index of each paper and its associated topic. From the index, he first selected those papers that focused on specific information about the Sudarium and the Shroud. From there he extracted information that he entered into his own journal, with his own comments enclosed in parentheses.

Following Pablo's directions, the subject of the first papers he examined were the early studies of the Shroud, starting in 1898. No scientific studies had been done in the previous two thousand years, because there had been no science and no instrumentation. To the naked eye, the image contained on the Shroud was vague and hazy, because the yellow-brown stain that formed the image faded into the cloth without well-defined edges, that of which made exact measurements impossible.

Measurement was made possible in 1898 by Secondo Pia from Turin, who took the first photographs of the Shroud that showed the figure of a reclining man with all his features—his hair, eyes, arms, legs, bruises, wounds, and blood flows clearly and sharply delineated. With striking realism, the injuries to the hands, feet, chest, and crown of the head could clearly be seen.

After that, in 1931, Giuseppe Enrie took photographs with better details of the face and blood stains. These newer photos greatly attracted the attention of outside medical experts. Even the initial photographs taken by Secondo Pia were detailed enough to enable Yves Delage, a professor of anatomy from the Sorbonne, to say to the French Academy of Sciences in 1902 that the image and the wounds on the Shroud were so flawless that it was impossible for him to believe that the image was the work of an artist.

Then, in 1931, Pierre Barbet, chief surgeon of St. Joseph's Hospital in Paris, started his experiments on amputated limbs and cadavers. He applied his knowledge of anatomy and forensic medicine to verify details that were made apparent to him from the Enrie photographs, and published his findings in an important book, *A Doctor at Calvary*.

Afterward, in 1988, a multitude of experts from England, Australia, Italy, and the United States formed a team called the Shroud of Turin Research Project (STURP), to conduct modern studies of the Shroud.

Lucien noted the important details of the Shroud with his own comments in parentheses:

The dimensions of the Shroud are a little more than 14 feet long by 43 inches wide, made of linen cloth, woven in a Z pattern, rather than the more common S weave of Palestinian linens woven in the first century A.D.

(The Gospel of Luke says that the Shroud in which Jesus was wrapped was made of "fine linen.")

The Shroud image is that of a well-proportioned male, from about 68 inches to 71 inches tall, that weighs an estimated 165 to 180 pounds. The man had been beaten about the face and head, causing a triangle-shaped bruise on the right cheek, a torn right eyelid and a large swelling below the right eye; the face on both sides, above the eyebrows, was swollen, and there was more swelling on the left side of the chin. The septum of the nose was broken. Profuse bleeding of the head occurred from puncture wounds caused by sharp, conical objects such as thorns, wound tightly around the head like a crown. The crown of thorns and the effects of a vicious scourging are evident on the posterior and anterior thorax of the man, and this was the cause of the most serious loss of blood. The severe scourging covered the front and back of the entire body from the shoulders to the lower legs. The whipping was done by two executioners, one on each side. Dr. Barbet's examination counted at least one hundred wounds, each wound having gouged out a crater of flesh, and believed there may have been one hundred and twenty strokes. (St. Paul said that He had been scourged five times, but each time with only thirty-nine strokes, because forty strokes was considered a death penalty.)

Lucien became very disturbed by what he had seen so far. Certainly, he had thought many times about Jesus on the Cross, but never in such detail. What he was learning was bringing those events of long ago closer to him, making the Crucifixion more real. He felt very unsettled, because his emotions were trying to reach the same place where his mind had already advanced. He was completely tired, having worked through the entire day, so he left the papers and his work on the table and drove toward Cádiz until he found the first beach. It was there when he stopped and contemplated the ocean for a while, then returned to his room and went to bed early.

He woke up alert the following morning, ordered his favorite hot chocolate and churros, and returned to his work to face a continuation of the agonies suffered by Jesus.

> Each strand of the whips used in the scourging had three lead weights that gouged out the skin and left a deep wound. (The total number of lashes must have left Jesus as if nearly flayed alive, since His protective layer of His skin had been so severely compromised. His entire body must have felt as if it were on fire, and every fly landing on Him, every stray breeze, every touch of the purple cloth that was placed on Him for the purpose of mocking Him, and the bruising of His body by falling several times while carrying his heavy Cross must have caused Him excruciating pain and exhaustion. No wonder that His sweat had been like blood.)

> The body has an elliptical wound, four and four-tenths

centimeters wide, on the right chest in the intercostal area, between the fifth and sixth ribs, which conform to the size and shape of a spear used in Roman times.

The exact cause of death of the man was asphyxiation as a result of a crucifixion. The body had been attached to a vertical post, with his arms affixed to a horizontal post at an angle of seventy degrees to the vertical, with the head resting on the right shoulder, tilted forward at seventy degrees to the vertical. The head had bled profusely from puncture wounds caused by sharp objects that had been wrapped tightly around the head. Other bleeding was caused by a deep spear wound in the right chest. Multiple bruises and contusions were present on the anterior and posterior surfaces of the legs and thorax. Nail holes were present in both wrists and both ankles, both ankles were secured by one nail. (Dr. Barbet confirmed that crucifixion victims needed to be affixed to the cross by nails through the wrists, not the palms, because otherwise the weight of the body would have pulled the nails through the palms. Dr. Barbet confirmed this fact with a newly amputated arm with enough attached weight to duplicate the weight of a man.)

Understanding this last piece of information had taken up most of the morning. Lucien rejected the thought of working longer, because he did not want to tire himself as he had done the day before.

He paused his work and decided to invite Mr. Hidalgo for lunch, finding him working in the bottling station. They left together for the café.

Mr. Hidalgo carried two bottles of La Gitana sherry with him, which they emptied during the course of their lunch. Lucien enjoyed his time thoroughly because the café, Mr. Hidalgo, the town of Sanlúcar itself, and the bottles of sherry all recalled Liliana to him.

After lunch, Lucien tried to work, but it was useless. He took a long nap on his chair, but awoke with no desire to continue working. He felt that his mind refused to learn more details of the Passion of Jesus. He returned to his place in Cádiz to rest.

Driving along the Cádiz waterfront, on the road that ran parallel to the ocean, he stopped when he found a beach that had concrete benches on the ocean side of the road that faced the open waters. Only a few people remained, but they soon left with the lengthening of shadows, leaving Lucien alone. His thoughts were of Liliana, missing her and wondering what performance she had prepared, and whether Pablo was with her to keep her safe. These musings, along with the repetitious sounds of the waves rushing onto the beach, then cresting and receding, calmed and comforted him.

As darkness deepened, Lucien saw more running lights of traveling ships sailing on the Atlantic Ocean in both directions, the smaller ships closer to shore, and larger ones farther away in deeper waters, which formed a continually changing pattern of dancing lights. Those changes reminded him of what Mr. Hidalgo had told him during their first meeting—that these waters, this place, had changed with time from the Phoenicians, to the Romans, to the Arabs who had brought Aristotle to Spain, then the present-day Spaniards. *How things have changed*, Lucien thought.

Stars began to appear in the sky above. He recognized Ursa Major, the Big Dipper—and Ursa Minor, the Little Dipper, with Polaris at the end of its handle. *Sailing out from nearby Sanlúcar de Barrameda*, thought Lucien, *sailors had used the Pole Star to find their way to continents previously unknown, and had found their glory. Some things have not changed.*

Lucien returned to his room for a restful sleep.

When Lucien went back to his work, he was fortified yet again by his hot chocolate and churros. He started by transferring the information concerning the Sudarium of Oviedo into his journal. This data was of particular interest to Lucien because of Pablo's involvement with the Sudarium.

He found the letter to him that was written by Pablo, which contained his forensic blood analysis stapled to the back, determining that the blood on the Sudarium was human blood type AB—a blood type that was rare in Europe and common in the Middle East. Pablo had made special note that the blood type was the same as what was found on the Shroud.

> The Sudarium is a napkin made of linen stained with blood, blood from direct contact with the face of Jesus. The napkin was first applied after His death while He was still on the Cross, used to limit the flow of blood while He was being taken down and transported, face down, between the Cross and the tomb. The dimensions of the napkin are 34 by 21 inches. The Sudarium contains no images, but the nose and eye sockets can be located by blood stains of prominent finger marks left by someone who applied pressure on the nose and mouth of the victim to limit the loss of blood while the victim was turned face downward during transport from the Cross to the tomb.

And then another paper:

> The crucified man spent approximately one hour in a

vertical position on the cross, then was lowered and placed face down for about forty-five minutes before he was laid face up on the linen cloth in the tomb. This information was determined by the angle of the flow of blood shown on the Shroud, and the known rate of coagulation of human blood. The blood pattern on the Sudarium can be aligned with the blood pattern on the Shroud by matching the location of the nose and mouth on both objects. The alignment is perfect and there are seventy points of correspondence in the facial area of the Shroud and the Sudarium.

And another:

The Sudarium arrived in Spain at Cartagena and was left with Isidore, the Bishop of Seville. The chest in which the Sudarium was stored was first opened in the year 1030 A.D. The chest was opened again in 1075 for inventory, and the inventory clearly describes the chest with an inscription stating: "Of the Sepulcher of the Lord and of His Sudarium and of His Most Holy Blood." It was not opened again for seven centuries, until 1765, even though in the interim, a bishop and a king had asked to see the Sudarium, but were denied. It was in 1765 when the chest was opened again, for the representative of King Philip II, that the Sudarium was specifically described for the first time.

Another study found:

The pollen study of the Sudarium found 141 pollens,

with ninety-nine percent of them corresponding to the Mediterranean and Palestine areas. (The pollens verify the travel of the Sudarium from Jerusalem to Alexandria and then to Spain.)

Lucien needed another rest at this point and stopped reading to review what he had learned thus far. He took note that each paper was the work of a competent, highly trained expert in their field of study, and that each paper had the validity necessary to stand on its own and make an important contribution to scientific advancement. But where were all these tests leading? What were the tests trying to prove? Was the purpose of the tests to determine how the Shroud was made so that they could duplicate it? So that the Shroud was a medieval forgery? Or were they trying to prove that the Shroud was *not* a medieval forgery? Lucien could not figure out the direction of where the tests were going, or where they wanted to go.

But the information that he had reviewed did present some difficult questions, of which Lucien had no answers to. If the image on the Shroud had been produced in the Middle Ages, how was it possible for that to have been done in conformance with the things that had not become known until centuries later, such as blood analysis and pollen analysis? If the Shroud was formed in the Middle Ages, why did it conform so perfectly with the Sudarium that was known to have been locked in an inaccessible chest since the year 616? How could the anatomical details of the Image be so perfect if such detail could not even be seen until after the first photographs were taken in 1898? How could the anatomical details match so exactly the biblical accounts of the death and crucifixion of Jesus of Nazareth?

Lucien began to feel that continued tests of the type that had already been conducted would not contribute to the questions that he perceived, and he felt discouraged and reluctant to carry on reading.

He sat for a while in silence, trying to come up with answers to his questions. He reflected more on the papers he had already reviewed, and concluded that many, if not all of them had something in common: each thesis proved one more way by which the Shroud had *not* been made. For instance, some papers proved that the Shroud could not have been created using paints, pigments, dyes, brushes, heat, radiation, or any other known method.

Other papers that had utilized modern methods in their study of the Shroud and the Sudarium had another commonality: neither object could have been created in the Middle Ages, because the technology had not yet been discovered. In other words, the Shroud and the Sudarium contained information, such as pollen and blood types, that became known only by modern methods—but had already been there centuries before the modern methods had been discovered!

But the papers had a third thing in common: none of them could state how the image on the Shroud had been created. No scientist had reached the conclusion that neither the Sudarium nor the Shroud were fake.

Lucien doubted again about his own ability to make any meaningful contribution to **EDICES**. He had already convinced himself that the Shroud was not a medieval fake, but he worried that his conclusion had come too easily and too early. He comforted himself by thinking that if the scientists had done all this work, they, too, must consider the Shroud to be authentic, for if they had considered the Shroud to be a fake, they would have stopped testing long ago. That made Lucien wonder all the more why the scientists had been unable to learn how the Shroud image had been made. The thought entered into his mind that the scientists could be following a path of diminishing returns, and each new test would yield only an increasingly smaller and narrower account of information. Could a totally new way of looking at the Shroud be needed?

Lucien decided to stop thinking about the papers as his mind recalled his previous visit to Sanlúcar with Liliana during their tour of this winery. He remembered asking Mr. Hidalgo how he could produce the salty flavor in his sherry, and that Mr. Hidalgo had informed him that the saltiness was produced naturally by fermenting the grapes open to the salty, humid air of Sanlúcar, instead of fermenting in closed containers. That reminded Lucien of the first miracle that Jesus had performed during the wedding at Cana, where He had miraculously turned water into wine.

Maybe, thought Lucien, *a new approach, or a miracle was needed to solve the mysteries surrounding the Shroud and the Sudarium?*

Lucien returned his focus to his work and reviewed the summary of the papers that he had made. He re-read the compilation of all the physical characteristics—particularly the wounds and bruises—that had been suffered by the man portrayed on the Shroud image. Dr. Barbet diagnosed the specific cause of death was of a man who had died in the position of crucifixion, and had been so severely beaten that his nose was broken, that his body was covered with wounds from a scourging, that a crown of thorns had been wound tightly around his head that had caused profuse bleeding over his face and upper body, that his legs remained unbroken, and that the right shoulder was chafed.

These physical details described the ordeal of Jesus of Nazareth so precisely, that Lucien immediately connected them with the Gospel accounts in the Bible. He made a serious effort to understand how the biblical accounts could match so exactly to the physical information developed by Dr. Barbet. How could the Shroud image have been made to make it correspond so perfectly to the Gospels?

Lucien considered the various methods in which this could be done, and concluded that the simplest way would have been to have an artist be present in the tomb—and using the actual body of Jesus of Nazareth, with all its wounds and injuries as a model, paint it onto a linen cloth.

However, that would not be as simple as it sounds, Lucien rationalized. First, he deduced that the artist would have needed to have the skills of a superlative artist such as a Leonardo da Vinci or a Michelangelo in order to portray a human body accurately, without a single mistake or erasure. *There are no such mistakes on the Shroud*, Lucien remembered. If such an exalted artist had existed, he left no other examples of his work.

The image on the Shroud is barely visible to the naked eye without distinctive edges, Lucien inferred. For that reason, the artist would have needed to portray the figure while essentially painting blind, because he would not have been able to see the proper place to locate the vague features. *There are no mistakes or distortions on the Image.*

The artist would have needed to be an expert in forensic medicine to successfully and correctly depict the flow of blood over the bones and muscles of the face and body, with the proper coagulation rate of human blood.

Even if it could be assumed that some truly gifted artist would have been able to accomplish all these seemingly impossible tasks, without a computer, without the knowledge of mathematics, without accurate measurements, without ever having seen the blood patterns on the Sudarium, how could an image like that have been put on the linen cloth without using pigments or dyes?

To go even further: If any artist had existed with the necessary skills to produce the masterpiece known on the Shroud, would he have abandoned it in an empty tomb?

These considerations forced Lucien to conclude that the Shroud could not have been made by any human artist, no matter how gifted, and could not have been faked in the first century, the fourteenth century, or any other century.

This line of thinking forced Lucien to try to determine what the studies by EDICES and the Turin Project were trying to accomplish.

What were they trying to prove? If the objective was to prove that the Shroud was *not* a fake, they already had overwhelming evidence to disbelieve the validity of the carbon-14 test. Lucien concluded that other reasons must be involved.

Could they be trying to prove that the figure depicted on the Shroud is Jesus of Nazareth? That Jesus of Nazareth really existed? That the Gospels are true? But Lucien decided that these were not likely objectives, since EDICES and the Turin Project were scientific, not religious organizations. Giving the matter more thought, Lucien decided that the scientists were still trying to determine how the Image was made, and would continue to test and experiment until they found the answer. But the more Lucien thought about all the tests that had already been conducted—tests that produced only negative results—the more he began to doubt that continuing to test was the way to proceed.

It seemed to him that the entire range of tests that had been conducted thus far had only yielded a negative, not a positive, solution— and that method was trying to prove the exception to the rule, instead of proving the rule itself. Each individual test had yielded the implicit, positive answer that the Shroud was authentic, but also produced a negative answer: that the Shroud had not been produced by a particular method, so although the research had provided a lot of information about the Shroud, the tests had provided no information about how the Shroud had been made. From that perspective, the harsh assessment of the tests was that they had not advanced the present state of knowledge much farther than the Bishop of Lirey's statement that the Shroud had been "cunningly and cleverly painted."

That made Lucien think about an ultimate proof that would show how the image on the Shroud had been produced. The ultimate proof would be to apply the "gold standard" of proof—one that would require an actual demonstration. Such a demonstration would require the duplication of the known initial conditions that formed the Shroud, and that would require the real Jesus Christ to present Himself, perform a few miracles to establish His capability and authenticity, allow Himself to be abused and tortured nearly to death as recounted in the Gospels, and finally allow Himself to be crucified on a Cross until He was dead. Lastly, He would need to be taken down from the Cross, His body wrapped in a linen cloth and be left alone in a tomb for three days. On the third day, He would be required to produce an image on His burial cloth that would exactly duplicate the marks of torture and death that had been inflicted on His body, and that would need to match the blood on the napkin that had covered His face while He was still hanging on the Cross. Lucien laughed out loud at the impossibility and absurdity of such a demonstration.

But why should scores of scientists continue to test if the latest scientific equipment had been unable to prove that the Shroud was a fake? And if the scientists did not believe the Shroud to be a fake, why should they continue more testing? Lucien could think of two explanations. First, if they announced that the Shroud was not a fake, a large number of people would be affected—so the scientists would want to make absolutely certain they were correct. They would also know that if one single test could prove the Shroud to be a fake, one test alone would negate all prior tests. Lucien deduced: *That must be the test they are all looking for. That must be the reason why they spent years looking for the one test that would enable them to say, "This is the way, the how, the where and when the Shroud was made."* The major result of such a test would be the separation of the Shroud from parallels to the biblical accounts with its religious and theological implications.

Lucien continued along his line of thought and came up with another reason for more testing: being true scientists, they had accepted the challenge of solving the mystery of the Shroud, and they could not stop until they solved the mystery.

Since Lucien was not a scientist and had no personal stake in continued testing, he felt himself free to try to solve the mystery in a different way. He took his first act upon doing so, and with some reluctance, some regret and some fear, stopped reading technical papers and stored them all back in their box.

The Awakening

After he moved the box of research papers away from the table, placing it on the floor against the wall near the door, Lucien returned to his chair and sat silently, staring around him. He remained that way for some time, his gaze shifting from the box loaded with the articles, to the bare working desk, to the other empty chairs. He needed this period of rest.

After more time had passed, Lucien asked himself, *What will happen if I stop thinking that the Shroud is a fake, and start believing that it is true? How would I prove that the man on the Shroud is Jesus of Nazareth?* After reading the papers, Lucien knew that to answer these questions scientifically would be difficult, so his mind shifted to something he was more comfortable about—the religious studies he had undertaken for his own pleasure, time that had formerly been used to prepare his assigned lectures. These extracurricular studies had given him much pleasure, and had been a reason he had secretly toyed with the idea of becoming a seminary for the priesthood. This turned his attention to the similarities between the Gospel accounts of the death and Crucifixion of Jesus of Nazareth, and the injuries shown on the image of the man on the Shroud.

His first step was to retrieve his own Bible from his car, and read once more the Gospels of Mathew, Mark, Luke and John. Lucien was a quick reader and already knew many of the passages by heart, so the process did not take long. He was particularly looking for information regarding the death of Jesus of Nazareth, specifically the descriptions that described how Jesus had been beaten, scourged, crowned with thorns, crucified, and buried. Those Gospel accounts confirmed that the wounds of torture and death narrated by the Gospels and the injuries shown on the Shroud matched each other exactly.

Is the fact of an exact match sufficient evidence to prove that the man on the Shroud can only be Jesus of Nazareth? Probably not, but it would explain why all past custodians, known and unknown, of the Sudarium and the Shroud always cared for them with mystery, respect, and wonder, for they believed them to be objects of priceless value because of their connection to Jesus of Nazareth.

Lucien returned to the Gospel of John, to the part when John entered the tomb for the first time, three days after the Crucifixion, and "saw the linen cloths lying," and, "He saw and believed." With his newly-acquired knowledge of Jewish burial customs, Lucien could more readily believe that John was aware of the need for secrecy that was prevalent after the death of Jesus, and was the reason why John explained in more detail about what he "saw and believed." If that was the case, then the purpose of John's vagueness would have been to prevent the Shroud and the Sudarium from being destroyed.

John's Gospel went on to say that inside the tomb, the "linen cloths and the napkin were lying apart." That "the cloths were lying apart" indicated that the cloths had been disturbed in the interim between the time of interment of Jesus and John's entry into the tomb, because at the time that the body of Jesus had been placed in the tomb, the napkin had been wrapped around the head of Jesus. That all the cloths were still in the tomb was also indicative that the body had likely not been stolen, because it would have been easier for thieves to steal the body if the linens had been left on the body, as it would be used to make the body easier to move.

Lucien then confronted the same question confronting the Turin scientists: *How was the Image put on the linen cloth?* Because Lucien had decided that more technical studies would not be able to provide an answer, he began to think about whether non-scientific means would help to find the solution.

Lucien then returned to the fact that the Sudarium had been on the head of Jesus of Nazareth while He was still on the Cross and while He was moved from the Cross to the tomb. *So, the blood on the Sudarium is the blood of Jesus of Nazareth!*

Lucien also recalled that the Sudarium was an ordinary cloth, with nothing mysterious or extraordinary about it; it was only a bloody cloth. The scientific tests showed the blood type was AB human blood that matched the type of blood shown on the Shroud. The Shroud image conformed with the Gospel accounts of the death of Jesus of Nazareth, and that was another confirmation that *the blood on the Sudarium was the blood of Jesus of Nazareth!*

Lucien's next conclusion startled him again. The blood patterns on the Sudarium corresponded exactly to the blood patterns and injuries on the face of the image on the Shroud. Since the blood on the Sudarium was demonstrated to be human blood—blood type AB that matched the blood type AB shown on the Shroud—and because there were seventy points of correspondence between the Sudarium and the face on the Shroud, he reasoned: *The blood on the Sudarium is the blood of Jesus of Nazareth!*

The Sudarium contained postmortem blood as well as vital blood, meaning that part of the blood of Jesus was deposited while He was still alive—and the portion of the blood, the postmortem blood, had been deposited after Jesus had died on the Cross.

Furthermore, it was clear that at the time that Jesus had shed his postmortem blood on the Sudarium, He was still on the Cross, but the image on the Shroud had not yet appeared! Therefore, the image on the Shroud could not have been made by the *human* Jesus of Nazareth, because *the human Jesus was already dead!* There was a time lapse between when Jesus was taken down from the Cross and the time that the body of Jesus had been placed in the tomb. Therefore, *the Image could not have been made by the human Jesus of Nazareth, because the human Jesus of Nazareth had already died on the Cross!*

Other tests confirmed that Jesus had died by asphyxiation, and that rigor mortis had already occurred when the body of Jesus was moved from the base of the Cross to the tomb. These facts supported the conclusion that the image on the Shroud could not have been made by the human Jesus, because that Jesus was already dead. *If the Shroud image was, in fact, made by Jesus, He must have made it as a glorified or resurrected Jesus!*

If the proof for that conclusion was insufficient proof, then all that could be said—all that remained—would be that the Shroud image was made by an unknown person, in an unknown way, at an unknown time. That conclusion did not satisfy Lucien, however, he could think of no alternatives.

Lucien then turned his attention to the fact that Pablo would want to know the reasons why he had stopped reading the technical papers, so he started writing an explanatory note to him. He did not expect that the explanation would take much time, but right now time was not important to him, since he had no clear direction of how to proceed any further.

Dear Pablo,

I feel a little guilty about having stopped reading the papers, but I have put an end to that because I think that reading all the technical papers will not answer the question of how the image on the Shroud was formed.

I will now try to answer that question with a different approach, applying philosophical principles and logic rather than scientific methods that have been tried. I don't think I will stray too far from the objective of EDICES, because we are trying to answer the same question, and I am trying not to work beyond my capabilities. If I stray too far, please correct me. These are my conclusions thus far. Please look at my journal that I am enclosing, so that you can know how I have reached these conclusions.

1. THE BLOOD ON THE SUDARIUM IS THE BLOOD OF JESUS OF NAZARETH.

2. THE FACE ON THE SHROUD IS THE FACE OF JESUS OF NAZARETH.

I know that these conclusions are nothing new to you, because you already know them through your work, especially through the conversations we have had, but they are startling to me. As I have mentioned, I am now using logical and philosophical principles instead of attempting to think about more instrumentation. But only to show you that I have done my best to keep an open mind, I have also reached the alternate conclusion, that is not very satisfying:

3. THE IMAGE ON THE SHROUD WAS PRODUCED BY AN UNKNOWN PERSON IN AN UNKNOWN WAY, AT AN UNKNOWN TIME.

Pablo, I have to admit that after I wrote this last conclusion,

I was really tired and discouraged, although the feeling of disappointment with myself was even stronger. I really felt bad for the scientists, too, because in a way, all the efforts of running all those tests had only shown many ways that the Shroud had NOT been made. A feeling of uselessness came over me when I began to admit to myself that I would likely be unable to be of any use to you and your work. When Mr. Hidalgo stopped by at closing time, I told him that I was finished with my work, and asked his permission to leave your papers in the study overnight. He must have sensed that I was feeling low, so he invited me to listen to a classical guitar group with him. That was exactly what I needed, so I spent the rest of my evening with him.

The diversion did wonders for me, because when I returned to my workroom the next morning, I felt more positive, not quite so ready to give up. I was not ready to accept the conclusion that the Shroud had been made by some unknown person at some unknown time. There were simply too many obstacles that demanded an explanation before I could accept that conclusion. I began to wonder whether it might be possible to find some answers by taking another look at the information I had available.

I decided to keep trying, and returned to the place where I had stopped the day before. I felt that the last conclusion I had reached would not surprise you, because I believe that it states the present state of our knowledge. All the studies of EDICES and the Turin Project have not been able to determine how, when, or by whom the Shroud was produced, even though they have been utilizing all the knowledge that has been developed by scientists over the last twenty centuries.

I began to wonder: If the origin of the Shroud could not be explained by scores of scientists using the new knowledge and instrumentation of the last two centuries, could it be possible to conclude that the Shroud had been made by a Divine Person, Jesus of Nazareth, after He was resurrected? I was not ready to quit, and I had nothing to lose, so I started to think whether that might be a possibility. Could that possibility be proven by science and logic?

After thinking about the information that I had in the box about Jesus of Nazareth, it was clear that He was not an ordinary man. He had survived beatings and tortures that were beyond the capacity of ordinary human beings to endure. He had survived so many lashes that He had nearly been flayed alive. He was so near death that His sweat had become like blood. He had suffered a major loss of blood caused by the Crown of Thorns—and the beatings and scourging that He received—and this trauma was verified by the presence of bilirubin in the blood. The very fact that He survived this mistreatment and remained alive long enough to have been placed on the Cross and left there to endure the unimaginable suffering of His Crucifixion, leaves no room for doubt that Jesus was an extraordinary human being—a superhuman. That made it easier to think that Jesus of Nazareth was not only a superhuman, but that He could be Divine, and that He produced the Shroud after His resurrection. The Church itself had believed and taught that Jesus of Nazareth was a true man and a true God, and had ascribed dual natures to Him, a human and a divine nature.

Pablo, what I have written so far are things that you likely already know. But this is all new to me, and it is taking me much more time than I had anticipated. Only one day ago, I thought that I could not continue doing what I had been doing, and if I had quit, I would have to fill in the rest of the two weeks that would remain…and I had no idea what I would do, but now I am intrigued by what I am learning, and realize that I am getting into some deep subject matter that will keep me moving back and forth between the reference books that I have brought, and the Bible. Because I am neither a philosopher nor a theologian, I will have to be jumping back and forth between *God, His Existence and His Nature*, the *Summa Theologica*, and the Bible, and I know that may take more time than I have left in the two weeks of my exile. Whereas before I was feeling quite discouraged and not seeing how I could contribute to anything useful, now I have become so interested in what I plan on doing that I have already asked Mr. Hidalgo if I can stay a few days longer! But my strong intention remains true and firm of returning to you and Liliana, so I expect to be back soon, on schedule.

So now I have gone back to work, continuing with the supposition that Jesus of Nazareth must have been Divine and that He had made the Shroud after His resurrection, and I started looking at anything indicating that Jesus had any powers associated with the powers of God.

One such power that Jesus possessed was the ability to foresee His own death. The Gospel of Matthew contains the words of Jesus that He spoke to his disciples: "The Son of Man shall be betrayed, and on the third day He will rise again," and, "Behold, we go up to Jerusalem, and the Son of Man will be betrayed to the chief priests and the scribes; and they shall condemn Him to death and shall deliver Him to the Gentiles to be mocked and scourged and crucified; and the third day He shall rise again."

The Gospel of Mark also contains the spoken words of Jesus: "The Son of Man must suffer many things and be rejected by the ancients and by the high priests and scribes and be killed, and after three days rise again." And, "The Son of Man shall be betrayed into the hands of men, and they shall kill Him; and after that He is killed, He shall rise again the third day."

In the Gospel of Luke, Jesus says, "The Son of Man must suffer many things and be rejected by the ancients and chief priests and scribes and be killed, and on the third day He will rise again." Jesus later tells His disciples that He shall be delivered to the Gentiles and shall be mocked and scourged and spit upon. That after they have scourged Him, they will put Him to death and the third day He shall rise again. In all four Gospels, Jesus foretold not only His death, but also the manner whereby He would be killed.

Jesus also foretold His resurrection, saying THAT ON THE THIRD DAY HE WOULD RISE AGAIN.

An even stronger indication of the divinity of Jesus of Nazareth is the response that He gave to two messengers sent by John the Baptist to ask Jesus this question: "Art thou He who art to come? Or look we for another?" Jesus answered not only by the use of His words, but also by performing a physical demonstration before the eyes of the messengers. The Gospel states, "And in that same hour, He cured many diseases and hurts and evil spirits, and to many who were blind He gave sight." Then, in addition to these physical acts that He had performed for the messengers, Jesus gave them the verbal reply to take to John the Baptist: "Go and relate to John what you have heard and seen: the blind see, the lame walk, lepers are made clean, the deaf hear, the dead rise again, to the poor the Gospel is preached." The miracles, the physical cures that Jesus performed for the benefit of John's messengers, were an important part of His answer because they demonstrated to John the Baptist that Jesus was in fact God, "the One who was to come." Jesus performed the miracles to prove that He was in fact God, because ONLY GOD CAN PERFORM MIRACLES.

Pablo, to be certain that we have a common understanding of "God" and "miracles," I need to define them, and will start by defining "God." We all use this word, but to some people, the word "God" refers to an old man with a beard that serves some vague purpose in the Universe. I use the term as defined in the dictionary that is consistent with its use by philosophers. In the dictionary, God is "a being conceived as the ULTIMATE PERFECT BEING, omnipotent, omniscient, the originator and ruler of the

Universe."

Pablo, I know that you believe in God, so I need not prove God's existence to you, but if you should ever need rigorous proof, I recommend the work of Garrigou-Lagrange entitled *God: His Existence and His Nature*. Garrigou-Lagrange's books contain five specific proofs and one general proof for the existence of God—proofs that are based on the *Summa Theologica* by Thomas Aquinas and *Metaphysics* by Aristotle. These two intellectual giants establish the basis of their metaphysics and theology starting with the basic fact of *being*.

The term "being" as in the words "is" and "to be," are the basic building blocks and the beginning point of human reasoning, because "is" refers to the first apprehension of an object by the human intellect when it makes the decision of whether the object perceived either *is* or *is not*. Does the apprehended object exist, or does it not exist? If it *does* exist, then the intellect moves to the identity of the object. That gives rise to the principle of non-contradiction, that limits an object from existing and not existing at the same time; whether it can be one thing and also be something else at the same time. Using these principles, Thomas Aquinas developed five proofs to prove the existence of God. The five proofs can be condensed into one general proof: THE GREATER CANNOT PROCEED FROM THE LESS. Based upon this principle, Aquinas continued to develop the attributes of God, and defined God as: "Pure Act, Absolutely and IN ALL WAYS PERFECT Without Imperfection, Omnipotent, having infinite power."

It is God's omnipotent power that gives Him the ability to perform miracles. A "miracle" is an effect accomplished by God outside the apparent order of nature, that is beyond the sphere of action of all created natures. That is the reason why GOD ALONE CAN PERFORM A MIRACLE. Therefore, when Jesus performed miracles in the sight of the disciples of John the Baptist, the miracles were important, because Jesus was demonstrating that He could do what only God has the power to do. Therefore, by His words and actions, Jesus proved to John the Baptist that he was God.

Since God is perfect, it follows that God cannot mislead or deceive. An example of this precept occurred when Jesus was being questioned by the Sanhedrin to determine if He had committed blasphemy, an offense punishable by death. The high priest asked Jesus, "I adjure thee by the living God, that thou tell us if thou be the Christ, the Son of God." Jesus, being God, could not deceive or tell a lie, so He replied, "Thou hast said it." This admission by Jesus that He was God was accepted by the Sanhedrin, and He was crucified for committing blasphemy.

Pablo, please excuse my digression about the power of God, but I needed it to be able to answer not only the question of how the Shroud was made, but also to prove that the Shroud was made by Jesus after His resurrection.

I could not accept the earlier conclusion that the Shroud was made at an unknown time by some unknown person.

Therefore, I am attempting to prove that the SHROUD WAS MADE BY THE DIVINE RESURRECTED JESUS. I am looking for a proof that is not based solely on faith, but rather one that is based on science and logic. I know that the biblical citations I have already used might be sufficient in the minds of many people for them to accept the divinity of Jesus of Nazareth, but that would depend on their faith, and whether or not they believe that the Bible is true.

Pablo, again I misjudged how much more time I will need to finish where I want to go. I have not only used up another day writing this letter to you, but I have also used up all the paper that I have. I will stop here for today, and return tomorrow morning with more paper.

Okay, I am back with more paper. I am glad that I did not work late last night, because it gave me a chance to rest and better organize my thoughts. The classical guitar concert with Mr. Hidalgo was exactly what I needed.

I had the time to wonder about whether biblical statements could be proven true by scientific methods. I believe that an affirmative answer may be possible, and should start with a thorough examination of the information on the Shroud and the Sudarium, starting with the Shroud. That information shows that the Shroud is a real, physical object that exists, because it can be seen, touched, studied, and analyzed. But the Shroud could not begin to be studied and analyzed until 1898, when the first photographs were taken. Before that, the Image was barely visible to the naked eye so it was of no scientific value. It was only after Pia's photographs in 1898 and Enrie's photograph in 1931 that the details of the wounds—the beating, the scourging, the crown of thorns, and the marks of crucifixion—could clearly be seen. It was the SCIENTIFIC INFORMATION that has been collected since 1898 THAT CONNECTED THE IMAGE, not directly to Jesus of Nazareth, but TO THE BIBLICAL ACCOUNTS of the life and death OF JESUS OF NAZARETH.

Of course, that raises the question of how the Shroud, in the interim between 1931 and the present, could have been made to match so precisely with a biblical account made two thousand years ago. That biblical information has been unchanged for centuries, so it could not have been written to match the information on the Shroud—the information has only been known since 1931! So, several reasonable conclusions follow: THE SHROUD IMAGE VERIFIES THE TRUTH OF THE GOSPELS BY A MEANS THAT DID NOT COME INTO EXISTENCE UNTIL 1898. THE EXACT MATCH BETWEEN THE GOSPELS AND THE SHROUD INFORMATION CONNECTS THE SHROUD TO JESUS OF NAZARETH.

THEREFORE, THE MAN ON THE SHROUD IS JESUS OF NAZARETH.

Furthermore, the Sudarium verifies the Shroud, and the Shroud verifies the Sudarium. The seventy points of correspondence between the blood pattern on the Shroud image and the blood pattern on the Sudarium is proof that THE BLOOD ON THE SUDARIUM IS THE BLOOD OF JESUS OF NAZARETH.

The match of human blood type on both objects is additional proof that the man on the Shroud is Jesus of Nazareth, because the Sudarium was known to be on the head of Jesus while He was on the Cross. And the existence and location of the Sudarium is known seven hundred years earlier than the Shroud.

The Sudarium, the Shroud, and the Gospels match each other exactly. The Gospels were separately written by four men over a span of forty years after the death of Jesus. The authors were eyewitness observers of the events and are consistent within themselves. Then, twenty centuries later, different men highly trained in scientific methods, by studying the Shroud and the Sudarium with scientific eyes and modern scientific instrumentation, have been able to establish the information that matches the Gospels so precisely, that it seems that the scientists must have used the Gospel accounts as a script! The information obtained by the scientists is scientifically correct, and the correspondence of the scientific facts with the Gospel accounts is also beyond question. The presence of the Shroud and the Sudarium in the tomb of Jesus is established by the Gospel of John and substantiated by the studies of the Turin Project. Nothing has been developed to raise a doubt about the truth of John's Gospel.

One element of doubt, however, does arise from the fact that modern-day science has been unable to prove how the Shroud was made, or by where and how and by whom it was made. Scores of scientists have spent decades of study and have used all the learning known to man over the course of two thousand years, but nothing has been able to explain how the Shroud image was made.

This was the reason why I stopped reading the research papers, and felt that more studies and more tests would not be able to answer the question of how the Image had been made. For that reason, I thought that an entirely new approach was necessary—an approach that involves attempting to prove the divinity of Jesus of Nazareth. That proof has two parts.

The first part involves the subject of *miracles*. If the image on the Shroud was created by a miracle, the Image is in and of itself miraculous. The Sudarium is an ordinary object that verifies the Shroud by the exactness of its correspondence with the image on the Shroud. There is nothing miraculous about the Sudarium, it is only an ordinary cloth with ordinary blood stains. By scientific means, that blood has been shown to be human blood, type AB, in an irregular pattern that corresponds exactly with the image on the Shroud, and establishes the connection between the Shroud, Jesus of Nazareth, and the Gospel accounts. That connection makes the Sudarium a holy object that is worthy of veneration, although there is nothing miraculous or unnatural about the way the blood was deposited on the cloth. The blood was deposited during the course of a crucifixion, so there is nothing mysterious or miraculous about the method of deposition. Nevertheless, it is entirely in keeping with the character of Jesus that He would leave only a small, humble cloth to verify the Shroud and verify His existence.

But the Shroud is something completely different. There is so much mystery about it that despite the time and efforts of the scientists, they have been unable to determine how it was made. This is made more difficult because the provenance of the Shroud is uncertain. Before the current studies of the Shroud were undertaken, there were only a few uncertain references by which to establish the existence and the travels of the Shroud.

BUT IT IS OF NO IMPORTANCE TO KNOW WHERE THE SHROUD HAS BEEN IN THE PAST. THE ONLY FACT THAT MATTERS IS THAT THE SHROUD EXISTS TODAY AND IS REAL.

But the question still remains: How did the Shroud come to be? All the studies on the Shroud conducted thus far can only establish that the Image was NOT made by human methods, NOT made in any known natural way, and NOT made by any known natural human process. Could the Image have been made by a miracle, by a miraculous process?

The dictionary's definition of a miracle is "an event that appears unexplainable by the laws of nature, and so is held to be supernatural in origin or an act of God." By this definition, the Shroud qualifies as a miracle. BECAUSE ONLY GOD CAN PERFORM MIRACLES.

If the Shroud is a miracle that has been made by God, then the Shroud, being the work of God, cannot be anything other than perfect. Thomas Aquinas says in his *Summa Theologica*: "Since God is perfect, and the perfection of all things are in God, something is said to be perfect if it lacks nothing of the mode of its perfection." If the Shroud is a miracle made by God, it must be perfect, since God cannot be false or deceive, because God is the supreme good absolutely. If these attributes of God are correct, and the Shroud was made by God, it follows that the Shroud can contain nothing that is false or fake. Therefore, it follows that EDICES WILL NEVER BE ABLE TO FIND ANYTHING IN THE SHROUD THAT IS FALSE OR FAKE. That necessarily means that EDICES will never be able to prove that the Shroud is a medieval fake, or any other type of fake, or find anything false in it.

Another philosophical requirement of a miracle is that it must comply with the principle that WHAT IS MORE PERFECT CANNOT PROCEED FROM THE LESS PERFECT. Applying this principle, it follows that MAN, BEING LESS PERFECT THAN GOD, WILL NEVER BE ABLE TO DUPLICATE WHAT GOD HAS MADE. MAN WILL NEVER BE ABLE TO EXPLAIN HOW THE SHROUD WAS MADE.

The truth of these last two conclusions explains why all the tests by all the scientists have failed to determine how the Shroud has come to be in existence. More testing may continue to be done, but the results will be the same: A HUMAN METHOD OF DUPLICATING THE SHROUD WILL NEVER BE FOUND.

I now believe that the Shroud is the result of a miracle performed by Jesus of Nazareth, who was Divine, who was God. That is why I have discontinued reading the papers, and why I am ready to return to Seville after I have fulfilled my promise to Liliana. But the conclusions that I have reached have affected me deeply, and I need to have you read them to see if they are correct or not. Although I have been unable to contribute scientifically, I have learned so much, and my entire life has changed for the better. I have always been religious, but I have not always made a conscious effort to follow the religious teachings of Jesus. Maybe I lived that way because I never fully accepted the truth of the Bible with all its miracles, and maybe I thought that Jesus was an ancient and remote being, too good, too wise, and too holy to have really existed. But what I have learned here from the research papers about the Shroud and the Sudarium has given me a new perspective on the Gospels, and my life. I know now that the Gospel accounts of the death of Jesus are true, and that the Shroud and the Sudarium are the physical evidence that Jesus left to prove the truth of His existence, His teachings, and His resurrection. Pablo, I am most grateful to you for showing me a way to a better life and for making me a better person.

I also believe that the reality of Jesus of Nazareth is a fact that has been proven scientifically and rationally by the

Shroud and the Sudarium. That is what the old priest in Arizona wanted to accomplish, and I feel that has been done. Now I can look forward to my own life with Liliana.

I am very anxious for you to read my conclusions, because I need you to verify what I have done, and to inform you about how future testing by EDICES may be affected. I will send this note to the place where Liliana works in case my liaison shows up at your apartment again. This way, Liliana can also see what I have been doing during my time away from her. Tell her that I love her and I don't want any more delays in our wedding plans.

Pablo, I earnestly and sincerely hope that you can agree with my conclusions.

Your Brother,
Lucien

Lucien placed his long letter to Pablo carefully in a large envelope he had purchased while buying extra paper. He wrote Pablo's name on the front in large letters, excited that his two-week retreat from Liliana would be coming to an end in a few days.

The Bell Tolls

Lucien packed the box in his trunk, and thanked Mr. Hidalgo for his generous company and kindness before driving back to Seville.

Along the way, he made the impromptu choice to stop at his Arenales apartment to shower, rest, and for a change of clothes. When he opened the door, he immediately saw that someone had broken in.

His clothes were strewn across the floor. He could see that in his bedroom, drawers had been pulled out of the dresser and laid upside-down at various parts across the room. The bed no longer had a mattress, for it had been pulled off the frame and left on the floor.

Heart racing, he went into the kitchen and found there was a man who turned to look at him with surprise. Lucien did not see another man who struck him from behind, on the back of his head, in the same place he had his prior injury. He lost consciousness.

Lucien awoke feeling a lot of pain on the back of his skull, on his wrists, and in the muscles of his legs and arms. He felt his own warm blood running down his back and down both arms, starting at his wrists. He was in a room without windows, dimly lit, that smelled musky and damp. He could see moisture seeping through the walls, so he thought that the room was probably located close to the river, below the water level. This very well may have been one of the rooms used by the Inquisition for its isolation and soundproof qualities.

Lucien felt his arms stretched above him, with his wrists tied tightly with piano wire to two iron rings embedded in the walls. There were other iron rings embedded in the walls at regular intervals. Lucien's toes could barely touch the cold floor, and the muscles of his legs and arms were burning from trying to raise his body enough to breathe easier, and to ease the pain from the piano wire cutting into his wrists.

He had no idea how long he had been unconscious, but he regained enough consciousness to see several people across the room. He recognized Mr. Mason, Peg Ledbetter, and two hard-looking men, one of them being the man he had confronted in his kitchen.

Mr. Mason was the first to speak. "Mr. Christopher, I'm glad to see you're awake. Listen to me! This is the most distasteful part of my job, and I'm glad this happens only on very rare occasions. I don't want this matter to go any further than it already has, so I will give you every opportunity to avoid more unpleasantness. Ms. Ledbetter has told me that she has made repeated efforts to meet with you in Spain, but all her attempts have failed due to your lack of cooperation. She also said that she made a specific effort to prevent you from visiting Oviedo. Is that true?"

Lucien managed to cough, and then speak. "All that is true. I have avoided Ms. Ledbetter for personal reasons that I don't want to discuss with you, and I feel that whatever I have done or not done does not justify my torture in this way!"

"*Mr. Christopher*—you are not here because of your personal conduct; you are here because you have violated your contract with UNITA. We know that you visited Oviedo with Dr. Pablo Penafiel as your companion. We know that he is an expert on the Sudarium, and his dossier is one of the largest in our 'Most Watched' list. If we had had the slightest inclination that you would be coming to Spain to meet him, we wouldn't have offered you the contract!"

Lucien made a visible effort to respond. "Everything took place by accident. Nothing was planned by me!"

"That is not why you are here, Mr. Christopher. You are here because you went to Oviedo with a traveling companion who is unacceptable to us. You undoubtedly went to Oviedo to see the Sudarium—and probably learned much about the relationship between the Sudarium and the Shroud of Turin, and you might use that information in a way that might be completely opposed to the goals and purposes of UNITA. Besides, you have given us no assurance that you will deliver your work product to us. Without that assurance, you are in gross violation of the terms of your grant, and I must act accordingly."

"I was free to do research on any subject of my own choosing, was I not?"

"Mr. Christopher, the value to UNITA is the product of your research, and by the terms of your contract, the work product belongs to UNITA. All that is clearly contained in your contract, which I have brought with me, if you want to review it."

Speaking with a conscious effort, Lucien said, "Does the contract contain a provision that enables UNITA to suppress whatever they don't like?"

"That power is stated in clause thirty-six, on the fourth page, and gives UNITA the option to do anything it wishes, with the material submitted. But you know that it is very difficult to suppress information for any length of time, so in some circumstances, we may choose to release particular information in the proper context, at the time and place of our own choosing."

Lucien mumbled in a weak voice, "Was UNITA involved in the release of *The New York Times* article in 1988, that the Shroud of Turin was a medieval fake?" Lucien had tried hard to say "forgery," but could only say "fake."

"Mr. Christopher, you surely don't expect me to answer a question like that, do you? Don't waste any more of my time; I've already spent more time with you than I planned, and I need to conclude this matter quickly. I want to give you one more chance to end our relationship in a more friendly way, so please give this last offer some careful consideration; it could have a major effect on your future with UNITA."

"Untie me and…let me…go on with my life. I care nothing about my future with UNITA." Lucien gasped for breath. "…I terminate my contract, and I will reimburse you for the money I have spent." He started to say something else, but was unable to.

Mr. Mason looked disgusted and disappointed. "For your sake Mr. Christopher, I wish we could resolve this matter that easily. Unfortunately, I must make a determination about your state of mind. You can resolve this difficulty by telling me the specific conclusions you have reached regarding the relationship between the Sudarium of Oviedo and the Shroud of Turin."

After making a major effort, Lucien managed to speak more clearly in a stronger tone of voice. "I have not reached any conclusions that I am willing to share with you."

"I was afraid it would come to this. Give me your journal and your notes. If I find nothing contrary to UNITA's objectives, you will be set free. Will you accept?"

"No, I do not accept your terms, Mr. Mason," Lucien stammered weakly.

"Then we will persuade you. Bring in the girl!"

Two men brought Liliana into the room; her hands were tied behind her back, and she was looking extremely frightened.

In a terrified, worried voice, she asked, "Lucien, are you all right? Why have they hurt you? What do they want?"

Making the best effort he could muster to sound calm and normal, he replied, "Don't worry, Liliana, everything will be fine. There has been a misunderstanding about my grant contract."

Sharply, Mr. Mason interrupted, "Mr. Christopher, this is no time for details; she is here to persuade you to comply. We are willing to release you to retrieve the information we want, but *Ms.* Liliana will remain here to guarantee your return."

Liliana almost shouted, "I won't go anywhere without Lucien!"

"Very touching," Mr. Mason commented. "Tie her to the wall!"

"Wait!" Lucien used all his remaining strength to talk. "Let her go and I will tell her where to find what you want. When she has it, she can call me here. If I know that she is in a safe place, I will tell you where she has left the information, and you can collect it. After that, you can do whatever you wish with me." Turning to Liliana and looking into her eyes, he pleaded with all his life. "Please do this for me."

Liliana faced Mr. Mason. "I will do as Lucien asks, but I won't leave without giving him a goodbye kiss. I have not seen him for two weeks, and we will be married when all this is over."

Mr. Mason looked thoughtful for a moment before he spoke to the men. "Untie her hands and let her give him a farewell kiss. Take her where she wants to go, and when you've recovered the information, call me here. After that, you know what to do."

As soon as Liliana's hands were untied, she stumbled over to Lucien as fast as she could. She moved close to him to whisper in his ear, and said quickly, "We don't have anything to give them. I was going to the post office to mail some things to my sister, and I had the envelope for Pablo with me. When I saw the men waiting for me to leave the post office, I recognized them as the men who came looking for you that night before you returned from Oviedo! I figured they were after the envelope for Pablo, so I added Pablo's address to it and mailed it to him, so we can't give them what they want. —I recognize the man doing the talking, he was involved in the killing two years ago of the man who worked with Pablo! They are planning to kill you, and if you die, I want to die with you. I am ready and not afraid."

Lucien could barely keep his eyes open, but he used his remaining strength to bend as much as he could to reach Liliana. Looking directly into her eyes, he told her, "Liliana, I love you!"

Liliana raised herself on her toes as high as she could. She reached up with one arm to pull his head closer to her, while her other arm moved in a motion as rapidly as when she had first met Lucien on the bridge. As before, Lucien, with his eyes half-closed, was only able to see the flash of a small dagger. An instant later, he felt a fleeting pain on the back of his neck, like a bee sting. At the same moment that Liliana's lips touched his own, Lucien's mind exploded in a series of images flashing by so rapidly that he could not separate them from one another. They slowed down, and Lucien knew that he was confronting his Death.

After that, Lucien found himself in a large group of people that was moving slowly and silently towards a brilliant light. A smaller group stood still as if searching the moving people. As Lucien came nearer to a young woman he did not recognize, she said to him, "My son!" He could see that she was crying. A little farther on, Lucien recognized the couple that had adopted him, the ones that he had thought were his birth parents. His mom greeted him with joy, "My son!"

He moved toward the light with the crowd, and saw the priest from Jerome, and Don Gabriel De Los Arcos. They said nothing, but they smiled and bowed in approval. Then, as he passed close to Juan Belmonte, Belmonte whispered to him, "*Será suficiente*; it will be sufficient!"

Shortly afterward, Lucien heard a familiar sweet voice behind him: "I hope I have not kept you waiting too long, *mi amor!*" Liliana embraced his arm with her own, and together they walked toward the Light. They reached the Light, and they entered together. Like St. John, the beloved disciple of Jesus of Nazareth, they saw and they believed.

Sit finis libris; quaerere non finis.

PostScript

Teach me half the gladness
That thy brain must know,
Such harmonious madness
From my lips would flow
The world should listen then,
As I am listening now.

—Percy Bysshe Shelley, "To a Skylark"

The meaning of Truth is under attack by modern thinking. In today's day, a single event is presented to us in multiple versions that often contradict one another. For example, one version is presented as "news" while another source portrays the same event as "fake news." "Facts" describing an event are usually followed by contradictory "alternative facts" of the same occurrence. So, we are left with: Which version is true, and which one is false? Can both versions be true, even though they contradict each other? How is a person to choose? What thinking process can we follow to make the correct choice?

In this state of affairs, the power of Truth is seriously diluted. Many don't know what to believe, and soon they will believe in nothing or will believe anything. The great writer of *The Gulag Archipelago, Aleksandr Solzhenitsyn,* who was imprisoned under totalitarianism, said that totalitarianism is preceded by the negation of Truth. I believe *Solzhenitsyn* was right.

The fundamental questions are: What is Truth? What is Reality? These are not easy questions to answer. If people become divided into different factions that cannot agree on the basic facts, and if they don't agree about the process used to make a decision, then reconciliation will not be possible. The factions can only continue to fight.

Unfortunately, the struggle to define Reality is not merely a local matter that has arisen only recently; it has been going on for centuries.

About fifteen-hundred years after Aristotle, Thomas Aquinas was born in 1225 A.D. at a time when the Christian faith transmitted by St. Augustine needed to be reconciled with the teachings of Aristotle. A philosopher of that time was Siger of Brabant, who proposed that two truths should be considered: one for Faith, and one for Reason. Siger's proposal was opposed by Thomas Aquinas, whose genius could see that Faith and Reason could coexist in the same Truth.

Aquinas started by asking a common sense question: Is there anything out there? In a deeper sense, he was asking: Is there an Objective Reality that exists outside of the human mind? The same inquiries can be posed differently: Is there a bridge between the human mind and Reality? He answered those questions with a resounding: *Yes!*

Aquinas knew the answers that Faith already provided: First, in the Book of Genesis, when Moses asked God his name, and God answered, "I AM WHO I AM, He Who Is." St. Paul later affirmed this when he said, "The invisible things of God…are clearly seen, being understood by things that are made."

But Faith alone was insufficient for Aquinas. He saw that "I Am" and "things that are made" refer to *existence*, or *being*, and went on from that starting point to develop his masterpiece, the *Summa Theologica*, in which he proved by logic and reason the existence of God and God's attributes. He also defined Truth as the conformance of the mind with Reality. However, the thinkers who refuted the questions that Aquinas answered with a "Yes," were not silenced forever, although it took several hundred years before they resurfaced.

"Modern thinkers" in the last five-hundred years have also considered the question: Does Objective Reality exist outside the human mind? It may surprise you to learn that most answered with a definitive

"No!" They believe that the mind has no "bridge" to an external Reality, so the mind need not conform to external reality, since there is no external reality.

In the modern framework of thinking, everything is subjective—within the mind—and that has led them to conclude things that seem absolutely absurd in the Aristotle/Aquinas way of thinking. Here are some examples: There is no God. There is no historical Jesus, but He is a useful concept, so we should create Him. Intellect is entirely divorced from the mind. Truth is the conformity of thought within itself. God is a projection of human consciousness. Nothing exists, everything is Becoming. Only when reason is dead will be born the new man of the era to come. All of these disputes will disappear with the rejection of logic and the principle of contradiction. Conclusions of this nature may be at the root of our present crisis of thought and disagreement.

In this new world of "modern thinking" that is prevalent today, contradictions abound. An anti-Christian can still be a Christian; man is capable of loving God and openly denying Him at the same time. The flaw of modern thinking is that its ideas fail to connect with Reality. That is why "news" and "fake news" and "facts" and "alternative facts" can coexist.

How is a person to choose between these two systems of thought: the Thomas Aquinas system, and modern thinking? How to choose between systems that are consistent and have been developed by very intelligent people? One way of deciding that may be helpful is to apply the rationale of both systems, especially when it comes to the Sudarium of Oviedo and the existence of the Shroud of Turin.

In modern thinking, the Sudarium and the Shroud do not exist. They are constructs of the human mind. They are only pigments of the imagination constructed by the mind to serve a useful purpose. In this way, since neither the Sudarium nor the Shroud exist, they can be either medieval forgeries or an imaginary sample of cloth tested by imaginary mass spectrometers—and if there is a result, it can be a date between 1260 and 1390 A.D., or something that dates to biblical times. Since either date is rather made up by the product of human imagination, either result is equally valid. Take your choice.

Then apply the Thomistic rationale of Thomas Aquinas: that the Sudarium and the Shroud are physical objects that validate each other and confirm the biblical accounts of the life and death of Jesus of Nazareth. These two objects do raise many questions that are inexplicable by ordinary scientific means. For example, the congruence of the Sudarium and the Shroud cannot be explained since the details on the Shroud image could not be seen by the naked eye until the Shroud was photographed in 1898, and the anatomical correctness of the Shroud image was not known until examination by a medical doctor in 1930. In other words, numerous tests by a multitude of experts using space age instrumentation have been unable to explain how the Shroud image came into existence.

One difference between the two systems also rests on the existence of a *"miracle."* The system of Aquinas both defines and limits miracles, offering a radical explanation of how the Shroud image came to be. The modern system does not deal with miracles at all, but provides no explanation of how the Shroud came into existence, other than saying it is something useful constructed by the human imagination.

The system of Aquinas provides a moral incentive, a moral imperative, to live a life in keeping with the teachings of Jesus of Nazareth. The modern approach leaves conduct, good or bad, truth or lies, open to individual choice. The world of Thomas Aquinas is a world of Logic, Reason, and Truth. Modern thinking leads to a world of Absurdity. May God bless the world with the right choice.

—Roberto Rabago
February 2022

Appendix

The following works were used as research for the material throughout the book and are accurate at the time of publication.

References are cited in order of appearance.

The Holy Bible: The New Revised Standard Version.

The American Heritage Dictionary of the English Language. William Morris Ed., 1973.

Shelley, Percy Bysshe. "To a Skylark." *Prometheus Unbound*, 1820. Encyclopaedia Britannica. https://www.britannica.com/topic/To-a-Sky-Lark.

Carrasco, Davíd. *City of Sacrifice: The Aztec Empire and the Role of Violence in Civilization*. Boston: Beacon Press, 1999: "On this fearful night, women were closed up in granaries to avoid their transformation into fierce beasts who would eat men," 96.

de Sahagún, Bernardino et al. *General history of the things of New Spain: Florentine codex*. Monographs of the School of American Research. Santa Fe, New Mexico, 1950-1969: Appendix B, 187.

Anderson, Carl and Eduardo Chavez. *Our Lady of Guadalupe*. New York: Random House, 2009: 59.

On public display at the Shrine of the Virgin of Guadalupe, Mexico

City.

Valeriano, Antonio. *Nican Mopohua: The Story of Our Lady of Guadalupe in Nahuatl.* 1558. https://springfieldop.org/wp-content/uploads/nican_mopohua_english.pdf.

Anderson, Carl and Eduardo Chavez. *Our Lady of Guadalupe.* New York: Doubleday Books, 2009.

Austin, Mary. *The Land of Little Rain.* New York: Houghton Mifflin Harcourt, 1903.

Erikson, Erik. *Gandhi's Truth.* New York: W.W. Norton Co., 1969: 230.

Merton, Thomas. *Thoughts in Solitude.* New York: Farrar, Straus and Giroux, 1997.

Juan Belmonte, top Spanish bullfighter in 1925, the time considered the Golden Age of bullfighting.

Suzuki, D.T. *Essays in Zen Buddhism.* New York: Grove Press, 1961.

D. T. Suzuki. Encyclopaedia Britannica. https://www.britannica.com/biography/D-T-Suzuki.

Suzuki, D.T. *Zen and Swordsmanship in Zen and Japanese Culture.* Princeton, NJ: Princeton University Press, 1970.

Charteris, Leslie. "The Making of a Bullfighter." *Atlantic Monthly* (1937).

Suzuki, D.T. *Zen and Japanese Culture* (rev. ed.). Princeton, NJ: Princeton University Press, 2010.

Wilson, Ian. *The Mysterious Shroud*. New York: Image Books, 1979 and Reprint Edition, Doubleday Books, 1986: 5, 96, 137, 132, 169, 11, plate 2, 6, 16, 20, 30, 24-26, 97, 17-20, 126, 10, 17, 50, 511, 36, 16, 30-31, 27, 47-48, 41-43, 94, head of Zurich's scientific laboratory for 25 years Dr. Max Frei 38-43, pollens identified by Dr. Frei 40-41.

Rubens, Peter Paul. *The Elevation of the Cross*. Triptych in oil on panel and oil on paper. 1610, 1638.

Beevor, Antony. *The Battle for Spain: The Spanish Civil War 1936-1939*. London: Orbis Publishing, 1982.

Bennett, Janice. *Sacred Blood, Sacred Image: The Sudarium of Oviedo* (Libre de Espana). Littleton, CO: 2001: 17, 70, 84, plates 13 19a 19b 20, plate 20 122, 66-71, 73, 96-97, 23, 30, 31, 33, 42, 44, plate 13, plates 17a 17b 73, 76, 71, 84, 196, 195, 67, 73, 77, 75-76, 68-69, 193, 84-89.

Off the Beaten Path: Spain. New York: Harper and Row, 1989: 284.

Robinson, Jancis. *The Oxford Companion to Wine*. Oxford: Oxford University Press, 1994: 869, 597.

The Gospel of John, 20:7, 19:34, 20:8, 20:19, 21:19, 18:17-27.

Acts of the Apostles, 7:55-57.

Barbet, Pierre. *A Doctor at Calvary*. New York: Doubleday Books, 1963 and Reprint Edition, Image Books, 1963: 179-180, 76, 107, 14, 121, 73-

74, 77, 76, 92, 46, 87, 91-92, 128, 110-111.

Durant, Will. *The Story of Civilization: Caesar and Christ.* New York: Simon and Schuster, 1944: 180, 544-45.

The Edict of Milan, 312 A.D. Encyclopaedia Britannica. https://www.britannica.com/topic/Edict-of-Milan.

The Book of Exodus, 20:14.

Lavoie, Gilbert R. *Unlocking the Secrets of the Shroud.* 1998: 5, 12-13, 61.

Hemingway, Ernest. *For Whom the Bell Tolls.* New York: Scribner and Sons, 1958: Preface, quoting John Donne, 16th century English poet.

Subjectivism: The doctrine that all knowledge is restricted to the conscious self and its sensory states.
Naturalism: The system of thought that all phenomena can be explained in terms of natural causes.
Rationalism: The theory that the exercise of reason provides the only valid basis for action.
Intellection: The act or process of exercising the intellect; mental activity.
Liberalism: Having views or policies that favor the freedom of individuals to act in a manner of their own choosing.
Subjectivism: The doctrine that all knowledge is restricted to the conscious self and its sensory states.

Aquinas, Thomas. *Summa Theologica.* Chicago: William Burnett Benton, 1952.

The Book of Exodus, 3:14.

The Gospel of Luke, 22:44, 23:53.

Miller, Vernon, and Ian Wilson. *The Mysterious Shroud.* New York: Doubleday Books, 1988: Frontal figure of the man on the Shroud, photograph of the unaided eye image, 6.

Barbet, Pierre. *A Doctor at Calvary.* Published in English by Image Books. New York: Doubleday Books, 1953.

Wilson, Ian. *The Shroud of Turin* (rev. ed.). Ogden, UT: Doubleday Books, 1979: 36-37, 24-26.

St. Paul, Second Epistle to Corinthians, 11:24. Encyclopaedia Britannica. https://www.britannica.com/topic/The-Letter-of-Paul-to-the-Corinthians.

The Gospel of John, 2:1-11, 20:8, 20:6-7.

Denzinger, Henry. *The Sources of Catholic Dogma.* St. Louis: B. Herder Book Co., 1957: 60.

The Gospel of Mathew, 26:38, 17:22, 20:18-19, 26:63-64.

The Gospel of Mark 8:31, 9:30.

The Gospel of Luke 9:22, 18:32, 7:20-27.

Garrigou-Lagrange, Réginald. *God, His Existence and His Nature.* St Louis: Herder Book Co., 1948: 246, 157, 252, 277-278, 161, 110, 162.

Shakespeare, William. *Hamlet*. 3.1. Encyclopaedia Britannica. https://www.britannica.com/topic/Hamlet-by-Shakespeare.

Hemingway, Ernest. *For Whom the Bell Tolls*. New York: Scribner and Sons, 1958.

Additional Recommended Reading

Percy Bysshe Shelley, "To a Skylark."

Ernest Hemingway, *For Whom the Bell Tolls*.

Thomas Aquinas, *Summa Theologica*.

ROBERTO RABAGO

"The Writer," illustration of the author by Annie Rabago

Roberto D. Rabago, B.Sc., J.D. L.L.M.

*Bachelor of Science, Physics and Mathematics, Fresno State University;
Juris Doctor in Law, Santa Clara University; Master of Law degree,
University of California, Berkeley.*

Roberto Rabago was born in Jerome, Arizona, and is married with three children. He was employed as an engineer on aircraft instrumentation and nuclear magnetic resonance equipment, and certified as a criminal Law Specialist by the State of California.

Roberto currently lives in Arizona, California, and Spain. He travels extensively in Latin America, Europe and Asia. He loves books, poetry, wine and life. *Awakened by the Hidden Poet* is his second book.